# Pure, unspotted.....

## By Inge Borg

I am grateful to Sharon Colback and A. R for their helpful suggestions.

Introduction 5

**One** Convent-girls 25

**Two** Life in Cape Town 49

**Three** Job in Stellenbosch 74

**Four** Wedlock 88

**Five** Rage in Johannesburg 126

**Six** New friends.... 158

**Seven** ....new ways 198

**Eight** Forces from hell 236

**Nine** Back in the Cape 257

**Ten** Journey's end 262

**Eleven** 298

**Benediction** 311

Vocabulary of Latin/ Afrikaans words 324

## 1994. Rondebosch, Cape Town.

I stand blinking, staring: our red-hot sun, dragged down by invisible forces, is about to vanish behind the mountain. 'Not long now', I tell myself, 'breathe in!' And then it happens: that disturbing moment, irrevocable, each time: a kind of dying. As one breathes out the warming red-gold glow lingers and consoles, but only for a while. Another day gone, and such a busy one! Now comes the dark night...seductive, with all its stars.

It helps to hunch one's shoulders, press both arms around one's back, stretch, twist and turn one's hands.... bliss, that's better! My weary eyes trace the expanse of lawn, now immersed in soothing shade: that gentle slope around the ancient oak...and yes, here they come again, the flock of Ibis, frantically pecking at insects and worms in the grass before it gets too dark. With ferocious squawks they crowd in each day at the same time, to strut about under our remarkable tree, at least three centuries old. Acorns, vines, these are just some of the clever things brought here from Europe hundreds of years ago...and this house was *her* place, home of the mysterious

Finuala. *She* will have seen the view often enough, stood on this very spot, perhaps, watched the dying shadows, for at least one third of this century.'

'Stop scratching splinters and paint from the peeling window frame,' I tell myself, while making a mental note of a broken catch: another one of these *real* things I'm supposed to be taking care of. Again and again my thoughts turn to *her*, this woman, who, less than a year ago, apparently flourishing, was felled by a pain in her back...neglected for a while, perhaps? Mercifully, almost before she could take it in, she lay in a hospital bed dying of cancer.

Why do I say 'mercifully'? I search my soul but find no ready answer, other than wishing her suffering to have been brief. And now, each day, as I delve into her past, still knowing very little, that is to say, almost nothing, her spirit makes its presence felt, haunts me.

Is this to be expected? Am I going crazy? Strange, it was her husband's bright idea he and I might clear the house together. Now it seems to have become more and more *my* task. 'Tidy it all up...of course, why not,' was my breezy reply at the time. Only later, too late, I re-considered my options. Now, greatly absorbed by this so-called task, I must admit I also feel increasingly uneasy... in all honesty... well, I'm no longer so sure. One-hundred year old houses are thought to be venerable, possibly full of ghosts, not only here in Cape Town. It might be wise to consult the great co-ordinator in whom good Christians are taught to believe, even better, a shrink, come to that...but let me say this: if Finuala were still around I would certainly not be here, now, anno Domini 1994, doing what I am, in *this* house, *her* home. Things, all manner of things, creep up on one. That's all. But I've been side-tracked...it's getting dark: I really should go in now.

'She had taste,' I must admit: 'curtains, rugs, pictures and classy pottery, that large leather sofa, battered but stylish, even her strange name: so many of her things please me. I share her tastes...and, above all, I have become fond of her husband, Julian. He appears to reciprocate my feelings. Would she have minded? Silly question! Last weekend, on a particularly scorching day, he was vain enough to pose for me naked, stretched out on his venerable old sofa. All I was trying to prove was I had talents similar to another artistic lady-friend of his. I trust he's taken my point. I plan to do more work on the sketch; it's quite good really. And now, here he is, perpetuated on my sketch pad, a man of sixty-five, with a body reminiscent of those ancient Greek sculptures in a vast echoing hall of the British Museum in London. I did, but only once, have the pleasure of wandering about in that venerable place, with ample time to examine such treasures, the kind one has no chance of seeing down here, on this southern tip of Africa.

Like many newly widowed men, ('ancient treasures'…unkind voices might say, after all Finuala has been dead for two years), he has a following of admiring single ladies of uncertain age… making a bid for him with caring meals and other entertainments I try not to think about, but cannot help imagining. Tall, enlivening and intelligent, good-looking despite his thinning white hair, his phone never stops ringing. The man is plainly in demand.

'My wife,' he informs, 'lavished much love on numerous cats; she adored them.' The last remaining one climbs on his lap, settles her paws on his shoulder, carefully, thoughtfully, then stretches her elegant body lovingly against his chest to claw his sweater. She purrs gratefully. I was wondering why all his sweaters are shredded at the top. She is the only one remaining: a pedigreed chocolate-coloured Siamese, spindly, aristocratic, talkative, seemingly starved, and occasionally, (selectively), overwhelmingly affectionate. I do value her company but *she* knows best, refuses to get used to me.

More than unacceptable are dried-up remains of cat-sick, cat hair, droppings of cats, under beds, behind furniture, where no-one has ever cleaned properly. Why did the elderly servant neither see nor smell these accidents? She needed better spectacles, perhaps? Finuala's only sister, Ailsa, who hurried down from Pretoria to spend painful final days with her sibling, to comfort, to reminisce and read to her, was so exasperated by the maid that she sacked her: the sullen coloured woman was paid off, sent away, told not to come back. 'The master no longer wants you here,' was the expedient explanation. I'm relieved this awkward moment was before my time. So far there's been no replacement.... unless of course, *I* count as one? Well, 'let's not go there', as people say nowadays.

Thank goodness Ailsa has already removed the deceased's clothes: the sisters shared the same build. Now it's me who is in charge: to tidy up this place, make it saleable. I am to bring in a professional cleaner, we've already hired some workmen, a painter and a carpenter. There *is* a budget...'

...'still, it keeps coming back to me: how Julian's wife would have hated all this: above all me, for disposing of *her* things, and also for being alive and taking care of her man,... not least for finding him attractive. What are my motives? I'm not sure. From time to time I remind myself I am merely trying to help. In one way, no, in every way it's none of my business and, thanks be to God, the woman is not here to pass judgement. Increasingly it becomes difficult not to get involved. A 'little voice' constantly reminds me to tread warily.

Finuala, her grieving children, that forlorn Siamese,... I now know a lot more about them all. Three daughters, having been and gone, seem to tolerate my presence with wry, polite smiles. I suspect they must be grateful I look after their father so they can get on with their own busy lives without too much disruption. I've pressed them to take away anything they value and they have done so, rather half-heartedly, I thought. It appears their mother was a fine cook, a wonderful gardener and also a talented photographer, as I see from dramatic and professionally framed photographs of harbours and plants. There remains a library of her 'latest' cookery books, going back into the mists of time, also shelves piled high with other worn books, ancient editions; this family plainly loves reading. *My* top favourite cache of reading material is to be found lined up on the floor of the upstairs toilet: twelve cloth-bound volumes of Harmsworth's Universal Encyclopedia, printed in London, England, soon one hundred years ago; someone must have shipped them all down here to the Southern hemisphere at great expense.

'They were my father's,' Julian informs, grinning from ear to ear, adding: 'they have made me what I am.'

'Strange,' I cannot help thinking from time to time, 'this man, so solidly in control, he shows no particular signs of mourning. He is either hard of heart or an expert in stoicism...'

I take things slowly, day by day, room by room. Ailsa, also Finuala's children, have removed most clothes; like an ant I 'trek' down the hill heaving further bags of unwanted things to Charity shops. Sometimes I use the car.

Poor woman, what a hoarder! To think we all leave behind a trail of belongings, objects which betray not only our joys, but also our secrets and our pain, all that ever mattered to us. There are things here no-one wants, not even her daughters; she was plainly incapable of throwing anything away. My own mother was just like that. Perhaps I am too.

It happens almost every day: I open drawers, or lift a flap-- and welling forth come letters, bills, ancient postcards, photographs, old drawings, scribbles done by the children, or missives written twenty years, thirty, even forty, fifty years ago. Interesting: I find a cache of love-letters, from some man, no, several men, all dead one presumes, but also hundreds of letters written by Julian to her, along with her replies in the late 1940's early 5o's. No doubt there is more to unearth in this parallel world around me; I would like to interpret the mysterious imprints left behind by my unknown predecessor.

I feel eyes, *her* eyes, Finuala's that is, boring into me. *What a shame I don't write: all this might make an interesting read.* Of course Julian knows about those letters. Eyebrows up he shrugged when I mentioned them. A few moments later he decided he'd better hang on to them, to give to 'the children'.

'Really' I asked, 'to your daughters? Are you quite sure?' 'Yes, why not,' he nodded, looking vague, unperturbed. 'Mmm,' he murmured a few seconds later, lips pressed together. Then: 'oh,...just put them in that *secret* drawer, masses of space, over there, under the mahogany table', pointing to a surface piled high with files, bills, papers, and offering no further explanation. I did not press him.

Most of us cultivate the opposite way: throw things out. Later we wish we hadn't. Either method can bring troubling results, I imagine. For now my brief is to smarten up this neglected home, soon one hundred years old and certainly in need of a make-over. Encouraged by Julian's confidence in my talents I make one bold decision after another. Under this very roof the lives and feelings of people I am gradually getting to know are being disturbed and studied, not to mention these objects which must have given them solace and pleasure over many years.

***

Now, in 1995, my new friend, lover, fanatical amateur pianist but scientist by training, reveals he wants to move, back to Europe, to the countryside, to live in a commune. I do believe Julian is just pretending to be a hippy at heart. I should add *I very much hope* he's pretending.

This was how *we* met: Having listened to each other perform at a mutual friend's house-concert we began to exchange (reasonably) polite remarks about each other's performances. I too aspire to know about music, enjoy baroque composers mostly and play the viol, with modest enthusiasm, but these days, only when pressed. This topic was soon exhausted. Besides, we barely knew each other, did not dare to say what we really thought. Changing the subject he mentioned he was hoping to sell his house, make a new life, go abroad and start afresh.

'Quite understandable', I replied. I did not know then that he'd already shared this dream with one of his numerous mistresses, the one who now gives me the evil eye every time we happen to find ourselves in the same room. (We belong to a club. I currently avoid going there as best I can.) Yes, mistresses, plural... he's quite unabashed by this, as if it were his rightful due to have a flock of them. This particular woman was, allegedly, part of his scenario for over two decades during the latter part of his marriage. They'd been 'an item' for that long! Some cataclysmic row now shattered former closeness. You'd think, after the death of a wife the moment for starting a new life with such a long-time lover had finally arrived. But no…it seemed to be 'all over.' He now relished his freedom, he told me. In the meantime poor Finuala's spirit hovers in every nook and cranny as far as I'm concerned.

A shame really, to sell this place! I think the house is lovely, a real home. Perhaps I can change his mind. What with Mandela and the big elections and everything changing here, this is an exciting and interesting time in South Africa. The world is watching. All Julian needs is a reliable maid, or a good house-keeper (like myself?), although, to be honest, I'm not sure about those other entanglements of his.

It is dark now. Tomorrow I continue with all this. I must rip out my oversensitive antennae and harden my heart for another day's revelations and hard work.

This is what I've gathered so far: Finuala was a small woman, but fat, apparently…'gone to seed' in later years. At first she'd been a gamine, sylph-like creature, delicate bait to every male she came in contact with. In her younger days men were drawn to her, moths to a flame…

Most beings have two existences, one for themselves and another for the eyes of onlookers. Finuala seemed, from the first, to have been unusually aware of her image. She did not wish to be conventional, ordinary. There is a snapshot of her, years ago, her hands in snow-white gloves at a school garden party. Surely no-one but the Queen of England would wear white gloves on such an occasion. White signals many things, not only fastidiousness but also spotless innocence, perfection, purity and possibly immaculate hands. Perhaps she liked being 'posh'? Carefully posed she is also seen seated by the edge of a fountain outside an ancient Cape Wine Farm, to remind the viewer that she was a 'cut above' ordinary passers-by, possibly to make one assume it was her ancestral home. Perhaps she did not care to be thought 'ordinary'. Her background? Modest, I'm told; parents came as penniless immigrants to South Africa a decade before the last World War...an Irish Catholic mother and a hardworking non-conformist father from the north of England. With self-discipline and sound business sense he started a firm supplying tyres to all manner of vehicles from a humble tin-roof workshop employing white and coloured workers on the outskirts of... Plumstead, I think, yes, that's what Julian told me. Exempt from the war effort on account of a bad chest and poor eyesight the father and his firm went from strength to strength.

Unlike her father Finuala had 'an eye,' she became excellently skilful with her camera. I know very little: in later years she travelled in Europe...Framed pictures of exotic harbours and foreign looking towns, all her work; some of these hang on the walls. Today I make a start on the disused, out-moded bathroom downstairs. It is the place of a mostly smelly cat-box.

Ye Gods! I must fight my way through floating tangles of cobwebs, dead bugs, peeling paint, dust, rusty tools, old newspapers, boxes of Christmas decorations, a grandiose mess of discarded objects, piled up in a scaly, rusty, claw-footed bathtub. Behind the cracked no-longer-in- use lavatory from another era I fish out a necklace, then realise ...no, hold on, this is no necklace: it's a rosary, partly tucked under a crumbling skirting board. A rosary! How did it get there? Finuala must have been a Catholic! I shiver, but feel an immediate bond: I know about such things, having lost all trace of *my* own rosary a life-time ago. A good convent girl then, perhaps, just as I once was. I never could throw away Holy Cards, or my rather worn missal: judging from *its* tattered condition I must have prayed long and hard.

Later, after clearing away all this, I sort out the tiniest room upstairs. At the end of a long corridor it offers a view straight into the crown of an unbelievably magnificent old oak. This, Finuala's study, I consider the inner sanctum. Here it is now. With barely enough room to stand up in I've just scraped my leg on the rusty metal-framed bed; the scratch bleeds. I press my handkerchief against it, emit a deep puff of held-in breath, sigh, frown... an ominous start, I've probably been poisoned. By the window stands a desk, on it an ancient Olivetti; files, slides, boxes and a well-used Missal are right at the back of a deep drawer, I almost missed it, stuck at the back, in the dark. Inside the prayer book I find a much folded letter, tucked into the back pages. Hm,....might as well get myself a cup of tea, nurse my wound while I take a look at it; a love-letter I guess, because it ends: 'I love you unbearably,' and is signed with a flourish, *'Julian.'*

Irresistible...may the Good Lord forgive me. To hell with tea! Guiltily I settle down to peruse it. And the date of this missive: *April 1948*...goodness, forty years ago!

*Darling, I am desperately lonely for lack of you.* (Should I really be reading this?) *My mind conjures up the most fantastic schemes so that we could be together. In books people don't seem to be at all tied down by the sort of things that deter us. If I was to leave home, throw up the university and live with you (under the aegis of the common law) meanwhile working in a coal mine or something… the world wouldn't come to an end. It seems fantastic to think of things like that, but I don't see why it should be. In fact, to cut loose from the conventions that twine around one's childhood is probably the best way of growing up. As I am so weak and incompetent a creature I haven't sufficient courage to take bold steps like that,* (bless him, how old was Julian then? About nineteen, nearly twenty, I imagine) *I am not working hard, only thinking of the next weekend… those two days, even if we are together every minute, is a pitifully short time. Since those two nights –I make no excuses- I have been obsessed by you. It is customary to regard physical love as, though eminently desirable, a rather inferior brand, not to be spoken of too eagerly. Well, where you are concerned I shall speak of it openly, frankly and unceasingly… and in case you are afraid that my intentions are not 'honourable' I only need to explain that there is obviously no question of the physical aspect being exclusive in my love for you. I feel in the sort of mood where I want to keep incessantly on all the glories both experienced and yet remaining- this is of course what led to the ugly stuff I wrote once before.*

One does feel a little guilty reading this. Still, no point stopping now…

*Then the circumstances were different- the ugliness due to incompetence and the fact that -comparatively, I hardly knew you. Now I try to describe how it was…as much for your benefit as for mine… because, when I write about it knowing that only you will read it, I feel closer to you:*

*I lay awake for hours - The housekeeper went to bed, all noise eventually ceased. Midnight. I must wait, longer yet, wait till they're all asleep. Now, at last, surely… The bed creaks. Another move- the bed protests horribly- one foot on the floor tangled up with shoes-careful, careful! At last, a patch of floor to put a foot on… the supreme effort of swinging myself out of bed. The bed makes a final complaint and I'm standing shivering in the darkness.*

*I put out a hand to feel for the door. The one place I must not touch is the latch. A horrible metallic rattle shatters the silence. I wait again, frozen with fear, and all the time the pounding excitement-what will you do? Finally: movement again. My door opens silently. I ease myself out, the floorboards creak …now your door, I touch it - gentle pressure - and a crack like a whip. I wait for the adjacent sleepers to drop off again. The only way to open the door must be to push hard and make one noise only. Infinite courage summoned up only by thoughts of you. The door is open, I stand inside the room, fear is forgotten. About to move when: 'who's that?' (Your voice, terrifyingly loud.) I whisper: 'It's me.' I hear you sit up. I reach out to touch you. Now, the moment of all…perfume, softness…terrified and excited, I hardly dare to breathe. I draw you to me and it is you I touch, not a vast amount of base clothing. I can't go any further- it becomes unbearable to think of it, yet I would much rather be thinking of it than not. I am impatient, darling and perhaps also very irritating? I will stop before being driven insane.*

*I love you unbearably, Julian.*

Well now! Small wonder she kept his letter, lengthy as it is, almost a short story. How well he expressed his tortuous feelings. Where were they spending the night?  One tries to imagine such bliss when they eventually got married, half a century ago.

Why was this letter in her prayer-book? Only a stony-hearted person would not give it some place of honour,…but in a liturgical book of worship? And then, why not, what more honourable place could there be? High time to return to my sorting, sifting, siphoning away of Finuala's things. My snooping soul, even more my fingers, have begun to feel dusty. I look around: the room I'm in is barely large enough for one frugal bed. More cat turds and vomit, solidly dried to this dusty carpet under the bed. I shudder. Everything must go, as quickly as possible. I remember, not that long ago, spending half the night in here, having decamped from Julian's bed, to his great irritation. It takes time to become used to sleeping by the side of a new body, one which makes noises and leads an independent life in its own world of dreams and feelings. I did soon flee back into his arms; the small room was so very uninviting. 'Maroon and gold wall paper, the peeling window frames, the smell, cobwebs,' was all I can think now...

I examine a dusty, ancient box camera, a Leica, and other less classy cameras, ancient and modern family photos, negatives, boxes of papers, impressive numbers of further old letters spilling from crumbling boxes and folders, collections of slides, stored for a considerable time, everything falling apart, forgotten, dusty and joyless... Julian must tell me what he wants done with all this. With a flourish I pull open the door of a tall built-in wardrobe, for inspection. What is this? My eyes dart from one thing to another. I will need a 'bakkie', at least!

Dirty socks, crumbling, flaky, powdery... mud still clinging to crumpled worn football boots; also a large box of seashells, nothing special, just ordinary shells, a few candles, candle-wax...matches. With the bin-liner ready I sweep it all into a bag, (....visions of using shells decoratively somewhere in the garden?) yes, no...not sure, keep the shells, also old socks, tattered children's books, I barely look ...just scoop it all away, into the bag. Why would anyone want such filthy old boots? 'Everything must go'...still my mantra, as quickly as possible, I tell myself: 'first thing in the morning'.

Days later came the revelation: that very wardrobe had been Finuala's 'shrine,' her own secret place in a room where she could do her work and also think about her son, Jon, the child who had died ..., something to do with the dosage of a prescription drug.

'Those boots were his,' Finuala's eldest daughter Vikky stated, with a worried frown, some days later. From the expression on her face I could almost read her thoughts, confused how to handle this situation. She mentioned she might have liked to take those very football boots to give to *her* own son...had she known.

Oh God. I did try, I really did, believe me... to retrieve them.

Too late: even the charity shop had thrown them out. They'd been binned, cast out, taken away. I wished the ground beneath my feet would swallow me up.   Why wasn't I more sensitive?  Mortifying...  what an oaf, what a bungler.... would I *ever* be forgiven?'

Now, as I leaf through Finuala's worn prayer-book, wondering in the back of my mind what Vikki and the other daughters were finding to say about me, my eyes fall on these words:

### Judge me, my God...

# One
## Rondebosch, **1946.**

'**F**in! Come *on*, we're late ...*and* I've been made to remove my nail varnish, can you believe it! Mummy disapproves, yet again, even though I am sixteen! Any one might think God would judge me. As if he cared. Besides, it's 1946, not the Middle Ages. We're almost half-way through the twentieth century!' Ailsa, grumpy, grumbling, not properly awake, stands on the veranda clutching her missal in one hand, also, draped over the other arm, a black lace shawl. This will cover her wild, curly brown hair during the service. Good Catholic girls are expected to conceal their heads in Church.

She growls through the half-opened window behind her: 'Mass starts at eight, as you well know, do get a move on. Honestly! Why is it always me who is ready while you stare at the mirror re-arranging your hat... *come on,* Fin-u-a-la. Do- me- a -favour! Even if we walk double speed we'll be late again. I can't bear it.' Then softly: 'God, you're so fussy... ever since you finished school, started at Secretarial College.

Hurry up, Mummy's in the kitchen, waiting, and her face like a thunderstorm.' The younger sister turns away, displaying a brow well furrowed for her age, frowning, groaning and sighing. Biting her lower lip, she shifts about, swings one foot backwards and forwards like an irritable, wild beast ready to attack.

Mrs. Goodkin, long-suffering but patient, *and* her daughters, usually did manage to get to Mass on Sundays, even if it was occasionally only after the *Introit*, or worse, the *Collect*. Death or deadly disease would be the only reason for completely missing the service. Wearing sensible shoes and keeping their heads down they, all three of them, were soon trotting briskly down-hill, crossing over, turning left on Main Road. Trying to get back on the right side of her bristling offspring Mama jollied them along with her best Irish accent: 'come now, my darlings, isn't this just a wonderful fresh, birds-chattering, radiant summer's day... only in winter or when it's really pouring, can we persuade our nonconformist *Daddy* to drive us... still, it's only fair, don't you agree: he likes to stay in bed on Sunday mornings, to have some peace. We three must stick together, do the praying for this family... keep on the right side! Just like the other good Catholics in Ireland and in England!' Would she ever stop missing her relatives? For a long time both daughters had been aware of their mother's homesickness, but also how *she* hoped to see *them*: her two obedient, old- fashioned, hoping-to - please convent-girls.

Now, 'almost there, girls', the entrance to the President's Garden and first right turn into Rouwkoop Road: there it stands, St. Michaels, patiently waiting: *their* rugged stone church (in the English style), with colourful tall stained glass windows...built about the same time as their own house, allegedly. And the Lisbeek River, rippling gently, sparkling in the sun, soothed all passersby, while trains to southern suburbs puffed along gently, like giant caterpillars, in the distance.

'Strange, isn't it ,'Ailsa, shorter than her sister, looked up, also trying to restore peace, 'imagining our aunts and cousins, way up north, up and up and round the top of the globe, bobbing off to church, just as we are. There they are, wearing furry coats, in blackest, darkest winter, lucky them, with snowflakes even, and ice to skate on. I'd give anything to see snow, have a 'white' Christmas just once.

I don't suppose we'll ever go, it is such a long way and Daddy hasn't got enough money. *Perhaps- one day,* is what he says. Still, there are quite a few Irish people here, in our own Rondebosch parish.'

Finuala looked back, craned her long neck, searching for someone. 'Stop looking around, Fin,' teased the younger sister. '*He*'s not even out of bed yet, besides *he* doesn't go to our church, you would have noticed him by now. I know who she is looking out for...Mummy, our Fin, she's fallen in love!'

'Come now, Ailsa, even if it were true it's none of our business. Stop annoying your sister', and, 'ignore her, Fin....' But then, after a pause, 'have you really? Fallen in love? At your age I *collected* admirers, lots of them: it's completely normal.' The older sister raised her eyebrows, refusing to join in such demeaning conversation and overwhelmed by the Sunday-morning effort to get to Mass the sisters remained, as ever, cantankerous.

They were not remotely late. Inside the dark, cool, stone church they resumed customary ways developed over years and years of Sundays: squeeze into a bench, preferably near the back, a few rows in front of the coloured people, then, with pious expressions which disguised the study of 'ridiculous hats'... a quick  flip through the Missal depending on just how early or bored they were: 'See this, Fin, the feast of St. Felix, priest and martyr, a holy man who died in 312,' Ailsa would whisper,...'look, seven other St. Felix's , should you be trying to pass the time, here's one who earned the title of martyr, although he did survive the cruel torments he underwent'....

How many times, eyes narrowed, had this mother leaned towards her girls and hissed: 'pull yourselves together now, show respect! I'm ashamed of you both!' Only then they'd move away from each other. 'What *is* happening to them', the mother wondered, 'they may be pretty, even intelligent, but somehow young girls, these days, they're so independent, so rebellious. Dear God!'

It did all seem so trying.

The choir, in the background, comically abysmal, was again near collapse, as usual....but the congregation was quite used to this.

𝕴𝖓𝖈𝖑𝖎𝖓𝖊 𝖙𝖍𝖎𝖓𝖊 𝖊𝖆𝖗 𝖙𝖔 𝖔𝖚𝖗 𝖕𝖗𝖆𝖞𝖊𝖗𝖘, 𝖜𝖊 𝖇𝖊𝖘𝖊𝖊𝖈𝖍 𝖙𝖍𝖊𝖊, 𝕺 𝕷𝖔𝖗𝖉... heard the parishioners. Finuala, a student of Latin, was always intrigued by the liturgy. *𝕴𝖓𝖙𝖗𝖔𝖎𝖙𝖚𝖘,* she read and *𝕱𝖑𝖊𝖈𝖙𝖆𝖒𝖚𝖘 𝖌𝖊𝖓𝖚𝖆, 𝕭𝖊𝖓𝖊𝖉𝖎𝖈𝖙𝖆 𝖙𝖚, 𝖎𝖓 𝖒𝖚𝖑𝖎𝖊𝖗𝖎𝖇𝖚𝖘...*and *𝕰𝖈𝖈𝖊 𝖇𝖎𝖗𝖌𝖔* *concípiet.* Translations provided were absorbed, imprinted in her mind. For years, ever since she was able to read, this had been her best pastime during Mass: guessing the meaning of those mysterious words. '*Virgo concípiet,* yes, she'd worked that one out....the chanted sounds and phrases had soaked in over the years, were now absorbed and part of her being. She felt like a member of a secret club. The sermon dragged on, as sermons do. The last words: '...and the Holy Ghost flows forth from the Word, bearing us all to the Father on the waves of his divine love', seeped into Finuala's mind, then out again. Kneeling, benumbed, passive, in a trance-like state, she was re-awakened by observing her wide-hipped mother easing herself out of the pew along with Ailsa, both now lined up with other church-goers to take Communion. They cast concerned glances at their Finuala, now so obviously abandoned...

'My sister looks back to see if I am coming too. I'm not. Now she and Mother wonder what radical failure there is in my virtue... not taking Communion.' She imagined her mother's thoughts: 'Fin, the *sinful* one, who is growing up so fast, who will not go to the priest, kneel down, open her mouth to have the 'body of Christ' placed on her tongue. What *is* happening to our Fin?'

Finuala sighed, her hands folded together in resigned contemplation. The truth was: she'd not been to confession for ages, certainly not since she left school. 'When did this start,...on my seventeenth birthday?' She re-lived the last time she'd knelt in that confessional, in the darkest corner of the church..... 'forgive me, Father, for I have sinned', that's how one gets the 'ball rolling', and then one reveals everything absolutely, minutely, while feeling contrite: things like 'I lied to my mother/teacher/sister' or 'I stole my sister's chocolate bar,' or 'I had unclean thoughts,' or whatever guilt-provoking offences came to mind. She sighed. 'I've just gone off all that. Nothing bad happens if one refuses... no, no more Confession for me. I've not been evil. Just a few rebellious thoughts... and besides, kneeling by a confessional, inside it a man, a priest, his ear glued to a tiny window covered with mesh, straining to hear, probably even recognising each sinner, God forbid: how embarrassing, just being there! How much do priests see through that mesh while we, poor sinners, make a clean breast of our grievous sins, or of...shall one say, rebellious thoughts?' Even thoughts can be sins…. the Church has rules for every moment of life. Priests could jump out from behind their confessionals and persuade you to come for instruction, to release all that pent-up guilt….'

Suddenly, Mass was over. The Parish priest prayed for those who had lost loved ones in the War while someone's unhappy baby, at first only complaining on and off, now screamed at full volume. Unperturbed, a calm beacon of sanctity in splendid white robes, the smiling 'Holy Father' turned to face his congregation, and, seemingly taking in each and every parishioner, calmly forgave and blessed all, believers and doubters, good and evil. What a splendid man. What was he really like, behind all that regalia?

One would never know.

Freed from confinement in dark pews, possibly even from sin and guilt, the congregation streamed out like shoals of gleaming fish, strengthened and cleansed, eyes blinking in that blinding Cape sunshine. Out in the refreshing sea air parishioners liked to stand for a while, to chat with others.

'This venerable oak… just like the one in our garden,' dreams Finuala, 'so old, so strong. When was it planted? According to our teacher, Van

Riebeeck brought oaks from Europe when he first came to the Cape....well, just the acorns probably.' Gathering under a separate tree, smaller and less shady, coloured parishioners stand apart, also chatting cheerfully among themselves. An elderly man, wearing shabby clothes, has unpacked a banjo, and now, crouching on the ground in the shade of another tree, he begins strumming, humming, mostly jazzy tunes. 'Clink, clink-clink,' occasional coins ring out as they drop into a tin in his up-turned straw hat. Black parishioners keep to themselves a little further away. There are very few of them. Everyone knows their place.

Mother and daughters have come to a halt by a Plumbago hedge. Behind them, in the near distance, loom over-powering, craggy, grey, mountain rocks. Soft morning air, suffused by gentle strains from the banjo, confidences, small-talk, queries: 'how are you,' 'have you heard of,' 'lovely to see you again' or 'back from your holidays', relaxed exchanges flutter gently like drunken moths, from group to group, everyone in their Sunday best looking forward to a day under clear skies; picnics, tennis, or a swim in Muizenberg, the Brighton of South Africa. Well yes, there might be sharks, but life in the Cape could be, usually was, heaven; and one had learned to be careful, even of those not so comical baboons near Cape Point, the most southern tip of Africa..... 'We are having one of our 'braais' in the garden, Mrs. Goodkin...you know where to find us, bring your husband, your lovely daughters?

*Do* come early, before sun-set, *do* have a swim!'

She nodded, 'why yes, how kind...'and overheard Ailsa whispering: 'good-eee, we're going out, to those nice people with their fantastic garden around the mountain stream, what shall we wear, Fin?' Already a stylish young female, she blinked at the radiant sky imagining the contents of her wardrobe. Both sisters owned the latest fashion, those wide skirts, well below the knee, under them, voluminous frothy nylon petticoats, worn with a crisp blouse, and a tightly belted waist. One had to be lavish with the lipstick- that was 'the New Look'.....the very latest thing.

'Don't know yet,' Finuala pretended to be blasé. She shrugged, and, hating herself, turned away...to stare at the grinning banjo player.

So, sanctified for another week, stimulated by social intercourse and, on account of this pleasing prospect, at last reconciled with one another, Mrs. Goodkin and her daughters set off in the direction of home, looked left, looked right and crossed the road. It was getting to be warm. Sunday was the day the coloured maid went to her own small house in District Six: therefore it was the day when daughters help in the kitchen. Tonight however, glory-be-, they'd be let off.

*** 

Mr. and Mrs. Goodkin had long been relieved to forget the social distancing which was once part of their earlier lives in the north of England. Here, on the other side of the globe, 'Europeans' stuck together, feeling they were all much the same, although there was increasing unease with coloured and black people who lived separate lives, mostly in conditions imposed by poverty, lack of education, but rooted in their own traditions going back for centuries. Whites, both Boers and Brits, and other nationalities invading and adopting this gorgeous land, generally stuck to their own rituals. Relaxing in exotic, scented gardens... around open-air fires roasting deliciously spiced meat, to be devoured around sunset, washed down with local beer, or wines....

such customs did, on the whole, belong to everyone. Of course there were white people who recognised the misery of the townships, the extreme poverty, but such truths, hidden behind South African life in the fifties, were not discussed all that often.

Having lived in the Cape long enough to join in pleasurable events: that uniquely South African, mouth-watering, out-door way of being together, the Goodkin family was learning to socialize in the knowledge that one must retaliate, throw similar parties, in all likelihood with a 'braai-vleis'. As for uneasy and divisive politics, well, 'so far, so good. Only time will tell, when Coloureds and black people become more educated, one day, when they get enough work.'

In most white circles this was about as far as discussions went.

*

On *this* Sunday evening, gazing at those grey 'backs' of the Twelve Apostles, looming large and dark after the sun set behind them, (the burning orb drops into the ocean on the other side, glowing red and gold, unforgettable, awesome), friends relaxed, enjoyed their wine, 'gesels-ing,' as one says if one assumes Afrikaaner ways, with fellow parishioners and other guests. A few lanterns had been lit.

With her passion for exploring the meaning of words, Finuala had, this evening, chosen *gesels* to be one of them: 'if one removes the *S* at the end it means a companion, and changing the stress (from the back of her throat came an explosive guttural *ggggh*) 'gésel'... becomes a scourge or a whip.   Strange, Mynheer, don't you agree?' Turning to an Afrikaans-speaking gentleman sitting by her side she'd plucked up courage to share this newly won insight: 'How curious language is! A slight change of emphasis alters ones understanding to gesels, to chat... which we are doing right now. Could this be a significant thought, Mynheer,' she asked, cautiously assuming maidenly modesty.

The man stared ahead, and then up at the mountain, after that, frowning briefly, doubtfully, at the young girl by his side, he attempted a wry smile. Munching dumbly, rhythmically, he nodded but said nothing. Had the penny dropped? No, it was all too much for him. Finuala's flickering flame of linguistic talent, her brave attempt at conversation had gone no-where. He swallowed, gulped, examined his empty glass, and nodding glumly left and right he fled, shuffling off in the direction of the bar.

'I've bored him. I'm no good talking to strangers. Especially not old fogies like that one,' Finuala whispered in her sister's ear. Ailsa, eyes closed, nodded vigorously. The girls sat in silence.

'A few, or even one misplaced word can completely mess up everything. Social life is so embarrassing... one never knows what to say.' Scraps of past conversations and misunderstandings drifted about in Finuala's head. Her thoughts returned to the vast rock-formations, the 'Apostles', were there really twelve? That mountain range she'd been gazing at, trance-like, since her failed linguistic attempt... 'it continues along the coast behind Table Mountain...and poor me, chained down here, in Rondebosch, unable to get to the other side, so I will never witness the end of the sun's trajectory, how it dips into the sea. On *our* side blackest night covers everything much sooner... but then, to console us, out come the stars, followed by (ruining everything,) crawling 'goggas' and mosquitoes beginning *their* own hungry search: namely us poor humans as we chew delicious Karroo lamb, beef and boere-wors...and then the blood-sucking insects go into action...beasts chew us, humans chew beasts.' Ailsa, by her sister's side, also gloomily silent, suddenly leaned forward  and whispered: 'Fin: quick, look, over there, that pianist boy you liked so much, by the entrance, isn't that the one, remember, him, and his brothers, those short boys, not as handsome, shy and sort-of, I don't know, out-of place? Shame: they don't even seem to have a car? Wonder what *they're* doing here, they don't go to our church, do they?' Eyebrows up, Ailsa studied her older sister: 'I suppose you still fancy him? Say something!'

Finuala has reached breaking-point. She can no longer bear her sister near her, no, not for another moment. 'You do grind on and on about things,' she hissed, pretending to study an insect bite on her elbow. 'What's it got to do with you? Just go away. Get lost!'

Looking peeved the younger sister shrugged and wandered off. Finuala had to admit to herself: 'she's right of course, damn her, I've also spotted him now: and he *is* the spitting image of that French cartoonist's 'Lover,' handsome, shy-faced with slender hips, long legs, broad shoulders and big beautiful hands.... and, yes, we *did* hear him play the piano *and* he is brilliantly clever: a Rondebosch High School scholarship boy, even. He must have left school a year ago, ever since I've been slaving away at secretarial school.' She looked across the lawn to see her sister alone, her skinny arms, hugging herself, staring in front of her. But soon enough she returned, carrying a load of goodies piled on a huge plate, having seemingly forgotten all former quarrelling. She whispered 'thanks be to God, he's not wearing a ridiculous round black hat like that French cartoon-man who's permanently in love with small bosomy ladies'. Finuala, pained, put-upon, completely silenced, shook her head, gave her sister a weary frown, then turned away thinking: 'it's because of our shared room, and our shared books, that's the trouble; if only,...if only Ailsa would disappear.' Only two feet away, Ailsa sat, swinging her legs and munching one delicious pastry after another. Then, she reminded her sister how... 'absolutely ages ago, someone was looking for gifted pupils from schools in the Rondebosch area... to perform, many terms ago, remember? And *that* very boy,' nodding in his direction, 'was the one selected for that charity concert. Seeing and hearing him play just that once...silly old Fin, you've never forgotten him, have you? You liked him didn't you? Is it because you're a mere five foot? You've got 'a thing' about tall boys? It's only Mother Nature ensuring your babies will average out to a more normal height...surely you know you'd look ridiculous next to such a tall man? A midget, with short legs..... I suppose he's already at University. And you? You've been going to secretarial college forever...he probably has a University scholarship... he must be the same age as you. He'll not even look at you.' Ailsa, aware of having put her foot in it, studied her sister warily from the side.

'*His* name was Julian', Finuala remembered, eyes shut. 'I don't remember the surname,' she thought, 'but I'd give anything to stand next to him...hear his voice, just once, very quickly, but far away from this pesky sister of mine. I'd better stop this right now.' At this moment both girls heard their mother announce, in that own special resonant Irish voice, something about 'the olden days, when there used to be a horse-drawn omnibus on the Main Road,...it belonged to a Mr. Cutler.' How embarrassing! What was this, 'why is our mother doing this? How embarrassing!' Both girls, dismayed, embarrassed, instantly transported back to real... life wondered how their mother knew all this stuff... It must have been long before she came to Africa? Which books *had* she been reading?'

Strangers had turned to listen; 'is that so,'.... 'how interesting, quaint...' they remarked, as both girls, mortified, looked down at their shoes, while their mother aired this unexpected conversational gambit, (drawing attention to herself, and probably to them as well, *why was Mummy going on and on*? Look how red *her* face has become!)

'Valiantly,'... that so known and yet suddenly alien voice continued: 'in the cold Cape winter wind the faithful had to trudge through driving rain and mud to get across the Liesbeck River to our church.'

The girls concentrated on their feet, trying in vain to keep their minds on the slender, awkward, adorable Peynet look-alike...and indeed, Finuala had managed, in her mind, to slip away, go one step further: she no longer heard her mother's historical reminiscences.

Instead she saw a river: and now a picture of that 'lover', (Peynet..of course...the cartoonist's name), his famous 'Lover', winding up his fishing rod, as he stood fully-clothed, hat and starched high collar in flowing water, a river, wet up to his knees, having ensnared, with a hook, a pert lady in a tight-fitting top and a flouncy skirt….flowers on her hat. Dangling from the fishing line between them was a vast red heart….*my* red heart! 'He's winding up his fishing-line, red heart and all, while I'm looking on, helplessly ensnared, drawn to him…and now', back to reality, dreams Finuala, 'that's exactly it! That's what has happened to me. Why, I wonder? Here I am, hooked like a caught fish. That Julian over there would never in his life wear silly hats, nor high starched collars. What can I do, go over and talk to him? I'd blush and stammer, not really knowing how to begin. And now… there's another girl, sipping wine, making eyes at him.'

Stuck in her helpless reverie Finuala accepted the pain, that pleasing ache of passion, the inexplicable longing. Longing for what, exactly? She was not sure. Sitting quietly she thought about the 'handsome one' who *did* look across, once, but only vaguely, and oblivious, in her direction.

'I even still have to learn how to kiss,' she thought. 'Like French kisses; what on earth are those? I will ask Mummy.' Finuala applied lipstick to her mouth while sending an avalanche of jealous loathing across the well-groomed lawn in the direction of the intrusive rival, that 'other' girl.

'Remember the French cartoonist, the one who can't draw terribly well...' Ailsa's little girl voice piped up again, out of no-where, just to annoy her sister: 'well, I can draw better than him... Still', she added, drawing a deep breath, 'where could one get hold of more of those pictures he does? I sort of like them,' she nodded, hoping someone helpful had been listening. But no-one had the faintest idea what the sisters were on about...nor were they listening.

'Scary...my irritating sister reads my mind. There's no getting away from her', Finuala realised, wishing she were back at home. The sisters glared at each other, one sipping Coca Cola, the other a small glass of wine, both too shy to join the younger set, but also not quite ready for conversing with dull adults. Soon, occasionally gazing up at the starry sky, a flushed and animated Mrs. Goodkin shepherded her morose offspring to be driven home by the unusually affable head of the family.

'What a splendid evening' he told them: 'I've made several new contacts regarding the business,' Lethargic, drowsy, seemingly not remotely caring, vaguely dissatisfied, his family listened politely.

Soon back on safe ground, inside his gleaming Vauxhall, they had to hear it yet again: how things were going better than he'd ever believed possible...life in South Africa was a success,...apart from, well, a few strikes... and sporadic boycotts lately and those daily difficulties with the Afrikaans language, and of course, finding the 'right' sort of coloured or black men to work in his firm. He liked them to have at least Standard 5 and to speak some English. There weren't quite enough of those....

'Ag man, jy moet mos *learn* to praat soos ons Afrikaaners,' Mr. Goodkin recited to his wife. 'It's almost the only sentence I know! Good people, the *right* sort of Coloureds, the ones one can trust, that's what one must look for. I could do with evening classes, you know. Everyone, even you, *and* my daughters, you all laugh at me. Are you asleep back there, girls? But then,' he lowered his voice, 'I'm just too old for new tricks now: speaking Afrikaans, especially to customers...ridiculous! Our daughters, well, it's different for them, they've learnt all that at school; Fin is almost through secretarial college, she's already got the skills; this means she'll soon become useful working for the firm.

But Ailsa,...I suppose we must get her off to Art School, with all that talent of hers, a waste really because soon after there will be marriage and all that. A shame we have no sons; grand-sons perhaps, one day. Still... girls, expensive as they are, they're nice to look at. Fin's quite bright, I know, she'll be able to do anything.' Looking up into the rear view mirror he proudly observed his 'young ladies', seemingly fast asleep.

'...our Fin...such a smart girl, have you noticed how men stare at her? Even though she's so tiny; well, they both are. Do you think she might grow some more,' he turned his head, whispered to his wife, 'she *is* seventeen? My God, or is it eighteen?'

'Eighteen, dear, almost nineteen....do watch the road...it's so winding, so dark, are your lights up, you're making me nervous!' Mrs. Goodkin's hands were pressed together tightly. Tense and tired, she now tried to speak quietly, instructing her husband:

'Our Fin is an asset, learns all these awkward things, shorthand, typing, quite naturally, but really, I'd prefer you not saying, well, you know, about growing more, and men staring, things like that. She is, they are both innocent and in-experienced.' Her voice tailed off….

Mr. Goodkin, wise enough to accept he may have put his foot in it, admitted how proud he was of his little family and only too embarrassed and lazy and old and tired to get his head round learning Afrikaans. 'And the wine…'he nodded prudently, and went on nodding until the next traffic light, not quite remembering what he could say next.

'All I can do is pray and cook for everyone', offered Mrs. Goodkin. 'A troublesome thing it would be', she added, 'to have to lock up ones' daughters. Didn't we go to the theatre once, a play, with that very title? Not so long ago?'

'Of course, dear…' turning with a flourish into their driveway, 'you're right. You're always right. Best thing is *you* do the praying and locking-up and I'll get on with earning the money.' Then: 'wakey-wakey, girls', he called out resoundingly.

Hair mussed, clothes crumpled, his daughters yawned, eyes shut they stretched like languid cats and slid reluctantly towards and out of already opened car doors. The habitual superfluous message: '…everybody out now and straight to bed …' was, as always, countered by:

'we think you bumped into the gate-post, again, Dad.'

Best to pretend he'd not heard the demeaning truth, he told himself. Having to accept there was yet another small dent on the fender, was not pleasing to a man in the motor trade. He insisted that things, all manner of things, remained unblemished, un-spotted, undamaged, immaculate: cars, reputations, even daughters.

Stretching and straightening his back like an attentive meerkat in the Kalahari, paws draped over a portly stomach, he peered up and down the quiet road before cautiously bolting the gates to his property. No doubt it would not be too long before he'd have a choice of grandsons to continue his business ventures. They would be equipped with degrees and diplomas.

Future family members would, he hoped, become wise and practical and filled with multi-lingual expertise and learning.

# Two

𝕭rethren: What things soever were written, were written for our learning...' Mulling over these words, (she'd come across them this morning in church) Finuala stared before her. 'I'd like to be a writer,' she thought, 'I've kept a notebook of my thoughts for some time'. But, for the benefit of her sister, she muttered: 'If only there was more time, just for learning! Yes, that's it. That's what I love best: thinking, reading, talking to *intelligent* people, becoming wise. What about you then?' She gave her sister a challenging look. The girl was stretching her legs, sat idling about on the 'stoep', doing absolutely nothing but looking at the birds, while waiting for sunset and supper.

'Ora et labora.... less of the ora, more of the other, these should be ones favourite things. Reading, working, improving, yes, pondering, poring over words on paper, thoughts written by others, letters,  and, of course, poetry,' Fin continued, but now mostly to herself.

'God, you're weird', hissed Ailsa under her breath, with a pained look.

Fin was rarely, even never, without a book. Each week she extracted, distilled and absorbed a steady stream of literary lives and thoughts from the Library: Jane Austen, Charlotte Brontë, Dickens and Flaubert, even Gide... oh, many more....right up to the present. It seemed she remembered every detail of the intimate history of society, of relationships gone wrong, of irony and humour in past centuries from faraway countries, as well as absorbing comparative studies of society, of the social ladder, of men and property. She found herself totally involved in the lives of women, daughters, those who seemed to be first the property of fathers then eventually of husbands...and those obedient ones, who seemed to be destined to morph into dutiful wives. She suffered with them. 'What is one entitled to, what should one expect? Work in an office? Marriage? What exactly is a French Kiss? I still don't know. I'd have to do all the things Mummy does, and then a lot more. I wonder, is *she* a contented woman? Now that she is so nearly old? Like forty? I should ask her.'

'Dear God!' Ailsa groaned, as she observed her sister crumpling her forehead, making slitty eyes and muttering to herself: 'Having babies! I'd be a neglectful mother, or worse, an over-indulgent one. Horrible, horrible! To say nothing of cooking; I'm not at all sure about that! Still, there are always nannies and cooks. Why is being a woman so demanding, so complicated....'

Poised on the edges of their deckchairs, still warmed by the reflection of that setting sun on the glowing red-polished floor, both girls were once again distracted by the throng of ibis pecking at worms on the lawn; they always came around this time. These were tough birds, with large bodies, long necks and short legs... creatures that killed snakes with one deadly blow of their beaks. The sisters stared at the creatures stretching upwards, beating the air with wide wings; and as usual both of them had already blocked their ears against the shrill triumphant 'haa-haa-dee-da,' that penetrating, squawking racket as the beasts soared overhead, at least seven of them, all shrieking 'haa-haa-dee-daa' full-blast in cacophonous sequence. What power, what freedom! Night after night, this was what they did, without fail.

'They are monogamous, you know, someone once told me,' the older girl informed: 'sensible archaic animals... I suppose you know what that means? ' Then she bent forward, resting her elbows on her thighs as she supported her head in cupped hands...until, more or less in foetal position, she pondered again how unready and threatened she felt by the above mentioned possible states of her future self. How *Strait is the Gate*? She swallowed hard, remembering the complicated contents of that slim copy by Andre Gide, just returned to the Library. Had she understood it? It had not been an easy read...

'Relationships, marriages, surely all these known and accepted states could be made to work differently, more like temporary arrangements? So much is expected of us women. And of men! To get through life with some sort of happiness, what a balancing act it must be! *Offer it up to God* is what the nuns used to say. And now Daddy has decided I must stop going to Secretarial College, start work at once, in his office! Here I am, vaguely wondering whether I might perhaps be accepted at Cape Town University and he actually said to me: Fin, you're a clever one, I need you in the office'.

'Do you suppose he'll pay?' enquired Ailsa. Fin's eyebrows went up. Feeling the after-sunset chill, she frowned, she shrugged. *Finally* Ailsa understood why Fin was so exceptionally bad-tempered this evening.

\*\*\*

Cape Town, huddled against its famous mountain, had, for three centuries, been a place of vibrant, colourful life.

From dockworkers to Afghan mattress makers, from St. Helena prostitutes and German detectives to Chinese laundries, Indian shopkeepers and Scots policemen, to say nothing of Jewish traders and English soldiers... there was never been a dull moment in this untidy city. To live in such a large and active society could and should be a stimulating privilege.

For the poorer and ethically diverse as well as the more established middleclass there was always the 'Bioscope' culture, that cheap and popular entertainment from America and England, welcoming and influencing large audiences all over the world. Numerous Odeons and Curzons absorbed five to six thousand people daily while more up-market entertainments like the symphony orchestra were enjoyed in the Town Hall. Outside the Town Hall, on the Parade by the old Castle was the famed, fantastic Saturday market run almost exclusively by Coloured people...where shoppers were drowned in masses of colourful flowers, in beauty and scent, while being scorched by the sun and bitten to death by fleas.

The 'Labia' Theatre, opened recently by an eccentric Count bearing the same name, was a great asset, right by the famed Mount Nelson Hotel, the classiest hotel in town. This existed for the most illustrious and wealthy visitors, royalty, film stars or top politicians.

Whenever possible the Goodkin daughters got themselves taken out to see plays and films; they attended concerts in the Town Hall, or at the College of Music, not far from their home. During these times of the two young ladies' maturing, just a few years before the 'apartheid system' began to put a ferocious strangle-hold on much of Southern Africa, Cape Town was still alive with influences from all over the world. The Cape of Good Hope...yes, there always had been hope, but now there were new signs: WHITES ONLY-SLEGS BLANKES. Some things were changing! 'On benches, on buses, in the cinema, those signs, they're everywhere!' Did anyone foresee the tightened reality of Apartheid, soon to overwhelm the entire country, and how it would challenge and harden the hearts of its people?

\*\*\*

Shy, analytical, ambitious, and totally unpractical: a second year University scholarship student called Julian savoured, devoured, relished, occasional piano lessons at the College of Music: they were his lifeline to the miraculous world of virtuosity and splendour of great musicians of the past three centuries. Off he went, to every recital in the solemn, dark, stone building near the base of the hill on which the University stands; this was where he most loved to be.

At home, in his parent's modest house he practised on a 'honkey-tonk' upright piano while dreaming of becoming as proficient as his teacher, a disciplined performer and composer, who had taken him on. The honesty of this exceptional extramural student, the fact that the ambitious youngster admitted he had his hands full with a demanding course in the Physics Department...it was this which had both intrigued and touched the teacher.

*** 

A recital was scheduled in one of the larger rooms, just by the entrance: a location spacious enough for weekly University Symphony

Orchestra rehearsals. Vaguely jealous, Julian got goose-pimples just being there, in that hallowed place, as *he* saw it, even when there was no music to be heard at all. In the meantime Fate decreed this young man, but also an attractive young woman, were seated in adjacent rows, his seat just behind hers during a piano recital given by his own teacher.

Dressed like a flapper from twenty years earlier, she, who had picked up a leaflet for this evening's event in her local library, and who had been dropped off by her father, was now on her feet after the applause, peering around to see who else had come - and found herself face to face, no, eye to eye, with no other than that handsome boy, *the* handsome boy of her dreams, still quietly seated behind her. He looked up, and she, standing, stared straight into his blue eyes. Could this be Destiny?

Perfumed, painted lips parted, she blushed to the roots of her hair (trimmed to perfection just yesterday by the hairdresser), and breathed a maidenly 'oh, hallo.' After a short shy silence, looking at her feet, there was no stopping her: 'I'm Finuala and you,' she paused, taking a deep breath,'...I heard you performing at a schools concert, years ago... you played really well, beautifully, just like the pianist tonight. Your name was Julian.'

'God, he must think I'm dotty,' she feared... after this outburst.

'Why, thank-you', he managed unassumingly, but puzzled, inclining his head, and 'my name, believe it or not, is *still* Julian. Julian Conley.' He could not help grinning. Then, at a loss, embarrassed, he changed the subject. Nodding proudly in the direction of the pianist the said: 'tonight's performer is my teacher. After a short pause he added: '*he* plays a lot better than I do.'

She turned to examine the artist, a man with short legs who was invisible, surrounded by towering enthusiastic admirers. Julian, who had got to his feet, turned to the enchanting fellow-enthusiast by his side and enquired:

'Did his playing move you? Don't you think he's marvellous? And did you notice his left-hand technique during the Godowski? What did you like best?' His sky-blue eyes glowed with proprietorial delight, plainly overwhelmed by his very own admirable teacher but also by the fact he seemed to have a 'fan', a 'little girl', as he saw her, at this moment gazing up at him. She made him feel powerfully in control. He smiled, despite the fact he was rarely all that powerful, and even more rarely in control.  He studied the young woman's face, gallantly giving her time to formulate a reply.

'Oh.  Those Preludes,  I  think.'  Finuala's immaculately groomed head nodded uncertainly. She checked her programme: 'yes, Mr. Chopin's Preludes, they were definitely my favourite.'

As  someone  who  knew  nothing  about preludes or indeed any piano repertoire, she could barely believe this was happening. The young man was holding forth enthusiastically on the merits of Chopin and Godowski while Finuala fixed her eyes on him in silence thinking: 'Wait 'til I tell Ailsa...or Mummy. At last I've a chance to talk to him. Has he noticed my new haircut, lucky I went this week...and will he walk me to the bus-stop?'

His face up there was out of reach, (she was wearing her low-heeled lacquered shoes on account of the longish walk to the bus-stop) but stretching up to look into his Plumbago-blue eyes she sensed his shyness, which however did not stop him from talking faster and more than any other young man she'd ever met before.... or was he just a young boy? He did look, well, dashing. Almost like a film-star....

'So, where do *you* live,' he managed, forcing himself to examine the well-spoken female creature. He noted her smile, her long neck, her slightly receding chin, her china doll appearance; could it be the fancy hairstyle that made her so special, or the wide-eyed, submissive, helpless look? She even appeared to be quite intelligent.

'Oh, it is just a little too far to walk, unfortunately. I must take the Main Road bus, then walk up Klipper Road, it's not very far...you know, opposite the President's Garden...and you, Julian, where do *you* live,' she chattered on, almost forgetting to breathe.

'Oh, the opposite direction for me... Mowbray, bad luck! Still smiling at her he was honoured to catch the eye of his teacher, so now, waving a discrete farewell, he could proudly guide Finuala out of the 'hallowed' building and downhill to the crossing. Bending uncomfortably to cup her elbow Julian escorted her to the bus stop.

'He really is very tall', she thought, gazing up at him, 'and so gentle, in that slightly absent-minded way!' She loved that. Hands in his pockets he now stood by her side. Embarrassed, tongue-tied, both stared into the darkness, unable to latch onto any suitable topic.

'Yes, unbelievably nice,' she thought to herself again. Then, after an  embarrassed silence: 'it's all so difficult, you and me, we live at least three miles apart. How can we keep in touch?' Written all over her small face was the worry she'd never see him again. He had just become even taller, feeling protective and immensely flattered. As the bus pulled up he managed, just in time: 'may I telephone you, Miss Finuala?'

'Oh yes,' she called, 'please do,' already dangling from the platform of the moving bus, 'in the phone directory, *Goodkin*, Klipper Road, that's us...' the bus rumbled on, then darkness swallowed her up.

They were not bright, those lights on Main Road. Had he really caught her name?

Still, *she* was the one all lit up now, sparkling as a five carat diamond.  She almost forgot to get off the bus only two stops on.  Her heart was racing. 'Physics, *and* a pianist: please God... make him phone!' Suffused with a glimmer of hope her as yet little life may have changed at last. On the next day he *did* call, but they would have to wait all week to be together: her tall friend, the Peynet-look-alike, was usually 'up to his ears.'

'My head spins after a few minutes in his company: this new friend, well, I just can't imagine ever losing him! This is someone special. There's *hardly* any-one else who matches such cleverness'. The thought of him made her feel small, vulnerable. This was a new and unknown sensation in her life.

But even just seeing each other soon became testing: they needed to be alone, to talk, to discuss books they loved, to hold hands, be close... go dancing. That was indeed on the horizon, a few months ahead, at the Rag Ball. The event promised to be truly special, something to look forward to, talk about, for months and months before it came to pass.

*** 

The big evening came. Unblemished, immaculate, in a pale blue, off-the-shoulder-three-quarter-length tulle gown, Finuala, flushed with excitement danced, in silver shoes, barely touching the ground, floated through air, as the hours passed at the Rag Ball in Jamieson Hall, that famous University landmark one sees from far and wide. She was in heaven. Whirled about by one student after the other, especially by an arts student called Julius who was stocky, compact and witty, with a coif of curly hair sticking up like a cockatoo, all this close dancing, all these compliments, this unheard of gallantry, who was *he*? One thing was sure: this young man was certainly more her size. When pressed he admitted he'd admired her from a distance 'for many moons... actually, since nursery school', he teased. They'd been at the same school originally, barely noticing each other, and 'I am a very old and dear friend of *your* Julian, the one who's only managed one slow and agonising waltz, not even that: dancing is patently not his thing...are you confused Finuala, surrounded by two admiring chaps with almost the same name? Julius grinned, gleefully rubbing his hands together. He was confident of his conquest.

'He mocks, he is making fun of my own boyfriend!' She looked across the heaving dance-floor: *her* Julian was nursing a glass of beer, presumably talking about Physics with a similarly 'afflicted' fellow student. Mutual suffering then: 'my girl is so in demand tonight, I rarely catch sight of her', was written all over *his* face, and 'that *Julius*, he'd like to take Finuala away from me. He's been my friend for years. Even so, I shouldn't think he can be trusted ...'

In the end the new 'lovers' did overcome at least one hurdle, they managed to go home together. They scrounged a lift with an heir to the South African peanut butter industry, who, in a posh car, was driving his own girlfriend home in the same direction. During poignantly sweet moments on the back seat Julian put an arm around the dainty 'Fin', his fairy princess drowning in tulle, while she allowed him to kiss and fondle her bare shoulders and to plant several shy kisses on her lips.

'I'm truly sorry I'm not a good dancer,' he whispered in her ear. Despite all that, for at least one whole mile, they were innocently happy, holding each other, minutes passing all too quickly. Soon, catapulted into cold reality, frustrated and defeated... she had to get... not only out of his arms but also out of the car which had screeched to a halt in front of her home, with, believe it or not, Daddy, arms akimbo, by the door, garden gate open, peering blindly into the headlights. How long had he been standing there?

When they met up on the following weekend Finuala launched an attack: 'Why were you too shy to dance? Drat! It's your own fault....why on earth did you invite me? Let's hope you got a thrill watching me dance with all the others...especially that Julius, your friend, who is really nice, by the way. He's invited me to go to see 'Waiting for Godot' at the Labia, and to an exhibition of lithographs, he told me it is the best one he'd seen for some time.....'

'Indeed. Is that so? My old pal, we were at school together!' There followed a longish silence, a silence which marks the beginning of some devastating or unusually important announcement; she clasped her hands, frowned and waited. He was taking his time.

'Now listen, Finuala' said Julian, looking very earnest. 'I refuse to be jealous, I want you to know that. Go out with Julius, or with anyone else, if that is what you want. Seriously,' he stressed, coolly. More silence. She was beginning to feel sorry for herself. Why did he behave like this? After a short silence she heard him say:

'We could of course go to that exhibition, all of us, together, your sister too, if you like?' This took the wind out of her sails.

Later she turned it all over in her mind. 'Why is *my* Julian not jealous? He doesn't care. I want him to care. He's younger than me.' More than one year younger and strangely pre-occupied...*and* we both still have to learn how to kiss. Properly, that is. Perhaps that's what it is. He is very wise. And so clever! Though there is never enough time to talk about everything...' For a few days she remained confused, uncertain. But then, later, it was *her* chance to give him a hard time:

'Daddy has agreed to release me from duties in his office; I've been accepted by a really well-paid organisation in Stellenbosch: a Centre for Higher Education, offering day and evening courses. Just imagine! No, no, silly, not to study, but as their secretary; although I might even be able to take part in some of the courses myself...in the evenings... in both Afrikaans and in English. Not for a few months yet, but then I will be living there.'

'Oh no,' was Julian's ill-concealed first reaction. But then, tenderly: 'Of course, Fin, you deserve something more interesting than writing invoices in your father's office,' was his second. Her delight at all prospects: responsibility, new clothes, going away, earning money, feeling important, all this, he knew, hoped, believed, would surely be a good thing for them both, in the long run. Now they did begin to find more ways to be together, more and more as time passed, especially on Sundays, after they had been to their different church services. Julian's family were Methodist and stern. Two older brothers, both short and stocky resembled their father. Finuala felt intimidated when she was introduced to them.

'You're not a chip off the old block then,' she told Julian after her first visit: 'Strange, to be and look so different from your father and your brothers, with those long legs of yours!' All *his* family had said: 'Look at them, they're inseparable… and so very young, only eighteen, both of them, how sweet!' Ailsa, who had been present, stiffly put this right as soon as Fin was out of the room: 'No, no, not at all, you're all completely wrong: my sister is a year older than Julian, she only looks young because she's so little…but believe me, she's bossy as they come…But don't tell her I said that!'

*** 

'A fine day, Julian, let's go to the park' or 'why not come to lunch, join the family and Daddy might drive us to the beach, Muizenberg of course, so much warmer than the other side.' Weekends were their special time for getting to know each other. Sometimes Julian took both sisters for a walk to the zoo, up by the side of the university, where they appeased the bored lions, commiserated with them: 'just big cats really, that's what *you* are...', or, they managed to hitch-hike up to the Rhodes Memorial and the cosy old tea shop behind it, to say nothing of a few drinks at 'Forries', their much-loved pub.

Soon followed more testing events: cadging a lift to the bottom end of Signal Hill, armed with sandwiches and bottles of water, wearing stout shoes: they'd made plans to climb Table Mountain from the Lion's 'rump' side, in order to walk across the top and climb down directly back home into the northern suburbs. 'Or are we the southern suburbs?' No-one seemed quite sure...

'Oh my God', Mrs. Goodkin exclaimed, not overjoyed by this prospect when she was first told about it. She'd never tried it herself. 'Everyone does it,' Mummy, 'except you! Don't worry about us. Julian has a friend, an experienced climber who is taking charge of the whole event, and that other nice Juli-**us**, he also wants to come along...you know, the short one, that would-be artist. I used to see him at school but we met again at the ball...'

'Safety in numbers,' muttered Mrs. Goodkin darkly, shaking her head, 'but Fin, I'm getting very confused with all these Juli-ans and Julius-es. Couldn't one of them change his name? Julian

Tall, Julius Small? And are you absolutely sure you will be safe? Without at least one experienced climber there might be some dramatic catastrophe; I can almost see the headlines in the Cape Times: *'students from Cape Town University tumble to their death on sweltering Cape day'*.

'Oh Mum, my two men are already so different...and of course we'll be safe, I've just told you: that experienced climber friend is coming along! We already know I must climb on his shoulders coming down...but just in one place. You could wave at us!'

Finuala's mother frowned, shuddered and worried even more.  She  also tried to imagine Julian's father's life, whose daily work, it appeared, was the task of having to print similar and often hideous news for Cape Town's Argus publication,... for this was what he had done, allegedly, for the past twenty five years.

'He's a non-conformist, he enjoys coaching a Temperance group to sing Temperance hymns', Julian explained, trying not to look embarrassed. He changed the slant by telling Fin's mother about his father's high expectations which had already been thwarted, or rewarded, depending on how one looked at it: 'my brothers left home several years ago, one a scientist, the  other a bomber pilot'. Mrs. Conley tried to picture this man with three sons, and now so proud of his youngest who was distinguishing himself in so many ways *and* who appeared to be quite serious about her own daughter.

Most weekends the young people found sufficient time and pocket-money to hop on buses, go to films, exhibitions, listen to music at each other's homes or at concerts. The 'artist' Julius, now also part of this ever widening circle, amused his friends with quick sketches of things, very clever, very skilled, while they all enjoyed talking into the small hours, discussing, agreeing on the need of a new vision...especially on the political future. In buses, in public places, on the beaches, there appeared ever more signs saying WHITES ONLY where black or brown people must remain separate and not only in designated areas. White people were slowly becoming more conscious of a not altogether new burden: resistance from other races in South Africa. Building up, unstoppably was a sense of mistrust, dislike, fear and foreboding.

\*\*\*

And the young men, Julian and Julius: was there any topic these two could not expound on? They sparred with each other, openly, endlessly, while Finuala kept an eye on them, which was, of course, what they'd intended and hoped for. For the time being the Peynet-look-alike had totally captivated, captured the much coveted Fin. They were soon known to be boy-and girlfriend, already almost in that most earnest, pre-nuptial manner.

She finally got round to telling her 'special' Julian that looming date of her departure in September: 'You won't *really* mind, will you? It's only 30 odd miles away, you know. We'll see less of each other, but weekends are free, we can write and telephone and I will become rich, because it is quite well paid. Tell me you *truly* don't mind.' She looked at him coyly, teasing, hoping to hear a confirmation. He stared at his hands. He smirked. In the end, getting little reaction from him she told him her mother's view: 'remember that old saying, Fin, *there's lots of good fish in the sea,...* and you seeing just one young man *all* the time' (she did say it, you know, but believe me, she doesn't know about the other one...) 'We do like your young man, the music one, an impressive young man. He *is* a bit younger than you. I know, I know, only by some months...oh, a whole year? Really? But why are you so single-minded? What about that short one, the artist? Look around, girl!'

***

Julian studied 'his' Fin's expression. He no longer found any clues about her feelings for him. Secretly he wondered if this upheaval would change everything.  There was to be a new routine to their lives: separated during the week, together only on selected weekends. And soon her increasing expertise, and gravitas: 'all that money she'll be earning. It will be years before I can contribute anything!  Once I have my degree it will be National Service next... and only then my music. The thing I love best! So? How *is* this going to work out?'

'Don't worry, we will write each day and meet when we can,' consoled Finuala, 'there'll be loads of holidays... Daddy can come in the car to fetch me, every weekend.  Well, almost. This will be better for us both, surely, you see that. And there is always the train.' She took Julian's hand, held it against her cheek, gave him one of her most knowing and compelling looks...while he finally came to realise he was counted on to remain clear-headed, reasonable, and sensible, also single-minded, easy-going, interesting, tolerant, exceptionally clever, constant, perhaps not quite of this world...anyway, that's how his Fin liked to imagine him. She had first-hand knowledge, after all. She was very sharp, and, well, a little older. It might just be true! At least she didn't seem to mind him being poor. 'And I must be completely faithful, true as steel, of course.'

She was certainly clever enough to have noted her 'beloved' still seemed content to be looked after, clothed and fed by his mother. And one so had to respect the father, that stocky, benign man who loved growing vegetables after he returned from work and then spent much time at the Methodist church on weekends.

He was not much in evidence.

Julian did promise: 'I'll be writing regular letters to you, my new, my only and altogether 'best' girl-friend.' At least independent enough to wink occasionally at other female fellow students, he did admit he might take one or two of them to the movies, or accompany them on the piano, if and when necessary. Finuala studied him warily.

One does learn to love from *being* loved.

'We are not going to be like *conventional* boyfriend and girlfriend, endlessly moping, writing letters full of sighs...are we, asked Julian, 'after all, there is also our other friend, who seems to like you a lot. How does *he* feel about your going off?'

Finuala shrugged. There was little choice for either of them. Finuala accepted her admirer as he was: the cleverest boy in town, with Plumbago-blue eyes: an unpractical dreamer, filled with ambition: simply to be the best at everything that came his way. Not conventional then. Two young men, Julian and Julius, but only *one* Finuala, would soon start writing frequent, even daily, letters.

This was conventional behaviour. They did still quite like to behave 'conventionally' but, at the same time, appeared to have a bee in their bonnets about the very idea.

One could, even should, no...:

One *must* not take anything for granted.

# Three

'Dear little Fin, wonder what she's up to now, at this very minute?' Such thoughts were fleeting. Julian had resolved to take nothing for granted but was in any case mostly absorbed in his own life. While letters and notes were flying between them it was only occasionally he moped and missed her. 'She's coming home next weekend...I know we will be together, and then...we will not.' Plain-thinking, busy, reading great tomes, practising, and not endlessly pining after this delicate girlfriend who nevertheless showed such mysterious strength,... that was his way. After all, he had seen her around since they were at school. He knew and accepted she may have other admirers.

'My physics lectures are difficult; killing even: I must work harder. Much harder,' he wrote to her. 'How much more pleasing it is to dream at the piano, and savour that contentment brought by each advance. I'm improving so much, all the time.'

But his piano teacher, dispensing the best advice he could give to this a-typical student, had not been convinced Julian might get a place at the College of Music after completing his Science degree:

'Still, if you really want it so much, Julian, well, I suppose, it's worth a try. Who am I to stop you? What snags can there be? I am as full of goodwill as the penniless man is full of generosity. That old crack about the large quantity of merit required to make a small success cannot have escaped you? You may, like T.S Eliot in one of his essays, believe you are improving your mind, reading that *the universe is expanding or else contracting*...and other such things; you want it all, Julian, science and  music, don't you,...and now this  girlfriend? Perhaps you should be grateful she has so sensibly found a job in Stellenbosch. And then there will be your military service, have you two thought of that?'

Firmness, that's what was needed here. It was not forthcoming. Not from any direction whatsoever. Julian drifted about in clouds of ambition. Multi-talented people easily fool themselves, become self-deceiving dreamers. In the end they mostly shoot themselves in the foot. Single-mindedness...well, it gets one a long way. Making choices, sticking to them: was that the ultimate test? He knew all this. No-one could save Julian from himself, least of all his clever girl-friend. Choices might, should and could have been made. Drifting on the other hand… might well be the downfall.

***

The picturesque city of oaks, Stellenbosch, ('die Eikestad' in Afrikaans,) lies almost surrounded by mountains in the Jonkershoek River valley.

'Daddy's dropping me off and I shall feel at home, right away, from the first minute' she told herself…. recalling '𝔖𝔱𝔦𝔯 𝔲𝔭 𝔱𝔥𝔶 𝔪𝔦𝔤𝔥𝔱, 𝔒 𝔏𝔬𝔯𝔡, 𝔞𝔫𝔡 𝔠𝔬𝔪𝔢 𝔱𝔬 𝔰𝔞𝔳𝔢 𝔲𝔰'…a line from her Missal at Mass read this very morning. Of course she was a little nervous…and her father could tell.

'Only thirty miles from home,' he kept saying, in his protective way, 'it's nothing… *and* a payphone on each landing. You just keep in touch, young lady, remember to give us a call each day. And then, on a lighter note: 'You might turn into a ….*boor-a-kee* if you don't!'

'Dear, dear Daddy, you *still* don't pronounce it properly!

Although, in a way you *are* quite right…and you know what: can I tell you, I wouldn't mind a bit, becoming a *boeretjie*; they are much less snobbish than Cape Town people, warmer, friendlier, not always pretending...not always putting on a show.'

**My private Notebook:**

Daddy and I had a light supper together; the housekeeper made us an omelette, and now he's' driving home. I'm alone. I've unpacked. I am on the third floor, near a bath-room, near a toilet and in one corner of my room I have a basin with hot and cold water. I love my small desk, easy chair and a lamp by the bed. (Thank goodness for that, I should be miserable without that: I *must* read in bed.) Large communal dining-room: all this will become my 'home' for years. At least, who knows. It really is a lovely old place.

I'm also close to the Church of St. Mary, near that ancient Coachman's cottage and the old Burgerhuis, the cosy part of the village, with many historical buildings and the 'Braak': the old village green which used to be the parade ground.

These Cape Dutch houses, full of mysterious Dutch spirits from the past! The caretaker told us, Daddy and me, that since 1880, when the foundation-stone of a new college was laid, there has been steady growth towards a university for Afrikaans speakers. Now it is almost as famous as the Cape Town one. Well, not quite.

I've had a peek into my office downstairs: desk, telephone, bookshelves and cupboards filled with files... just an office, really. My predecessor is retiring. Tomorrow I spend time with her to ensure a seamless hand-over. As from Monday week I will be in charge of residential arrangements for visiting lecturers and students, and for the timetables of classes, to fit in with rail and bus transport from Cape Town and other outlying smaller towns.

There will be weekly 'conference' meetings, keeping an annual schedule of stimulating lectures under planned control. How-the-heck did it happen *I* got this job? There must have been loads of applicants? I'm good at *both* languages, that must be it. I will be safe here, nothing can possibly go wrong. 'Cool as a cucumber' that's how I feel. What a beautiful place it is! I must write to Julian. I've brought stamps...all I need is a post box.

A committee had checked Finuala's typing and bookkeeping skills, had discreetly observed her ability to switch from English to Afrikaans and her commendable manner of communication. Instantly streets ahead of other contestants due to her 'communication skills', along with an unusually quick and quirky mind, pleasing manner and accurate book-keeping, to say nothing of her typing and short-hand: she had it all, just what was needed: a star, a winner! And the consensus of other staff: 'easy on the eye...confident, and so well turned out'! Those outfits of hers, all handmade, not the usual stuff from the shops... this petite new person is quite something!' 'So well-dressed, and well-spoken, organised....' the staff conferred behind her back. 'What a doll'!

There was only one complaint from Miss Goodkin herself : her office chair: 'I need two, even three, maybe four cushions to be seated at the right height; I'm so sorry, I should have warned you!' There was nothing but warmest admiration and affection welcoming her.

*** 

1st Sunday, <u>Stellenbosch</u>.....September 1947

My dear Julian, I am in Stellenbosch... (as you see from the postmark.) Would it be *conventional* to hope you are missing me just a little? I trust the last two days haven't been too draining, and that you have worked hard. I am overwhelmed, you can imagine. It will be a while before I become a proper 'boeretjie.' I have unpacked. My room is quite cosy. In the office my chair is much too low. As you know, this is not a new problem. The caretaker must take care of that one! It is 10.30,

I am tired.  Will get this posted tomorrow and write when there is more to tell you. Remember: I come back on Saturday. All my love, but also send a tiny bit of it to our 'gang'; tell them my news and that I will have little time for writing letters.

Jou beste vriendin, … yours, (hopefully), Finuala.

### 3rd Tuesday….<u>Cape Town</u>

*Dear 'vriendin', is this really you?*

*Well it must be, but not in the conventional way, of course. Conventional, conventional, conventional! Will that suffice for this letter's ration of our most favourite word? Looking back on that conversation on the day before you left I have come to the conclusion that we each said it about 10 times in as many minutes and you even introduced it into the second sentence of your first letter. I have been trying to fathom out its popularity- could it be that we both fear conventional behaviour and hope to exorcise it whenever it rears its ugly head by loudly and vehemently calling it by name? (First prize for psychology, however, enough of this introspective nonsense). I understand the 'conventional' thing in answering letters is to go over any points raised in them, so here goes: It pleases me, and does not,… that your room is 'cosy'. Just so long as it is not <u>so</u> very cosy you will not want to come back to Cape Town very often. Several large books for sitting on could perhaps be found in the library? You will surely have discovered it, always your favourite* place, by the time you read this letter, although you do not speak of it. How can this be? After you left I was much occupied (until about 8 pm on Sunday) in playing the organ, an unfortunate ordeal. But it pleased my father.

Nevertheless I am still puzzled by your behaviour before you left and am no more able to account for it than I was when also losing much sleep at the same time as you were. In time, perhaps, we will understand the mysterious recesses of each others' characters.

That covers your letter, and mine too. Very little has occurred.

Only one problem remains to be solved: how to close gracefully and again it's the fear of convention that has me in its grip. Yours------ly? I'm running out of convenient adverbs. If I was writing to my bank manager (if I had a bank manager) 'yours sincerely' would be admirable, while to a maiden aunt (if I wrote to maiden aunts) 'best love' would no doubt fit the bill. As it is I am in a quandary so perhaps it will just have to be ....Yours, blank-ly, Julian.

Ps. I trust you haven't already met several more Julians/Juliuses. Your current 'other' boyfriend bumped into me two days ago bemoaning your absence. I realise, imagine, we do not see you in the same light. Or do we? You mean more to me, and I suppose, to Julius, than I can safely say, more than any other girl at any rate on the immediate horizon. Why I should choose to tell you this now, by such roundabout means instead of the more *conventional face-to-face I don't know (perhaps it is conventional cowardice) but I throw myself on your mercy. This attraction you hold for Julius/Julians is all very well but I fear it dispels a lot of idyllic illusions about platonic trios. Of course you never entertained any. The choice is up to you. Phew, a sigh of relief. Reading through what I have just written I wonder whether perhaps a certificate of sanity ought to be attached to dispel any qualms you may have. This is your opportunity for a withering retort, almost too good to forgo, but I hope you will.*

*Yours- apprehensively,* Julian.

Stellenbosch: Dear Julian, I have done my best to reassure you, although speaking on the public phone on the landing is not ideal. I am unbelievably busy for the time being and think it best to wait until Saturday, when Daddy will pick me up. Do come over and have supper at our house. Or for Sunday lunch. I'm sure Mummy will understand. In this way I can tell you all my impressions and when we are finally alone, perhaps after I've been to Mass on Sunday, we could go for a quiet walk to be together for a while. Enough. In haste, must go.

We can have a lovely long 'talk' in a few days, be patient. *Your* 'Fin'.

Cape Town: *My dear Fin, I am so sorry, it is impossible not to write once more. We are told that the* sincerest emotions are expressed in the simplest language. On that account our sincerity can hardly be in doubt....

I find it very difficult to be serious. I suppose one should be. At 17/18 I should be looking even more eagerly into the future I suppose, full of ambition...on the threshold of a brilliant career... planning to shake the world.

Hand me my book of clichés!

Actually, I daren't take a thought for the future, but just grab what glories the present can offer. It is quite impossible to realise that some day...we (who now know even more how we can hardly stand less than a week's separation) might have to cease to see one another. We are but children (physically and even more mentally)......
Are we justified in saying we are in love when we never see any one else? Even just socially? I was the first person to kiss you while my experience in that direction is hardly wide. All the rules say we are foolish.

It is almost as difficult to write 'kiss' as 'love'...they are horrible words, cheap, vulgar and disgusting. Here imagination is certainly required. Physical appeal is a peculiar thing.

I mentioned my incoherence earlier. Here it becomes very apparent....

Ps. Your last letter was scented again! There is surely some feminine secret here, learnt at an early age: When writing letters always sprinkle with scent before dispatch, or dust with powder, or press to one's face or *whatever the secret is. However, the seductive aroma provides delightful hopes.     J.*

*Dearest Fin, your letter came this morning and as I was reading it I was gradually filled with horror at my pompous statements yesterday. You really must disregard what I wrote- I think I must have a Teutonic taste for the 'kolossal' and can't quite realise as you so obviously do that a letter should be spontaneous, conversational and should not demand morbid introspective probing. You must regard yesterdays' letter as one of my frequent absurd lapses.*

* * *

Frantic letters from Julian were usually consigned into distant unreality, (into a folder, actually). They were piling up in an impressive way.

Only one of these, marked April 1948, received a special place: folded into the correct size to fit into her prayer book, it now went to Mass with her on Sundays. It was her favourite letter from her best boyfriend, written after they'd spent a whole night together in a cheap hostel in Stellenbosch. She now presumably knew a lot more about the mysteries of French Kissing. Having savoured the letter many times, carried it around (uncomfortably) in her bra for a few days, she now planned to keep it for ever.

Familiar routines back at home were reassuringly re-enacted. They even included going to confession on Saturday afternoon, (well, just once,) and chatting cheerfully with Mummy and Ailsa who were asking endless questions about the unimaginable change in the life of 'their' Fin. This brought the Goodkin family unit back to its accustomed solid closeness. Sharing a room with her sister for a few nights seemed not so bad after all. Even Ailsa was growing up.

Of course Finuala spoke to Julian on the phone and yes, he would love to come to supper and there might be time for a little walk alone, that is, just the two of them on the following day, after Mass perhaps, and 'your father will not mind driving you back in time for the evening-meal with the Stellenbosch staff, (although, perhaps next time, you might try using the train?)' 'It's all a bit tight, but that's the way it is, when one is a working woman,' Finuala, smiling affectionately, told her best boy-friend.

'Some time soon when you are home I will get all our friends together, the whole gang...perhaps we can go to town on the bus, see a show, or get ourselves to the Sea-Point drive-in, with a new friend I have, he has a car, I understand. I'm already feeling the strain, with you going off again. Still, letter-writing is good for focussing thoughts', Julian suggested, looking down at his 'vriendin', so fragile, with her 'friend'-ly face on that slender neck; how appalling, she must be off again so soon. He longed to hold her, which was never easy because she was so very short. Instead he took one of her hands, stared at it lying in his … and feeling masterful he suggested:

'If I saved some cash I could come again, by train as before, we could spend another night in that student hostel…why not look into that Fin, then we could be more alone, just for a while? Perhaps? Something to look forward to, then? We'll work on this, tell some white lies…. I mean, just think of the eternity it will be before I graduate. Another year and a half…. I shall be twenty. And then I suppose there will be military service for another two years. We may not even like each other any more by then. Who knows?' They sat quietly, thoughtfully, staring. He could almost *see* her thoughts, perturbed, disturbed, un-easy.

Settled in their daily routine of letters, calls and visits, during which they learned to cope with turbulent feelings, Finuala and Julian were becoming ever more separated.

'One thing is sure, if we go on writing letters at this rate we will need a special trunk to store them all,' she noted drily.

They tried to look into the future.

The years really were hurrying by.

# Four

When a strong man armed keepeth his court, those things are in peace which he possesseth. But if a stronger than he come upon him and overcome him, he will take away all his armour wherein he trusted, and will distribute his spoils.     Luke 11, 14-28

*My Private Notebook.* Fearsome tidings, that's what the weekly Sunday readings in church revealed: I read St. Luke's text this morning and felt afraid: what if other girls are making eyes at *my* Julian? It would serve me right. It's hard to be so far from home, the years are speeding by. Although there is time and dedication to sit here and read *all* gospel stories it is probably best to go to church regularly and get the benefit. Just to get out, even. Occasionally I go to church gladly, and to confession (once). Faith can bring consolation, when one is in the right 'mode'.

All my best friends are in Cape Town. Jul*ius*-the-artist; at least *he* is not going away to the air-force. I do sometimes wonder: it is surely not a sin to enjoy being held tightly by Julian, or even by any other lovely young man come to that? Is or is it not a sin? What would the nuns/priests say? There are many interesting men here attending courses. They invite me out. I think I know how they feel: I see their eyes and their expressions. It is irresistible to *feel* their reactions, when they press themselves against me, flattering and frightening…how strange to be a male! They become so impassioned, as strong as lions, they want to go all the way… one must be careful. They need restraining and often they would rather die than stop. Lust, what a human muddle: It's nature, of course.

Julius the artist: he's told me he cares very much, too much. I have less longing to hold him or be close to him. He is amusing, we laugh a lot, he is more open, more direct, than my special Julian. I miss them both, in different ways.  Girls must remain virgins until they marry. I certainly don't want babies, not yet! I've known long ago how it all works. French Kisses will have to do. They are quite enough! One learns to savour the waiting. It does seem dull, these days, sitting through church…so much better going with Mummy or even with my sister. Am I imagining that? It feels so false here, all on my own, in Stellenbosch. Very soon, Julian will be called up for two years of military service. Still, he'll be home regularly so we can time our visits.  For now I must curl up in bed with Madame Bovary.

'Oh, everyone reads that, certainly,' our librarian advised: 'you'll love it.'

*

Finuala has to admit on several occasions that 'it's been a rewarding week… but sadly I can't get home this weekend, I am behind with my office work,' while Julian confesses on the phone that he too has catching up to do. So, 'thanks God, for that phone on the landing, I become very happy and lively when I hear your voice,' she flatters her gentle lover.... but the truth is they were both, increasingly, immersing themselves in other things.

On the whole Miss Goodkin had drawn the longer straw: day after day she had time to attend lectures and courses in the arts, film and theatre amongst other topics. Surrounded by young and interesting people, she even joined long queues for popular events: her life was filled with stimulating events and discussions.

'Day courses are overbooked; my predecessor must have been dreaming before she left,' she wrote to Julian, 'still, all in a day's work, and I really know what a privilege it is to be here, with so many interesting people to meet. I take my meals with the resident visitors, I am able to attend lectures in the evening; good thing I'm so small, they can always fit me in! Interesting talks on music this week...Julian, you might have liked those. (I think.) But next week there will be lectures on official policy introduced following the General Election two years ago...I wasn't really interested in politics in those days and things haven't changed, I mean it's not really 'my thing', but my general ignorance is embarrassing. When I was very little, we came here from abroad, so I still feel excluded somehow, strange, as if I don't quite belong. If I am not careful I will belong nowhere, neither here, nor England nor Ireland, where I really come from. Other Irish can see from our names where we belong: Ailsa and Finuala...no-one else here has names like that! In the 1800's, my father once told me, huge numbers of enterprising Irish came to the Cape: there was an Irish Diaspora. (I had to look that word up, it is very meaningful.) I expect you know this, since you always know everything. One hundred years ago one third of the Cape's governors were Irish, as were many of the judges and politicians. Upington, that dreary dump on the railway line going north towards the Karroo was named after the Governor Sir Thomas Upington,... also the wonderful Sir Lowry's Pass...another Irishman. So, tell me, Julian, did you know all *that*?'

*\*\*\**

Months slipped by and National Service loomed for Julian. Julius however, the frizzy-haired school-friend, now at Art School, had remained close by, taking whatever chances he could, no longer repressing his own powerful feelings for Finuala. Letters from this young man also express hope and longing to see her whenever possible. At this time Fin, the 'queen-bee', began to store both suitors' letters in her large box.

Here is a sample of the scientist/musician's style:

*Dear Fin, brief but rather trenchant- I was distressed at the attitude revealed in your letter...I must forgo the temptation to be scathing as that would probably give the impression that I was annoyed...which of course I was not. But it is so easy and enjoyable to write with righteous indignation, however for the sake of peace I'll confine myself to mild expostulation...I think the appropriate tone of voice would be a piteous whine.*

- *As anticipated you found something to quote back at me as 'significant'- and of course as usual you missed the point: <u>unwise</u> to be alone together all the time, not <u>undesirable</u>...you appreciate the distinction. I was only voicing something you have frequently expressed yourself. I can write it in a letter perhaps easier than act on it when you are available.*

- *Why should I rant of duty involved…simply other people's convenience.*
- *This is most insane of all: '…second place in my affection…second place to what, in all conscience? If by that you mean 'accompanying' at silly concerts, the absurdity of the idea is revealed by simply expressing it. If you mean on the other hand playing the piano 'in general'… that is a not very bright remark of mine that were better left forgotten. Affection for a person and devotion to do one's work are so obviously different (and can quite easily exist simultaneously) that comparing them was a silly idea in the first place.*
- *There, Tuesday today, and I must go to my music lesson now, probably the last before I am tied up with Military Service. I trust you will sharpen your nails for Saturday… your favourite, 'Julius-the- artist', and several others of our 'gang' will be waiting to meet us in The Gardens as planned.*
- *Next weekend may <u>prove everything</u>…..Love Julian.*
- *XXXXXX*

The near namesakes Julian/Julius as well as several other young friends, hoped to spend time together just one more time, now that real life was slowly driving them apart. A tentative outline was hatched: to find days, in the near future, next year, perhaps, for an excursion involving the whole group… for a long weekend to St. Helena!

That shouldn't cost too much, surely? The time had come to open up, see the world, remember the past and be strengthened for what lay ahead. Yes, St. Helena. How would one get there? A canoe.....? Whose idea was this anyway? They were all so hard up.

***

Dear Julian, I've just had a call from Daddy asking exactly what time I shall be arriving on Saturday. His solicitude was rather amazing, I soon found out why- he wanted to get a word in before I see Ailsa. Apparently mother went away last weekend when I could not be at home, and on Sunday afternoon my 'little' sister and Daddy came to blows, (something to do with her smoking, perhaps?) He seemed to be affecting an amused attitude but I am sure he didn't feel like that really. I don't think I ever remember him thrashing either of us, although I've had one or two cuffs on occasion. I don't know what attitude to take. In theory I think it's shocking, but Ailsa is such a sour and irritating wretch on occasion that I wonder it has never happened before. Of course Mother has not been told. It must have been quite a set to...I'll bet Ailsa gave as good as she got. It makes me feel sick to think of it. Thank goodness I wasn't there.....Help, how late it is: as I am attending a course for fifty eligible men between the ages of twenty to twenty-six...all about to take their final Chartered Accountant's examination, I must present a powdered nose and lipstick-ed mouth in the dining room. See you on Saturday afternoon, <u>all will be made</u> <u>clear</u>!

Love, and <u>still</u> yours, Finuala.

*Still* mine?' Was she being endlessly propositioned by others? Julian was too proud to enquire.

\*\*\*

## More than just a year later:

Still obsessed with music, with a B.Sc. in Physics to his name, Julian has been languishing a fair distance away in the world's second oldest independent air-force, doing national service. As officer in uniform he cuts a dash, has become even more attractive, if such a thing were possible. The slogan, Per Aspera ad Astra (through adversity to the stars) seemed in every sense appropriate to the South African Air-force, but also to him.

Letters he's written to Finuala are both filling and spilling out of a size-able suitcase. She, almost two years older, already out in the world, in all likely-hood the more practical of the two, is the more restless one. During a few days on home leave, it is Julian who actually telephoned old friends to arrange the long-planned meeting. Two are still studying, everyone is probably still on good terms. 'It might be interesting,' he tells himself, 'best to humour this whim: none of us really know what the future holds, what to do with our lives,...' seemed to be the general idea behind it all. Planned an eternity ago, almost forgotten...the reunion is to take place in the open-air Tea-shop, one of Cape Town's most appreciated historic meeting places in the 'Gardens', van Riebeek's own famous park behind the Parliament buildings, right by the feet of the looming 'Grey Father'.

Fin, Ailsa and Julian have caught a bus, are travelling through 'District Six'... for once able to take in teeming, threatening squalor of colourful life, unlike anywhere else in town...bustling with Malay and Coloured people.

'Why are we doing this? People say it's not safe to go this way,' Ailsa whispers. 'Bad things happen here. White people are sometimes attacked…..'

While seven young, white South Africans travel safely towards the centre of town they are filled with doubts about themselves and the world around them. At last, having managed to find time to meet, they huddle around a table in the shade of pines and ancient eucalyptus trees, order tea, and, grinning happily, only a little estranged and embarrassed, they now study the faces of old friends.

'Hey folks, this huge plan: our own little 'conference'… what an achievement: we've made it,' comments Julian, drily. First there was small talk, eye-ing each other, pleased to be together… almost like long gone school days. Everyone looked a little older, of course. The dreaded 'South-Easter' was beginning to blow dust at unconcerned pigeons, but also at Julian and Julius, Fin and Ailsa, along with Donald, (the only one entering the world of medicine), Michael with his ambitions in the world of politics, and then there was Fred, the historian. Apart from Ailsa, they'd all crossed that fine line into responsible near-freedom.

It was surely impossible not to glance at the 'tablecloth' of cloud flowing over the edge of the mountain, but they barely took this in: to locals this was an unremarkable sight, besides, being with old friends was totally overwhelming!

Assuming the role of 'leader' Julian clinked a teaspoon against his cup, cleared his voice and announced the obvious: 'Here we are... all seven of us...welcome dear, very dear friends. The trouble with friends is the time and effort one must expend to keep in touch! Still it's wonderful to be together! The age of discretion and wisdom is allegedly upon us...but not even one of us has shown any idea of the distance between Cape Town and St. Helena. Shameful!' He moved his shoulders in a doubting way and said drily: 'Are we really still going there, then?'

'Why not,' muttered Ailsa, the youngest. 'But, you know, St. Helena is only a ridiculous speck of rock stuck in the middle of the Atlantic.' 'Quite right.' Muscles in Julian's cheeks had tightened. He was leaning back, his hands tucked away in his pockets. Whatever they'd been trying to say was entirely drowned by seagulls. 'Hear, hear', cried Fred, who liked to believe himself the most knowledgeable in their midst. Everyone stopped grinning, looked more attentive. What was this fuss about St. Helena? In an attempt to appear stolid and impassive, Julian raised one hand, a leader wishing to make a serious statement, studying everyone in turn. Then, after a dramatic pause he spoke: 'friends, we've been dithering about this for so long, could someone make a move, or at least a suggestion: we must resign ourselves, find a more suitable place than a speck of rock on which poor Napoleon died. It's absolutely miles away and very expensive to get to.'

'Right. Something not too remote, then, but relatively civilised', muttered Fin, 'where we can read, relax and get to know each other again'. In a responsible, grown-up manner she glanced at 'her' rival lovers, Julian/Julius side by side, as ever the best of friends, nodding agreement. 'Hear, hear' they said, like puppets in unison, after which she announced, in a throw-away manner, unable to hide her displeasure: 'Ailsa- wants to, well, hm, join us, come along too.' She made no attempt to hide her resentment.

Ailsa, elbows on the table, had covered her eyes with both hands.

'Don't be so *kali,* Fin,' scolded Fred, the history graduate. He'd spent time chatting with Ailsa and found her refreshingly forthcoming. Sensing his approval the younger sister rewarded him with an angelic smile while fumbling for cigarettes in her handbag. Her courses at Art School had begun and she was more than conscious of being the youngest, an intruder. 'Should she be smoking at *her* age,' muttered Finuala, hoping for support from at least one of the friends. No-one spoke.

Fred, elbows on the table supporting his chin, enquired with a leer: 'and so, mense,: what will we be allowed to expect other than drinking, talking and smoking during this proposed...hm, long weekend,' he paused...'given we *are* grown-ups, out in the world  now?' 'Most likely explore ourselves or even each other', feared Fin, keeping this thought to herself....

'I was thinking of exchanging ideas,  having at last learnt to be decisive and independent from, well, whatever... probably an optimistic expectation with *outjies* like us...'but by now she was muttering, head bowed, hands demurely folded. She was not the only one studying her fingernails. It all seemed so false, so forced, didn't it? 'God, I sound pompous, 'she thought. A long silence followed. Julian felt uncomfortable.

'Once we've made up our minds our excursion needs to be structured' announced Julius in a calm voice, over-riding the awkward silence. 'How about this: up, into the mountains, to Elgin?

Hire ourselves out to an apple farmer. It's beautiful there, we could go for walks, study rock formations...I could do some sketching,...' he turned to Finuala for support, but she was scraping away at some substance stuck to the table. Donald waited for a while, then broke another drawn-out silence: 'Hm, no... not if our backs are aching from picking and packing apples into boxes.' He knew about spines and back-ache. This proposal was vetoed by all as 'too much like hard work': slave labour, even coloureds wouldn't do it, 'we're on holiday. Remember?' Instead Donald came up with 'a few days spent quietly by the Indian or the Atlantic Ocean'...and how about discussions on 'other races', you know, what we know about black people in our country and the future of the whole of Africa, not just our own little bit?' 'Actually, folks, we're by these oceans already,' interrupted Ailsa, braving a withering glance from her sister. '*My* sister, again,' thought Finuala, but managed to say nothing for once. Ailsa cleared her throat, gazed modestly at everyone in turn, and seeing no signs of displeasure, or conflict, she launched herself into *her* proposal:

'People used to travel all the way from Victorian England to take the air in Hermanus, more or less where the oceans meet! Why not find a cheap boarding house by the beach, or rent a cottage... and sit around fires cooking massive 'braai's, take ourselves for long hikes and picnics, discuss life, and the future ....get to know each other properly.' Ailsa sat back and studied her sister's friends in turn. 'Hm, interesting', muttered Donald, 'practical...and not so far away.' Almost everyone nodded,... some sighed.

'We've all changed...we have very little to say to one another,' passed through Finuala's mind. 'Here we are, in one of the world's most complex societies, with all these problems about the rights of other races, and no-one has a single suggestion worth considering.' Flushed, she  glanced at everyone in turn and suggested: 'we could do more than that, take a more creative view....how about each of us choosing a subject, *one* topic, work on it, then present it to the group, and later, at a set time, we could make a study of it, pull it apart, appraise it. During a long weekend, there would be time for two or three discussions each day, of course only on topics we are truly interested in...' She'd had her say. She was hoping for an encouraging nod from someone, anyone. No-one moved.

'We could call it 'Summer-School', like those ancient, grey-haired alumni do, up at 'varsity...you know, every year, in January,' Ailsa added, feeling sorry for her sister, 'and I'd be happy to organise a timetable for us...I'm good at that,' she nodded.  For once, the sisters seemed in league with one another.

'How daft is that! Besides, why would old people want to go to 'Summer-school',' offered Julian. 'For the same reason *we* are planning this weekend', replied Finuala, in her best throw-away manner...The discussion was definitely livening up.

'You've been at your Adult Education place far too long,' Ailsa played devil's advocate, jabbing a finger at her sister, 'you don't have to talk down to us.' The others turned their heads, dreading a sisterly row.  Everyone was getting involved, but at their own pace. Finuala tapped the table with her fingers while studying all faces in turn. Holding back for a while she then broke the silence: 'Right! I'll do Victorian novelists in England, Julian can talk about composers or performers or the air-force and 'artist- Julius' will give an illustrated talk about cave paintings or Pre- Raphaelites or whatever and so on....'

'Call that a holiday,' Fred groaned...'and then what, politics?' Several heads, even at neighbouring tables, had turned, were looking at the presumed leader of the group: Michael. He already had a few grey hairs. Among friends he was admired for his radical views. Finuala turned to him: 'you'd want to talk about Malan, am I right, Michael?' He shrugged. He spoke quietly: 'of course. You know me. It's about time someone did,' then, lowering his voice: 'but not here, at this table....one needs privacy for that sort of thing.' He looked furtively at neighbouring tables: 'one must be careful these days...there's a hair in the soup, if you get my drift.' Almost whispering, he added: 'Have you guys heard about that student, a Catholic boy called Don Lowry... he dyed his skin brown, wore shabby, dirty clothes like a poor coloured and then spent two days and one night selling newspapers, sleeping rough in the harbour. He's at 'varsity' doing a PHD on race relations. His friends were afraid for him, having been sworn to secrecy. I heard he had much to say abut his deeply unpleasant experience. We should get *him* to talk to us...'

Julian, languid... Julius, fidgeting, doing battle with his ungovernable coif of curly hair, both nodded thoughtfully, while the rest began to rock to and fro like men attending a Jewish prayer meeting. Eyes fixed on the table before them everyone was absorbed in their own scenarios. Pigeons, squawking, fluttered, picked up crumbs, looking for anything at all edible, and not far off was the never-ending hum of traffic, honking cars and shouts of vendors around the Gardens. 'Are we actually thinking, or is it all a front'... passed through Fin's mind. Avoiding the eyes of the others, she'd begun to fear she might have over-reached herself, with those adult education responsibilities in the dark hinterland of Stellenbosch....

'Ag man, kinderkies'! What kind of a holiday will this be with our kinder-speletjies'? Fred shook his head from side to side, frowning: 'Our plans boil down to nothing but timetables of lectures. What fun! Remember, we're grown-ups now, we're free!' Somewhat peevish, fretting, he had a habit of blinking his eyes after he'd made a statement. He rarely seemed quite sure of himself. Undermined but undeterred Finuala glared at him and now also at her sister: 'as for you, Ailsa, representing the youngest of us, what might *you* actually have in mind?' Not expecting an answer, she opened her handbag and rummaged about for *her* own silver cigarette case. Like a 'femme fatal', Fin hid behind a plume of smoke, while blinking, waving away the smoke she gave her sister the 'evil eye'. This theatrical event demanded an appropriate reaction. Ailsa, who'd been twiddling her thumbs, now hoped all attention might be back on her... with one exception: Donald had winked at a pretty Malay waitress and was ordering beer. The remaining four males, called back to life by the sound of the word 'beer', followed his example. Despairing, Ailsa, with eyes wide open, stammered: 'we..e..ell, maybe, *praps'*...(since Julius was a third-year graduate art-student who presumably knew every single thing about *her* own subject), I might like to discuss...she took a deep breath: *'Religions of the World'*....or even...*'morality'*, yes,...'why not talk about things that stand in our way...holding away fairness, freedom, free choices, creating grievous sins from lack of humanity....' her question tailed off uncertainly, into a stunned silence. Everyone looked dismayed. 'Goodness? What's got into her? Is this to be encouraged? She's meant to be interested in Art. Little Ailsa, who's only been at Art School for a short while?' She continued, stammering apologetically: there was this book called *Guilt and Forgiveness,* she had found it interesting, 'well, up to a point...about other races, quite scary really.' Her gentle voice tailed off into another prolonged silence. Communication was in any case drowned again by swarms of gulls signalling to each other in their most deafening, squawking, angst-ridden way.

'Guilt and Forgiveness, hey..,now that has a ring to it! Very good.' Finuala looked around, pretending not to admit she knew she'd been upstaged. 'Before we know where we are my 'kinderkie' sister is becoming the star of our proposed weekend! Guilt, Forgiveness'...what do we think... on the earnest side, yes, but then, why not? Well? What do you say, people?'

Pensive faces turned from a study of the plastic tablecloth to the faces of both sisters. Gull-noises were reaching a dramatic climax. Fred raised himself, clambered to his feet and intoned: 'This high-minded, proposed excursion has taken on another dimension, but,' stretching even taller, 'could we be practical now? First of all: Hermanus! Three cheers for our clever girls: Fin and Ailsa... they are both dead-right. That's where we must go. The place has fabulously clean air and we might just be able to think straight! Secondly: Guilt and Forgiveness: we will throw open the windows of our souls. God will help us.'

'Fred. Sit down. No more waffle. Oh, for a rational existence! All this will of course have a bearing on real life....' Fred's throw-away manner was generally admired. Both Michael and Fred, hoping to become politicians were clear-sighted men who, together, would sort everything and everyone out. There were not nearly enough of those in South Africa.

In the meantime the Hermanus idea had taken root. Undeterred, as there seemed no other suggestions, Fred was allowed to ramble on about one Hermanus Pieters, a Dutchman who came to South Africa in the early 1800's, found a wondrous spring west of the Mossel River. 'No, we've not heard this story, carry on,' everyone assured, although they were only half listening...and Fred, back on his mettle, at last, had *his* chance to show would he could do. Guests from adjacent tables guests immediately looked up: that was certainly the *right* voice, the right sort of tale:

'Well,' he lingered, 'this Dutchman, you know, not so long ago: he found an elephant trail leading to an area which seemed the best possible spot to graze his sheep, where he felt he had to go:....now it's become an easy walk through Fynbos: a place where there is a lookout point over the village, which people would soon call Hermanus; only a small place. Archaeologists think,' he lowered his voice, adding weight to this information, 'it is *becoming* an important area for finding traces of the earliest inhabitants of this area. Rumours...about caves...there really *are* caves, you know...' he explained, and 'that Raymond Dart, (a 'prof' from Jo'burg,) well, he's found fossils in a quarry up north about twenty years ago, bones showing human and ape-like features, ...yes, quite likely human...with posture and teeth and brain-shape like our own...so, our early-early ancestors may have roamed about by the coast too, living on healthy seafood. 'At last: a spontaneous round of applause! 'Students of course', other guests leaned forward whispering to each other, 'Cape Town is full of them. Our future! Showing off, they are, as always.'

'Impressive, Fred! At last! ' Julian studied his friend. 'You confirm our ancestors were furry and black? Do scientists know that now? You are getting us in the mood for history.... the next thing will be politics. In other parts of Africa things are changing rapidly. People say there must be huge changes here. If we had any sense we *should* spend the entire weekend just on this single worrying and impossible topic! 'Guilt and Forgiveness!' No, wait, how about this: 'Guilt in the Fynbos'…? They grinned, they shrugged. All this was only moderately funny. Should anyone tackle such uncomfortable thoughts? This topic, ever-present, gnawing, was gradually invading every-ones' conscience. Eyes averted they nodded, groaned, and at the same time tried to measure reactions and feelings….but also still smiling at the 'Fynbos.' Cape Town students liked to show enlightened concern. Finuala, back in her practical mode, announced: 'So, yes,… this is quite amazing, but do tell us, how might we be getting *to* our so-called *summer-school*'?

'I just happen to know that Hermanus has a railway station' claimed Julian, 'but, wait for this, folks,' he paused, mockingly,' 'ha, ha…there are no tracks to it.'

'Don't be absurd, Julian, now *what* are you on about?'

'You heard me,' he snapped. 'Remember Sir William Hoy, Head of South African Railways ….filthy steam trains would ruin the good clean air? He over-ruled the railway line from CapeTown! Hermanus is the only town with a railway station which has never had a train arrive or leave! That article in the newspaper, folks, not so long ago... don't you read the papers?' 'Yes, yes, in all fairness, he did set up a horse and carriage service between Cape Town and Hermanus,' added Fred, inclining his head with a dramatic gesture to Julian, 'but.... my God, how long would that take?'

Amused... the group had come round, were bonding even. All seven were finally involved. 'Fin and I will work on Daddy to get us there in his car. Who else has an amenable parent? We could probably fit in two more. One further parent with a car is needed. Do you think there is a Catholic church? We *must* go on Sundays, you know.'

'Ailsa, don't be ridiculous! But we'll find out,' Finuala added quickly. 'Yes, yes. We'll look into that, don't worry...this is the university of life! Solutions will be found. To everything, worry not. It's only two hours' drive, isn't it?' Practical suggestions followed: monies gathered in reasonable quantities might just finance a long weekend with all the necessities. Even Julian joined in...but with a sinking heart: he'd so much rather be practising his Chopin studies. Cold water was not his thing, and in any case he'd never learned to swim. Fin, game for adventure, hoped she'd be protected by two admirers quietly locking horns for her attention, one possibly more morosely than the other. She had to accept, with some regret, that her sister was included, but parents insisted: 'It will be best not to be the only woman. So much more proper, you know.'

'Arty' Julius, whose frizzy hair stood up even more stiffly in salty sea breezes, immediately began planning best routes and pros and cons for wandering, bathing, and cooking boere-wors over open fires. Life in the raw, putting up with nature's foibles, no more pretending, but above all stimulation and improving thoughts...how earnest, how serious, how important it all seemed.

'Such an opportunity, this tryst, to separate the sheep from the goats', feared Finuala, 'and hard work, although surely revealing: to have my two favourite men so very close for a few days...'

And so it came to pass: Rucksacks packed, individual lectures prepared by candidates for presentation; uplifting, inspirational acumen and sagacity was to flow like a pure clear stream. Friendships re-affirmed and unforgettable inspiration would surely follow. There might be no Catholic service, regrettably. They would admit their guilt, and *have* to be forgiven. A few days before Hermanus, Finuala received a surprising letter from her most practical admirer, 'cockatoo' hair-cut-Julius, the unstoppable artist:

My dear Finuala, I do hope you can make some sense of what I intend to write. It's the sort of thing I chew over in those awkward silences and pauses that must annoy or at least embarrass you- the times when I dry up completely and look like a simple country buffoon; incapable of expressing himself; sheepishly eyeing his *faire milke maide*...I am in a dilemma, or rather a whole bunch of dilemmas. The first might be expressed something like this, (I quote from M. Sartre):

'Many people think that in what they are doing they commit no-one but themselves to anything: and if you ask them 'what would happen if everyone did so,' they shrug their shoulders and reply, 'everyone does not do so.' But in truth one ought always to ask oneself what would happen if everyone did as one is doing; nor can one escape from that disturbing thought except by a kind of self-deception. Sartre calls that sort of thing *anguise.* My particular anguish resolves itself into something more complicated. *My* reasoning is conditioned by extreme emotional vacillation. For instance, when I know I shall see you I am terrifically elated, when I do see you that elation is dulled by frustration of my failing to express adequately what I feel about you. That failure is due partly to an inherent dislike of anything that might be called mawkish (more so to the fact that you might consider a lucid eulogy glib and insincere) and finally, when you go, I am extremely miserable.

But then *your, our,* romantic Chopin-addict may have exactly the same feelings as myself. My taking advantage of perhaps a temporary cooling of his ardour (although the assumption that his ardour may have cooled is really an impertinence), is something which I find unpalatable. But there it is. At the risk of sounding utterly, damnably, grotesquely prosaic I can only (after weeks of introspection and armed by the knowledge that after this coming weekend I won't see you for a fortnight) declare a whole-hearted affection for you. It's taken me some time to write this...the culmination of several abortive attempts. I must dull my higher nerve centres in anticipation of an entire weekend without being able to express my feelings other than by affectionate glances! What I really want to say is this: whilst I'm now sure of my attitude towards you, dear Fin, there is still the question of your Julian to be debated. Please tell me what you think and PLEASE burn this drivel immediately you've read it.'

Finuala kept the letter, put it with all the others he'd written to her during her years in Stellenbosch. Touched, but also alarmed, she was now conscious of trouble ahead. She was aware of the need for more than one existence: one for herself, and another for the eyes of those around her...

Only in the evenings was there peace in the modest beach hostel. Hot showers, the simplest of meals after each of three long days, lively discussion and high thinking, along with daily walks, dips into the warm Indian, (looking out for tell-tale sharks' fins) or is it still the Atlantic ocean... (where does the one stop and the other begin...no-one knew or cared) as they shivered in wet costumes lashed by southerly winds from Antarctica. Solitary, dry beds waited for them in the hostel. As long as only minds met...and they did, for every one had diligently prepared papers and thoughts, even the youngest of them. They were on a roll.

The proposed topic, 'Guilt and Forgiveness' was accorded highest praise: for some days they became a spectacular, politically advanced, supportive, lofty-minded bunch. Their thoughts were not without danger, politically speaking. After all the 'high thinking' private passions were not forgotten; they *were* there, but smouldering quietly, imperceptibly. Rival lovers, mostly distinguishable from one other by their height: both liberal, (high-minded, talented, intelligent, good-looking, one simply ran out of epithets) lively young people, who had known each other from their schooldays, for at least six years, finally had to accept they *both* had more, far more, than just an eye for the same woman. Ever since their arrival in Hermanus, Julian and Julius had been uncomfortable, in dread of all this 'togetherness.' Julian calmly observed his artist friend kissing Fin as the two waded into the ocean, holding hands. They dipped, they ducked, shrieked and laughed, while he, turning away, told himself: 'I refuse to be jealous', and 'good luck to them'. He had noted the expression of bliss, of love on Fin's face, decided he would not allow himself jealousy, no, he did not even *mind* that Fin, (yes, *his* own dear Fin,) and her admirer were experiencing an apotheosis in the lapping waves, blinded by the setting sun...an inexplicable vision of the fusion of life within the present and the future, the living, the loving and the dying together, leaving the past behind and looking to a new beginning...or something lofty of that ilk.

'Guilt and forgiveness, indeed', he thought while reminding himself to shrug it off... not just in politics, it is everywhere, in everything.'

The group's behaviour remained impeccable throughout three stimulating days.    Finuala admitted: she was powerfully drawn to Julius, the artist. More gregarious, far less inhibited, his lecture and post-lecture discussions had been, to her mind, the highlight of those three glorious days in Hermanus. And he, ah, the artist, how he adored her! Now she knew, for sure. Had the appeal of her accustomed friend paled? And why? Everything felt different. When the 'former' lovers returned to Cape Town, they did not even try to pick up the pieces. For many months, unbelievably, all contact between Julian and Finuala was severed.

An unconvincing correspondence began several months later, long after Finuala returned to work in Stellenbosch. While the 'sobered' Julian had gone back on duty with the Air Force she'd apparently spent much time with their artist friend who was now so passionately in love with her. But some months later she sat at her desk, wondering how to begin this letter to her first love:

'My dear Julian, I have been regarding this blank sheet for at least ten minutes, partly because I am doped with codeine, partly because I am very tired and chiefly because I feel so completely divorced from you. I shall at least give you a list of facts: that holiday in Hermanus, stimulating as it was, ended in agony on the whole. I had told you before: I was never *physically* attracted as far as Julius is concerned. But this time it was much worse...I have a feeling that meeting up with him beforehand began it all. I couldn't bear him near me. I conquered it once or twice but apart from that. Of course that didn't improve *his* moods.

The worst times were the nights of that weekend in Hermanus, now such an eternity away. All those talks we devised were wonderful.... and, needless to say, the claret, white wine and general boozing added to my veneer of pleasantry. But I was wretched I'm sure. The only time I felt cheered was when I received an extremely amusing poetic composition from Julius.....

Last Saturday he came and we went to the pub where we met Donald and other friends.... who seemed to be spying. I also went to Julius on Sunday, by invitation...just after I got there his mother muttered something about a bath and escaped. He and I rushed out to do some gardening. At quarter to five I said I must go (since I was almost hysterical) and he said he would escort me, so we got away, in a state of collapse. I dread our next meeting.

But I am ashamed. I still can't get round to *my affair* with Julius... There seems nothing to tell you. You know my affection for him...of his for me. What else? I don't think my love for you has decreased...but perhaps I am to suffer more physical revulsion. I can hardly imagine it. I am extremely miserable away from him. I am more used to being away from *you.* And so it goes on. Your own attitude towards me is equally mysterious...can you throw some light? To think you and I were once decided to get married. Farcical!'

Julian kept this letter, studied it, over and over again: 'I could not bear him near me, but I conquered it once or twice'. *Her* words! He stared at them for a long time, trying to understand their meaning.

Veni, vidi, vici' was all that popped into *his* mind. 'Once or twice' he read, again, and again, 'I conquered it once or twice...' and 'my affair with Julius. Was she hedging her bets?

Eventually, only eventually..... this was his reply:

*Dear Finuala,*

*Thank you for your long if rather desperate letter. When I was confronted with the problem of replying I hesitated for some reason. You seem to rely so much on my 'shattering logic' or clear decisions, whereas my woolly mind evades the issue.*

*I must say....your affairs develop rapidly...one day you are encouraging our mutual friend in a mild flirtation, the next you seem to be contemplating marriage. At any rate I suppose he must get rather frantic, from your description. But I don't seem to be playing the right part sympathising with rejected rivals. Still, it isn't difficult to imagine his despondency, he being what he is.*

*It's a great pity our trip to Hermanus was so miserable for you though. It shows you can't rely on enjoying places and events if you allow yourself to get so involved with others. As to Julius, however, having written that, I find there is nothing to say. Though I hadn't imagined your attachment so great that you were miserable away from him .More than from me. Ah, bitter fate. If you prefer him to me I can only be logical (unsatisfying?):*

*Take him and I hope you will both be (sob) as happy (boohoo) as you deserve. It seems I can't be serious. I suffer from some strange affliction that makes me earnest and solemn at all times save when I get a pen in my hand, then flippancy triumphs, which must be very annoying. My old friend's attitude is strange...taking advantage of the supposed cooling in my ardour... when my attitude has been unchanged for years...*

After this reply Finuala decided it was worth her while to continue the correspondence, trying to clarify her own feelings:

'Dear Julian, when I told your rival that you were aware of my attachment for him he was horrified...afraid to look you in the face from now on. I must have been melodramatic in my information. His first letter stated that YOU were a restraining influence. So I wrote back and said: ignore YOU. Are you surprised?

Here is one interesting piece of information: Did you know that when we are in company I devote my attentions to any other male in order to combat your very obvious indifference to me. Intriguing. Had you noticed it? I must be naturally promiscuous. I told him you were the opposite of possessive. The situation has not changed. You knew I was *attached* to our artist friend; I suppose he is quite well disposed towards me, but my affection for you remains the same. However I do think he is surprised by *your* un-possessiveness.'

\*\*\*

After three months of relative coolness, with the distance between the couple greater and times of leave infrequent, letter-writing  eventually revived flagging emotions. Then, out of the blue, Finuala informed Julian she needed to have some minor operation in hospital (the nature of which was never made clear, but she remained there for at least a week). On the morning after the operation a nurse brought her a newborn baby to feed with a bottle. Whose baby was this? Was the nursing department understaffed? No light was ever cast on any aspect of the mysterious event.

During this unexplained episode, a whole week in a 'Cottage Hospital' away from home, (but near her place of work,) no mention of supportive relatives, and all without one single helpful word or explanation, Finuala sent a letter to the cast-off Julian in an effort to restore the status quo, pleading he might come and visit her in hospital. Alluding to this event Finuala wrote the following words to her mystified friend:

'I am no longer *pure and unspotted'*.

What was this?

'Pure? Unspotted? Julian was puzzled. He read it again. Poetic concealment of this sort was not something he could unravel. Some sort of feminine logic, some evasive equivocation? There had been no relatives or other friends visiting? The entire episode, seemingly hushed up, swept under the carpet, was destined to remain an enigma for all time. That very same time....the one which is known to heal wounds... but then perhaps there weren't any?

<u>Officer's Mess. Royal Airforce.</u>
*My dear Fin, of course I will come and comfort you on the 16th: Visitation of the sick is a very good excuse; there is nothing I would like better. ......I was altogether very glad to receive your letter, for some reason I was beginning to feel that you had spurned me, though it isn't really so very long since you last wrote. Perhaps it is because I have been*

reading 'Cass Timberlake' (Sinclair Lewis) a book to recommend- I am sure my enjoyment of books is always at a very childish level of identification- in face of all the evidence I can identify myself with anyone if necessary. So the mere difficulty of converting myself into a middle-aged Middle West judge, clever, industrious, a love of his home town, but not without a poetic streak, in love with and eventually married to a mercurial, intelligent young beauty- was as nothing. And when, after a couple of years she left him for his best friend, a smart 'shyster,'(whatever that may be) his desolation and mine was so complete that I was unable to relax until I had hurried on to the, fortunately comfortable, solution. So I was quite prepared to hear from you some awful confession that all was over between us. The fact that I am still relied on as a source of solace in distress, instead of being cold comfort turns out as a source of great delight.

By the way, I was telling Tommy of the string of weddings you mention in your letter...your unwonted mention of these can only be interpreted as a not very dark hint that it's time I made a move. Not an unsound idea perhaps, but I don't think *you would be quite so coyly allusive if that was your meaning?*

The time was ripe. Usually men need only a very small push in the direction of a pulchritudinous maiden.

# Five

Tota pulchra es, Maria: et macula originalis non es in te.

<u>My private notebook:</u>

Pulchritude: ripe perfection, beauty, a swan, a flower…I've looked it up, and am at a loss. The only way I can prove my commitment to Julian now, (after all that has happened) is to allow *him,* freely, to make love to me. But we are not married. Of course I still want him. When he comes I must see if I can persuade him sufficiently to agree to a wedding date.

We'll manage, even if he were still away. It can't be much longer, this Air Force thing. If I became pregnant I could give up work and Daddy has already said he'd help us finance somewhere to stay. We both have some savings. And that dream about studying music: it would be cruel and probably impossible to try and talk him out of that. I will have a word with my Father…and Julian must take instruction and promise to become a Catholic... Everything becomes so complicated. I don't quite see how all this will work out, but still…

December, 1950.

Friends for almost eight years, (if one counts eyeing each other on the school playground), foes marginally so, albeit only for several months, are about to tie the knot, that strict Catholic one, which entails special instruction for 'heathen' husbands-to-be and further patient waiting for the bride. The most unobtrusive, modest wedding is planned, two days in a tiny hotel in Hermanus, then instant return to reality: air force training for the groom and Secretarial services in Stellenbosch for the bride. All manner of complex problems  must be solved first: 'dispensation' from the bishop: *something* must be sent to the archbishop by Father O'Doherty, there are suggestions one can also obtain *this* from Father McLoughlin and all would be well without bothering about the  archbishop's Exequator. Whatever that might be?

*'Having left it to the last possible minute'* writes the bridegroom from Officer's Mess to his Finuala, *'I sent off my entry form to the College of Music scholarship exam this morning. I see no prospect of getting anywhere with it, but no despair allowed.* Now, before anything else, the bridegroom must undergo training in the immutable truths of the Catholic Church.

*'Well, I bravely sought out Father O'Doherty on Thursday evening and arranged my initial session on Saturday. It was, I'm afraid, a far from shattering experience, but a charmingly illogical exposition of the party line which I feel I must*

reproduce. (It has not shaken my intentions, you'll be glad to hear, since I was fortunately prepared for most of it).

Father O'D. is a square-faced squat, grey-haired Irishman (of course) who looks rather harsh but proves to be quite genial in an Irish Fatherly way. The lovely brogue he utters, con brio, such things as 'this age with its superficial sophistication' or 'unthinking supercilious atheists and agnostics' I wish I could do it phonetically. It could produce quite an outstanding flow of inconsequential oratory, sentences tumbling gaily over one another and finally disappearing into a few mumbled fragments. No doubt he has been well trained in the confounding of unbelievers:

'Young, sometime protestant scientist (so-called) and unthinking supercilious agnostic, seeks instruction....Now, to shoot him the works: 'Do you believe in God?'

'Well-er-yes or-in a sort of way- I suppose, according to how you define God-yes, I think I can say I do.'

'And do you believe in the divinity of Christ?'
'Well, er-, I don't think one can answer that question- one doesn't know...maybe, maybe not.'

'Ah. Doubtful about the existence of God...Doesn't know about Christ. Right. First we must prove the existence of God.'

(Heart sinks: which of the traditional methods- ontological, teleological?)(It proved to be the 'Existence of Law in the Universe, and therefore of a divine Law-giver.') Of course, I may be giving the impression it was all very high-powered and brisk- no doubt the method according to the book would be, but fortunately father O'D. is no tense rapier-witted Jesuit, but a discursive, intolerant, genial, illogical Irishman, so that the sharp edges became a trifle blurred and the cold all-too-logical basic argument barely survived among the mass of verbiage.

So we moved on to God, the Law-giver, which went on for a disproportionate time, but a glance at his watch convinced Father O'D that we must hurry on to the Divinity of Christ, proved by his 1) miracles and 2) prophesies.

What is a miracle? A sensible fact produced in a divine way. (I shall soon know the rules better than you, Fin. It's like a piece of mathematics). A man claiming to be extraordinary must give evidence of extraordinary powers etc.

2) I got lost somewhere......

*Christ formed a Church which provided seven sacred parallels to the different stages of life which are: birth, growing-up, taking sustenance, marriage, or becoming a priest and death and something else. So there are seven sacraments, one corresponding to each. Marriage is one of these. What is a sacrament?' A means of obtaining grace, a channel whereby grace may flow into a person.*

*Even in English Law marriage is defined as indissoluble. Did you know that?*

*And the first object of marriage: the procreation of children…no contraceptives! I hadn't the heart to bring up the hypocritical use of safe-periods (or coitus interruptus or whatever). The secondary objects are two: first, that husband and wife may prove a solace to each other, and second, to provide a legitimate outlet for the desires of the flesh. (The Latin word 'concupiscence', since you so love Latin)….*

*That was about it. Next Tuesday we move on to 'moral Law'. We have already agreed that this modern age with its shallow sophistication has abused the word 'immorality' so that it only means breaking the seventh commandment, whereas it should include stealing bicycles.*

*Meanwhile I have some literature to devour, a novel Bruce Marshall, a rather low-brow Graham Greene.*

*I brought forward the suggestion that the attitude of some converts must be embarrassing to the Church since they produce semi-heretical doctrines.*

*This pleased Father O'D —he agreed very happily Alfred Noyes was such a one: he wanted action, a Catholic party mixing in politics. Or Eric Gill- take his case now, he was a convert but in his autobiography published recently - or, just before he died, the poor man stated that 95% of men in England practised self-abuse! This I thought a trifle strange, so pressed for an explanation; well, how would he know. It is unscientific, misleading innocent people. I suggested he perhaps asked 100 people, or read his Havelock Ellis and was simply quoting his findings.*

*'Ah now, if he said that, then it would be scientific, it would be reasonable.' Which is probably not what the Church was fulminating about...I don't know, I couldn't understand it.*

*After all my learning we shall be able to have interesting discussions no doubt. The eccentricities of father O' D. have little to do with the doctrines...I don't think he is their best advocate. However, more on Friday: perhaps I will learn the fate of my children then. Wonder how long this course lasts?*

*Little else to record: the choir has reorganised itself to sing carols, the Little Theatre held a party yesterday evening which I attended on rather feeble grounds. I also wrote to Fred and Donald foreshadowing a possible convention some time over Christmas...There will be a passing out parade on the day before the wedding, which I may have to attend. If so, I will not be able to get to Cape Town by late afternoon. I also have a letter from my Papa, saying rather brusquely they will come if he can have another day off work.'*

The event of 'tying the knot' could not have been more low-key ... which is exactly how the couple wanted it. No-one there, no friends, just parents. The bride denied herself any ceremony, agreed to enter the married state wearing a tailored jacket and skirt with a small bunch of flowers in her arm: 'The suit will be useful for work', she stated, in her matter of fact way. The groom, an officer in uniform, married at last, posed for the photographer. One sees him seated, with Finuala standing by his side in high heels, gazing steadfastly into his blue eyes. Had they stood side by side in the customary way they might have looked like father and daughter. It was a muggy day, that third of February, in 1951.

'Yes', they'd both said, 'we will', 'I do,' or whatever it was that seals ones fate after being the closest of friends for so very many years. None of their friends were invited. Not one single one. The church must have felt empty indeed. Curious! Was there something to hide? Why, of course not, they simply hated any fuss was the explanation, but above all there should be no expense.

Very well, so be it: on then, to the long awaited apotheosis: for him a life of bliss, studying music, a gradual rise, achievement, closeness and strength... and for the bride: the wonder of life with her belovèd who combined so many admirable qualities, a brilliant mind, his degree in physics, and that most desirable of all things, a pianist.

Even simple truth can sound like a compilation of clichés.

There was little talk about earning money: Julian returned to the Air-force, Finuala to her tasks in Stellenbosch. They were doing their best.

Now married, they might even meet up every other weekend.

On the 7<sup>th</sup> of March she reports: 'I thought my end had come this morning- or a junior kind of miscarriage! So, following instructions I lay with my feet raised and it went away. Gory, to say the least. What have your excesses done to my delicate mechanism? I think I must see the doctor. After all, we always use condoms'.

9<sup>th</sup> April. 'When will you know about your future? I hope it won't be long- for a number of reasons. Perhaps you can guess: the normal monthly cycle seems interrupted. How has this come about? I have a lot of pains but nothing happens. I can't help worrying what I shall do, where I can go, how we shall cope. I need your reassuring presence. In desperation I went home to my parents at the weekend... wanted to see Charles Chaplin in 'City lights'. It was very good- one of the best of his I've seen. I bought some shoes, too, with your cheque. They cost £3.19.0.

In the evening I went to the Foresters Arms and became very merry through drinking there. Ailsa came along and Donald and our dear Julius, and (misery) Elsie and Whacko, (ancient school friends, remember them?). Donald took me to one side; he knows of my difficulties. I dimly recall seeking poor Julius' reaction to our marriage-but hardly remember what he said, unfortunately. He now seems to avoid me.'

'If you do come home this weekend I think you should tell your mother that we will have Sunday meals at our house- we shall ruin her otherwise, staying two weekends together. I am afflicted with perpetual sickness, no 'morning' about it. Jolly! Papa has bought a new red Morris 21. Now that's what I call Opulence....'

30th April. 'Went again to the pub, this time with Donald, who hinted at medical aid to dispose of my condition... Do you mind that I refused it? Now I learn that alcohol is poison in the veins of a mother and must turn to lemon squash.'

\*\*\*

12th of May: 'I've still not found sufficient courage to tell the Warden, even though Papa is considering renting or even buying a small house for us!' Finuala agonises about when she might leave work, when to become a lady of leisure, when she should return to the big city. The weeks in Stellenbosch were dragging. Working life would obviously have to come to an end sometime soon. Somehow she feels dejected although 'Mama is making stacks of useful utensils to hand on to me as soon as I can return to Cape Town. All manner of things are taking shape in more ways than one. I've written off for furniture catalogues' she wrote on the 5th of June, 'and I couldn't write in time for today's post because I visited Cape Town in order to be measured for my maternity belt. Mother arranged all this. You will hate it, I'm sure. Laces and things...'

'Friends have come forward with many offers: we now have a carry-cot, a pram, an eiderdown and, if by any gift of God (!) I produce twins, we would have two cots and two high chairs.' In June she informed her husband: 'I have actually started to knit, very awkwardly: a cardigan in chaste white wool. Daddy still intends to get us a house.'

On the 21st: 'A new Secretary starts of the 15th August...I leave on the 28th July. The new girl is 29, name of Muriel Large. (Needless to say she is small.) I am sure she is also prim... a member of the primitive Methodist Brethren and Christian Holiday Fellowship, and the like. But this is only conjecture. She also comes from Cape Town. Alec and Duncan will work on her.'

These two young men are staff at the College and have figured greatly in the past three years of Finuala's daily life. There had been earlier events, shrouded in mists and conjecture...a particular one stands out: rooms in College were often let to visiting students and Finuala, unable to find lodgings elsewhere, spent a night in an allegedly large bed inhabited by Duncan *and* his wife...an emergency measure which, allegedly, proved to be unexpectedly pleasurable.

Lucky Duncan! An insubstantial account, a fantasy, a figment,... but how amusing for them all. Could there have been an incident, a quiet hint of scandal then, sometime in middle to late February, when Finuala was newly wed? Surely not! Please note: *this* gossamer thread, gossip, made light of, blown away in the mists of time, may re-appear and linger in mysterious ways. But to return to practical matters: the account:

5th July. Finuala leaves her job. 'I shall devote a week to house-hunting,' she informed her husband.

30th July. 'I have found a house. We have been washing (Mother's maid has done most of the work but I am the wearier). And yesterday for some reason my back was agonising- in the end I went to bed at 4 o'clock, got up at seven, had a meal and went back to bed. I quote my woes to explain my failure to get the house sorted out. I had an enormous quantity of things to bring from Stellenbosch. Thank goodness mother can't see my front room. I must buy a bookshelf quickly, books are all lying in the hall. And these boxes of letters, I suppose I must keep them too. Perhaps one day you will read them all, even those from my other suitors! I am sure I can feel a stirring within me: quite a leaping, in fact. My first day of domesticity has been endurable- but day after day after day- God!'

28th August. 'Your mother said we can have the old stair-carpet from your house. The one she has had since 1919. It will cover our nakedness very well. My mother is in generous mood too. I shall be as charming and as scheming as I can. But I am so bored I must confess. The weekend was all right. I was with Donald and Julius on Saturday and Sunday. Donald and I also went up to Julius's last night. I was captured by his mother, who is in bed. I heard all about her illness etc. etc. on and on. She was however, full of praise for her son, so understanding, even-tempered, so gentle. I suppose she feels there is no danger now from my scheming. I escaped at 10.15 but we stayed until 12 o'clock. Julius' mother did seem to welcome a new face though. Will you bring some money at the weekend- or you can give me a cheque to cash? Now for the first time I know what it's like to depend on you for money. Are you offended that it displeases me so very much? I want to contribute, too.'

December 1st.

Finuala eases herself into a bath. 'Ah, this feeling of floating, of lightness, of buoyancy, this protuberance... pushing up from inside against the stretched dome which was once my stomach, what can it be... a fist, a foot, trying to get some space, weary of confinement? Blue lines, red stripes, air-brushed bruises decorate this terrifying, tight tent, the temporary home of my child. Will my poor stretched skin ever be tight again? What have I done? Only days from now a new human will come out, kicking, trampling, for all I know howling, wondering how the land lies. Emerging from the dark it will shout for a mother and father... and that all day long. We might even make it in time for Christmas. Now *that* would be something!'

'Puer natus est nobis, et filius datus est nobis...' she mutters to herself, another flash of Latin text embedded in her mind... 'such a long vigil, this waiting for the 'begotten'. How dreary it is. Well, not exactly that, more like an attentive wariness but feeling worn out. Of course I'm not afraid, even though I am so little: with any luck the baby will be little as well. Dear God, how I wish it was all over...ecce virgo concipiet, well, in all fairness, I was no virgin. It all happened so quickly. ☩ God, who makest us glad, grant that we now receive my only-begotten...' Finuala tries to pull herself together: 'This must stop; I am becoming maudlin, here in this little house. Still, thanks to Daddy we have a roof over our heads; I'm not exactly riding about on a donkey looking for shelter, and Julian has arrived. We'll work all this out together. I can't bear to look in the mirror. Gross!

La 'grossesse', say the French. No connection, I know.

I want to do this all alone: no mother, no sister, just me and a nurse. I'm doing my exercises. I'll concentrate on my task and connect with whatever my Creator has planned for me. I haven't been to Mass for months. Do I still want to go? Is this what is known as a 'displacement reaction? What is your plan for us, and for this infant, God?'

'And so it goes: when I am alone I *do* talk to him. It might be wiser to address my thoughts to

'Our Lady', under these circumstances. She surely is someone to hang on to under these circumstances. Perhaps I'll go to church again when I'm settled, after the baby. There'll be a christening.' Finuala stares at the ceiling, holds, strokes her tightly stretched stomach with both hands. The water is getting cold, the hot tap is out of reach.

'Mothers having babies feel very alone…. Mummy did say that and offered to come to the hospital when the birth starts. I said no, no, I prefer to be alone. Better, surely, than having all sorts of people around staring at the relevant bits. I wouldn't want Julian there, nor my mother. Nor Ailsa, perish the thought! Just me, and the midwife. What if I died or bled to death… should one go to confession before it happens. The infant and I could be buried together…..

And now, I'm really getting cold, high time I got out of…the…slippery bathtub…not so easy, really, with this protuberance…whoops…good thing I was holding on …Mummy did say I shouldn't bath when I was alone in the house. Oh well. And now… water all over the floor, is this bathwater… or what? Julian will be back later tonight, he'll have to dry up the mess. Didn't he say he'd like to have a son called Jonathan… perhaps just a bit too unusual? I quite like it.'

\*\*\*

Julian, having hurried home from work earlier than usual, called his father-in-law to drive Fin to the hospital; the waters had broken.

The men dropped her off. Finuala was adamant: there was to be no-one hanging about. Superfluous, vaguely lost, they drove back to their respective homes…where, on the next morning quite early, indeed extremely early, the phone rang: a son was born: Finuala, as always, had triumphed, a few small cuts and stitches but both 'mother and baby are just fine'. Julian heard these simple words, could barely take them in. Going to work, (a short-time occupation in an organisation to do with electronics), he tried not to arrive late despite managing an early morning appearance at the hospital. His wife and their newborn were fast asleep: he was permitted a glimpse of each in turn. He left a bunch of flowers by his slumbering wife's bedside.

'A son, I have a son. I am a father… I *must* earn money, yes, I need money, time, a job, and what about my music… the world has changed, our lives are topsy-turvy, everything has a bright glow to it: I have seen a tiny, purple, wrinkled, son, and he was fast-asleep.'

Julian, still the dreamer, was unable to see or move towards any firm goal before him; his safe, set days of military service had ended in a situation he could not handle. 'Here are the facts', he told himself: 'twenty-three years old, father of a son. Some potential...but no immediate prospects. Professional music...fat chance. I must give up this whole foolish idea!'

After work they came face to face: the crinkly, red-faced, grizzling Jonathan, already learning to suckle, usurping his father's favourite place. Julian melted, overwhelmed with tender feelings he never knew he had. With a sigh of relief he said to his wife: 'Step by step, thanks be..., it's all over: Christmas in a few days and when you come home, Fin, we can have a peaceful time, and make new plans, just you and me and this little crumple-face person.' Gently, cautiously, he stroked the tiny warm head; the new father's long fingers felt cold, awkward and clumsy. Marvelling at nature's miracle Julian forgot all previous misgivings.

\*\*\*

By chance a notice in the Physics department in Cape Town caught his eye. He'd dashed off to return a book to a former lecturer and noted the Bernard Price Institute of Geophysical research was looking for graduates. Just for once the new father made a quick decision: one telephone call, an appointment for an interview...and yes, there really *was* work on campus of the University of Witwatersrand...he must go immediately to Johannesburg, but only on a three month trial basis...to laboratories which had been involved with important research during the war, radar and such matters.

There was considerable consternation at home.

'We need the money, Fin, you know we do. It's not a hundred miles away...well,' the young father pulled a face, thinking. 'Ok, it's ten times that, but leave it to me, I'll look around, find temporary lodgings, and if it all works out you and Jon can join me. Plans to study music will have to wait until we are settled. It's all for the best, just a postponement. A pity to leave  our little nest here; but think of it another way: it's handy to have a toe-hold in Cape Town, and your mother, so close to you, will help you over the first few weeks while I look around.'

One week later they stood on the platform, arm in arm, heard the piercing whistle, then the first tentative puffs of the locomotive, felt torn apart by Julian's hasty leap onto the train, that cruel slam of the door, and then his upper body hanging from the window, barely touching fingers one more time, they had both convinced themselves: 'we're so used to being apart, ...just one more time, just one more time, just one more time, one more............puffing, clanking, noise receding, white handkerchief waving, ...all was well. How was this going to work out? Her eyes were damp.

It would surely be for the best. It had better be!

Two days later he telephoned from Johannesburg: 'I know no-one here. It is a monster, this city, lacking all grace, God help me. But Fin, the money will soon build up, good enough for the three of us! And the university buildings: so like the ones in Cape Town, at least there is that. Very strange.'

Back again, to their former ways, letter writing was resumed:

*....this place seems to be planned on regular lines: Market Square has the Town Hall, the Post*

office and the market buildings, also the Law Courts. There is an Art Gallery, there are theatres, parks, a zoo, churches, and even two racecourses. We could be perfectly happy here. I am a mere 900 miles away from where you are! I have found lodgings: a sort of boarding-house, owned by a woman, about thirty, American with a small son. Soon our Jon will be like him, friendly and trusting. She usually has students to stay, it is modest, but she is kind and allows me to use her piano...so what could be better. Not that I have much time for practising. The circumstances here are a bit odd- I only moved in yesterday. The ground floor is subdivided between Mrs. Bercott and her four year old ...she is thirtyish, very lively and pleasant, 'artistic', verging towards divorce from her husband in UNESCO somewhere in Europe....there is also an earnest physiotherapist and I have a small room at the back of the corridor. It seems I will be having breakfast with Mrs. Bercott and little Stevie...I expect I will have to find other meals myself. I don't want to be thought a scrounger. Mrs B. did say I could have meals with her if I want. She insists things must be cleared up (she's a bit casual, haphazard, which is quite a blessing).

*A coloured woman comes in twice a week from Sophia-town (the oldest coloured area, a bit like our District Six, I gather) to do the house work and even my laundry. If the other flat were available (it is bigger, two rooms and a kitchen) we might be able to rent it for ourselves, but it is not available now.*

*Once I've settled at work, I may be able to make contact with other young people, even musicians, and after a few months, with some accumulated cash we can find a place for all three of us. Be patient, darling. I'm sorry for this separation, but at least you are close to your parents and old friends. Here you would be alone all day long.*

*Anyway, this is my new address.*

Just a few days on and here they were, at it again: slotted into their accustomed, regular postal exchanges:

*Finuala darling, I feel reproved by your letter. I'm not sure that you are not dismal. Because I often am, though I'm sure I shouldn't be- I am at least getting so as to have plenty to do. You will again be accusing me of neglect, but I was only waiting for a letter from you.*

*When you and Jon have settled into your new routines you might be able to get on the train to* spend a little time here with me....and we can reconsider our options. I am reasonably well paid, well looked after. After all, we've had years of practice at being separated. Just keep those letters coming and please tell me all your thoughts.

Only a little while longer and we will have enough money to rent a bigger place of our own. As far as my career is concerned this step is one in the right direction. And although it is sad you are not here it is an incentive for me to make money to enable you to come here. HOW ARE YOU FINDING FINANCE? Keep praying; this separation might become more harrowing before many more weeks. My final want: YOU. But retaining reasonable spirits... I hope you are too.

Halfway through March Finuala reads:

...why did I feel, when reading your last letter that you were beginning to hate me? I hope the feeling was an absurd one: but I have been away from you for so long, to have done so little for you and Jon (my child too, you know, though I can understand your attitude)... this mustn't last long: it must be shocking psychologically! Jon-Oedipus... as for his vaccination, I don't know. Why did you decide against it? '

Their bond was stretched to its limit. How often did Finuala feed her baby, while brooding about his father? Friends, relatives did call her daily, feeling helpless: 'have you heard yet, when are you joining him,' concerned for the young mother and their child. She tried not to feel bitter, but she was trapped. Was there resentment taking root in her psyche? No, not yet.

There was much staring into unusually damp March mornings, massive clouds hanging where one usually saw grey mountain crags. She had a baby, a radio and the cat for company. One day resembled the next and all the ones before. Each day she counted every penny, all her 'tickeys', despite frequent help from Mum and Dad, while the daily-ness of hearing mostly her own voice mixed with Jon's squawks for subsistence was gradually wearing her down.

Condensation formed on the window where mother and baby stood; mesmerised by raindrops rolling down like tears on the pane outside, Finuala noted the grimy streaks...she'd not thought to deal with the windows since she moved in. The wall-clock ticked. There was a great silence around her. She shut her eyes. The child had fallen asleep on her shoulder.

'If I move slowly, carefully, I might be able to put him down and get on with that long-overdue washing, nappies each day but also other things... the trick is getting them dry outside, later, when the sun comes out. Mummy's maid is coming over to help for a few hours tomorrow...but, dear God, how one day resembles the other. I seem to have no time at all, even though I'm home night and day... unbelievable, without concentration to read, and if I did, it would only be Doctor Spock about the tyrannies of babies, or their diet and how to cope and things, like not running to the baby as soon as it cries; sticking to one's schedule, and to be strict. That's so hard!'

Once or twice a week old friends would drop by after work, to cheer her up. To feed her guests Finuala made use of simple recipes from her mother's war time recipes: skillet supper: chopped cabbage, chopped onion, chopped Corned Beef, one spoon of flour....fried up in butter, it took only two minutes, quite amusing that, a bit pongy, but people seemed to like it and it cost almost nothing. Social life seemed inappropriate now: only very few of Fin's former clothes fitted. Eating less might be all to the good, but the baby needed his regular feed... 'mustn't starve the poor mite', said Mummy, 'eat up Fin, eat as much as you can, your baby needs it.' So she obeyed and, of course, it was as well Julian was not able to see how depressed and formless she looked and felt.

'Which reminds me, I've yet to answer his last letter...he sounds less confident now: that new set-up, with the thirty year old woman who has a child, and who's husband is away too, or seems to have left for good. Do all husbands find ways to overcome parenthood....like simply not being there? Makes sense, when you think about it.' Fin, like most women, nourished a patient conviction she could change her man, if and when she discovered this to be true.

Of course it wasn't true. 'If this were the story of *our* love and our future lives... how would it end? It's just, well,... it's just so much more unglamorous than I'd imagined.'

Soon Julian also wrote dejected letters:

*My dear Fin,*

*The days are long and I feel out of touch. Has the money question been raised in some disastrous way? It may well have been, I must confess to feeling conscious of it now-all too late I suppose. What on earth am I doing, the months pass and I'm getting nowhere.... my ineffectual behaviour seems now to have been the utter-est, the most* ludicrous folly. I don't seem to be earning quite enough, it is not building up significantly, we must be patient a while longer.

I bumped into an old friend here, Harvey, (I'm sure you remember him,) quite by chance when I treated myself to an outing to hear the Johannesburg Symphony Orchestra....there he was, amongst the first violins, and when I managed to catch him during the interval he told me he was not much impressed with this orchestra, 'all amateurs, you know,' he informs me, and apparently the oldest symphony orchestra in Africa, founded in 1934. The first conductor was a pupil of Schoenberg.' All I had to tell him was that I had bought a French horn, something I have been dying to own and play....it was quite cheap, second-hand in a music shop. I imagine its former owner passed away. Harvey has taken this orchestral job on board for 'experience'....he teaches, but he too needs to earn more serious money!

It was when I came to tell him how I had spent the last months I realised how little I seem to have done, in spite of everyone's assistance. (Not least your father and the house, of course, surely he must be pretty fed up!) I seem to be betraying fatal

*bitterness, with little excuse, it is you who should feel that, I am sure. At least you must be certain'*
…Which of the two was manipulating whom?

By now, in the Transvaal, Apartheid had become entrenched, slowly saturating and choking life-processes. Johannesburg overwhelmed. By contrast Cape Town, curled sleepily around its mountain, seen from where Julian was, felt like a safe, sleepy hollow.

Soon enough Julian explored Sophia-town: shacks, squalor, dirty streets, houses falling down, gradually becoming one of the rare places where blacks had permission to own land. Just like in New York's Harlem cultural processes were intensified, along with the poverty. It was the cradle of that story about a famous boxer and brawler, which became the King Kong musical.

'It all began after the Second World War' a new colleague informed Julian, 'gangsters and *tsotsis,* young ruffians who speak a mixture of Afrikaans and English (tsotsi-taal), make walking about in old Sophia-town an uncomfortable business. They are the day to day reality, those city-bred gangsters, they still admire Hitler because he had taken on the *whites* of Europe! Nowadays their motto is: pas op…. watch out! Julian, those tsotsis, they will follow you, taunt and obstruct your path, especially around areas you don't know, do be careful. If you must go there, try the Odin cinema...it's vast, holds 1200 people. That Mr. Odin, a man of some renown, makes the place available for political meetings, parties and also stage performances. Close by is Freedom Square, famous for political meetings: Ghandi had law officers here, in Rissik Street, when he was a young man....'

Out exploring somewhat nervously Julian passed by the famous oak tree in Bertha Street, the 'hanging tree'. Suburbs like Westdene and Newlands, adjacent to Sophiatown, he learned, were thought by most whites to be too close to coloured people. Different races were now segregated under the Immorality Act, just like everywhere else in South Africa. But at least trying to feel responsible, brave and intrepid Julian felt the need to prepare his wife for her arrival:

'Not only the cleaning maid, but also some of South Africa's famous musicians, politicians, writers are *emerging from this feared and mistrusted area.* Cape Town has a different feel to it; the more I see the more I wonder if I've made a terrible mistake...Jo'burg can be an uncomfortably dangerous place...'

But he did want her to come. Julian was doing the best he could without getting her too alarmed. Their correspondence flew across the Karroo: his letters down to the clean sea air of the Cape which now seemed like a haven of sanity, while hers fluttered back to his primitive hovel. Perhaps she barely admitted to herself her man was hoping she might stay where she was... just a little longer. He, however, wary of revealing too much, feared she might refuse to come altogether: and now there was an added complication: unpremeditated closeness had developed between him and the older, more experienced landlady. What was he doing, and what was he going to say to his wife? This young husband had become a troubled man. *'Men like Father Trevor Huddlestone and some forceful black chap called Nelson Mandela are speaking out, in an effort to make justice prevail. Who are these people, have you heard of them?'* wrote Julian to Finuala...covering his tracks with stimulating up-to-date political speculation. *'One of the ways to find out things is to buy The Drum, a weekly magazine which expresses the voices of anguished suppression'*, he told his wife, *'a new magazine known for high literary standards in both fiction* and poetry. You will enjoy it. Being you, you probably know it already. It is available in Cape Town. But these gangs in Sophia-town, the crime and violence... well, you'll be unnerved by all that. But then this can't be an ongoing reality... It may be better for us to relocate to Pretoria. All this is not pleasing; although I hope it doesn't put you off coming. There are numbers of interesting people in Johannesburg. The latest addition: a young photographer from Berlin, who has become fascinated by that 'invisible wall', as he puts it, 'between races,' when certain races are not treated like citizens. Perhaps, Fin, you could get some work, find something you can do from home, once you get here, at the Drum magazine, with those office skills of yours... you might even meet Trevor Huddleston who is a close friend apparently of the Drum superintendant of St. Peter's School: everyone is talking about Huddleston these days, an influential man. Yes, we live in interesting times. The big thing is to make up one's mind... where it is one stands in a place like South Africa. PS. Jürgen ... the name of that young photographer I keep hearing about. He has come here straight from Lesotho, after that country became independent from Britain. It must be *strange for Europeans like him to set foot in a country like ours. PPS: One of his claims to fame: He has photographed the first horse-race in the Kingdom of Lesotho!'*

# Six

Johannesburg, June, 1952.

Sunshine...but that famous Transvaal winter nevertheless: Julian galloped down the stairs for work really early, seemingly in a great hurry, not saying a word.

'I really must get out of here!' Finuala has bundled up her child hoping she might be distracted from her heart-swelling rage and disappointment. She is shivering. Out in the fresh air the temperature is a mere five degrees Centigrade....she's glanced at the thermometer stuck to the windowsill... last night there'd been a frost, puddles still frozen over, 'but they've probably begun melting in the winter-weakened rays. There, a frozen puddle! She stepped on the ice to crush it. Again and again the angry grinding sounds helped to fuel her fury, her niggling, mortified pride. 'Sins are attempts to fill voids,' some female French writer had said that. 'All sins?' she wondered. 'Does this apply especially to adultery? Still, what help is that?' Shoes sodden, feet ice-cold, Finuala hardly noticed nor cared. She was re-living her arrival twenty-four hours ago, with her baby, two cases and a push chair. The rest, sent from Cape Town, would follow in due course, may even have arrived by now.... 'and this landlady, apparently out of town...thank goodness, may she stay wherever she is.' The young mother sighed. 'This chill, not only in the air...but also in my feelings, I'll never forgive him', she muttered, blinded with misery. In freezing Johannesburg morning air, pushing her son in the push-chair, Finuala nursed her pain, felt deeply betrayed....how he'd not even managed to appear at the station, how she'd stood and stood and stretched, peering, on her toes, everywhere she could see, through gaps in the passing crowd, searching, hoping, increasingly desperate, embittered and abandoned. What sort of a husband was this? In the end there'd been no alternative: buried in her bag somewhere she'd found an address Julian had sent her. She'd got a taxi, with difficulty. Even then she was still hoping. On arrival: no-one answered the bell. Julian was nowhere. And then, in that squalid tearoom, all those thoughts, possibilities, crowding her mind, while clinging to the squirming infant on her lap, baggage scattered all around them. Close to tears, a lump in her throat, the baby whimpering, she'd stared out of a smeary window, hoping that man of hers might appear. 'What's wrong with my husband,' she'd even said to the waiter: 'He's hopeless. He couldn't have forgotten we were coming?'

But Julian *had* gone to the station. Tall as he was, towering over almost everyone, he'd missed her in the crowds, simply failed to see her. Rushing about, jumping on a bus, he eventually tracked her down, forlorn in the café next to his 'lodgings'. A poor start for a mother with a cranky six month old baby. And all that baggage! What a bungled beginning of their new lives together! His explanations, her accusations, clouds continued to gather. And then, to crown it all, once they'd gone to the apartment, after that first cup of tea together, as if he'd been nurturing some death wish, he ineptly 'spilled the beans:' he and his landlady had become close. 'But' he added, 'I thought it might be more honest to tell you straight away; it was nothing serious, we were drawn to one another, not really love or anything... anyway she's gone away for a while and it's all over'. 'How *could* you,' was all the young wife found to say, tears welling up, stunned by the shock. There followed a long silence, the kind before an impending disaster. Finuala could barely take in what she'd just heard. A numbness around her lips, a dizziness, as if she was about to faint...she clung to little Jon on her lap....she closed her eyes. Now came the questions, she spat them out, in a rage, one after the other: 'you went to bed with her? Why should I be here, with you, now? Why did you make us come then, to *this* place, to be with *you*?'

Sitting opposite him Julian saw a medieval oil painting: a bereft, pale Madonna, her eyes lowered, tears streaming, holding an innocent child, looking first at him, then at his mother...frowning a little.

Penitent, leaning forward, practically on his knees, the young husband pleaded for forgiveness. He explained as best he could, with constant assurances of love and gratitude, adding further pleas for understanding,... allowing nature to take its course, extenuating circumstances, all these many, far too many months, 'it didn't mean anything...really, Fin, do believe me, it was nothing.'

She glared at him: 'Of course it meant something. Nothing you can say will ever repair this damage: a deep crevasse has opened between us. I'm going back tomorrow.'

Julian, hovering uncertainly by the brink, still tried to find at least some acceptable clarification: 'She had troubles of her own,' he tried, 'she's gone for a while. I have no idea where she is, nor when she returns... please let me get this off my chest: it just happened, Fin, unpremeditated, it was *her* idea, she meant no harm, nor did I, believe me, she'd got the 'flu and I nursed her back to health for a week or so. Nothing happened between us for a long time. Please Fin, try to understand? I'm so very grateful to have you here and with Jon too, I've been longing for you both. I do so need you. Believe me, it was nothing, nothing at all, really, truly. Look at me, please, Fin. Please!

Look at me!'

She could not. With venom, she spat out: '...and now you've got me here I'm supposed to accept it all? I wish I'd never set eyes on you. I'm going back to Cape Town. What a hateful liar you've become.'

Clinging to her child, Finuala retreated behind activities necessary to keep the baby comfortable...while thinking, in a haze of pained hate: 'the bastard, I can't believe he would do such a thing.' Tears were streaming down her face. She was aware it was the first time Julian had seen her weep.

'Oh... please Fin, I had no wish to make you unhappy'. And then, 'I've learned a lot, you'll see'… She heard him prattle on, tastelessly, she thought, his trying to appear so debonair, on top of everything. Nauseated, drained, and ever more furious she managed to spit out: 'Indeed! As if I cared. Why should I want to have anything more to do with you, stay with you? You are too young for me. Who do you think you are?'

They sat, staring hopelessly at their son, crawling about on tacky linoleum which had seen better days. Suddenly the child came to rest, determined to pluck off one of his knitted bootees. During this prolonged silence thoughts of both young parents swirled about like angry hornets against the backdrop of their child's puzzled and aimless noises. Wide-open baby eyes kept looking up for reassurance, while Julian, elbows on the table, large hands covering nose and mouth,  stared helplessly into the cracks on the wooden surface. Fin was already considering the now inevitable fifteen-hour train journey, all the way back to Cape Town.

'Hey,' Julian tried again after a while, looking her straight in the eye, 'come on Fin. It doesn't mean I love her,' and, still searching for a plausible explanation, 'it was meaningless, why can't you understand?  Look at me. Please, Fin. She was lonely, I was lonely. That's it.  Besides, she's much too old for me. Don't be like this, really, it meant nothing! Be reasonable. I'm so pleased you are here at last...and she's gone for a while, so we can use the apartment as much as we like. I don't even have to pay her: I'm the care-taker. You and me, we could even find another place together and move out before she comes back.'

Finuala, face to face with her man's aimless drifting, his ability to do nothing, and burdened with her own rage, gasped, glowered, and glared at this monster, who was now her husband. *He was a man and he's done her wrong,* she vaguely heard in the back of her head.

'I too am older than you', she reminded him.

Embarrassed, Julian tried again: 'Don't be hard on her,' he pleaded 'she is a *much* older woman, very experienced. Believe me, I am overjoyed you're here, at last, you *and* Jon, you two are all that ever mattered. She's letting us stay free of charge...she's being very generous really. She and I, we were both lonely and unhappy, but I always, always missed you, never felt even remotely disloyal ...'

Finuala's rage now turned to pain: a physical hurt, this searing jealousy, like a festering wound. Whatever *he* said turned into *her* torment, but also revulsion. It welled up again and again. She could not stop probing in her wounds. There was no relief, nowhere to turn, she felt trapped. She'd known jealousy only by observing her own friends, usually men who had suffered on *her* account, and she never could quite believe them. Now she knew what this felt like. She wondered if she was going to throw up.

Julian, as ever, did a great deal of talking. He was more than simply good at that. She'd switched him off... she barely heard him droning on. Trapped and, still overwhelmed with loathing, not wanting to see or hear him, she certainly never wanted him to touch her again. The baby clung to her legs, trying to climb into her lap. '...and now,' she heard him say, 'I've been offered slightly better pay, (a promotion already), it was to have been a surprise for you.

We can find a place together and start all over. Look at me Fin, please, darling, I beg you, don't turn away again, try to forgive ...I'm so glad we are finally together. At last! It's been such a long wait! When we have a place to ourselves, we can do as we please, even have people round...I've been waiting for your arrival to invite that German, you know, the photographer I mentioned: you'd like him, he already knows so many interesting people... he's in with the Drum crowd, and may be able to help you find something to do... I bet you haven't had any work or social life for the past six months. Well, all that could be over now, if you just let it go, your completely understandable anger. Please, please, please... be reasonable. At last we can bring up this little boy together and enjoy our lives again.' The baby was now clinging to his father's trouser leg, staring up at him. Julian's blue eyes were fixed on Fin's grey ones as he cautiously pushed one hand across the smeary tabletop. She frowned. She glared at him briefly, then turned away. Nothing was said for some time. The baby still clung to Julian's trousers, puzzled eyes moving from his father to his mother...

'Look at me, Fin. Please. I'm sorry you are hurt. I love you, believe me', he forced himself to say, yet again, embarrassed, but also perplexed she should be minding quite so much.

'How *am* I going to put this right,' he wondered.

Gently, patiently, he extricated himself from his tiny son, stood up, rummaged around and returned with a bottle of cheap South African sherry and two glasses. His ashen-faced wife had turned to stone. Staring dumbly at his familiar hands, she began to shiver. He poured the pale-brown liquid. She felt the hurt, just looking at those hands of his.

Jon, nestling peacefully on her lap, now stretched out one tiny fist and knocked a glass over. His mother, still locked in her grief, did nothing. Julian turned his head from side to side, took a deep breath and got to his feet ...to mop up the wasted golden painkiller.

***

'Strange, for a woman who owns a suitcase stuffed with letters from admirers... all on their knees begging her to marry them, to feel so much pain after hearing my one, modest confession', thought Julian. Several former contestants for her affection had been exceedingly suspiciously, closely attached to *her* over long periods of time...with repeated affirmations of undying devotion, and offers of marriage, matching those of Julian's from 1945 onwards, right up to this day. And she'd always been quite open about *her* '*friendships*'.....

Meanwhile Finuala wondered why it had all seemed so urgent, her resolve to marry this man; now that they were actually together.

'Let there be spaces in your togetherness', a quote from some Middle-Eastern sage popped into her head. 'How does one learn to do that? Can, could there ever be any togetherness for them now? But here it was: that long planned future, the marriage she had hoped for, dreamed about, for more than six years and which had so far led to nothing but misery.' They were both aware of this.

In the end, they accepted the challenge.

'𝕰𝖌𝖔 𝖙𝖊 𝖆𝖇𝖘𝖔𝖑𝖛𝖔' is what a priest might have said. She was no priest. Absolution is forgiving, not forgetting and 'I, Finuala, have no choice, really. Wounds like these leave painful scars. I will be licking mine for as long as I live.'

A clever woman listens to myriad voices in her head, voices that assure all is well (or not), that such things are natural, (or not), what does it matter, men *are* like that, just let it be- consider the mysterious sexual appetites of most men: he had not relished living alone, and of course, sex could be seen as almost the opposite of love, just an appetite. *He*'d said it was nothing. Nothing.

So, '*let* there be spaces', like some poet said... 'but, you know, the wound, the scar, it really *is* there, and probably for ever. Why? It's not logical? No, I know. But that's how it is with those so-called spaces...and that togetherness'...

On and on she reasoned with herself.

\*\*\*

In some such cases relationships grow, in others there remains irreparable mistrust, especially when the victims are still so very young. Unexpected places in the mind open up, caves to hide in, or high look-outs to seek escape routes, and then, sadly, there comes a hidden store of permanent doubt, mistrust, distrust, blank unbelief, even spite. Although demands of a baby and penitent assurances of a husband kept despair at bay, reality took its toll.

Finuala was an intelligent woman. After this conflict... confrontation, on the very next freezing morning, she found her way to a church. She didn't even bother to look if it was Catholic. She told her God, *any* God, quietly and firmly: 'Rid me of this pain, release me from all routines, regimentation and prescriptive traditions. I will be generous, I will be sensible, do my duty as expected, and from now I will follow my instincts, just as men do. I too will be free. Free as I've always been…….' When she stepped back outside into the sunny bustle of life she felt restored. In *her* mind this notion of freedom was in brackets, a proviso, a loop-hole.

And why *had* she felt she needed to keep all those old letters, that extraordinary record of admirers but also of her own unbelievably lengthy and sometimes clouded, shrouded courtship?

Flatteringly sweet memories, dalliance of one sort or another, might they become a crutch and reassurance after shocks of this sort?

\*\*\*

Once the couple managed to move away from the 'tainted' rooms of the American landlady Julian made an effort and invited his colleagues to their new apartment in the centre of town. Finuala and Julian now lived right over shops, up a few shabby steps, close by Woolworths, quite near Lewis' Shoe-Store. That, sadly, more or less summed it up. Their new home was dark, dilapidated, noisy and dusty. For a while, until the bank account built up, they were right in the heart of town: trams, traffic, shouting and whistling, screeching brakes and hooting, especially during the day. All this, so very different from somnolent, 'oak-tree' Rondebosch, on the other side of that patient Table Mountain, became 'home' surprisingly quickly. The young couple found it unexpectedly stimulating, an adventure, bonding, possibly even exciting, with at least one pleasing, 'flowery' park reasonably close, and Julian's work only a short bus-ride away.

***

Citizens of Johannesburg had to be tougher than people in the Cape. Julian's new colleagues and acquaintances soon provided welcome distraction and stimulation. There was resilience here; even a youthful German émigré felt that, since *he* recently arrived from Berlin. Claiming to be sick and tired of hearing about Germany's Nazi past he understood soon enough he'd emerged from one monstrous struggle to find another.

With a heavy German accent he explained: '...apart from all zat it eez also difficult to make a living when you are 'Fotograf'. The Drum, a specialised literary magazine, has only four people on the staff ...also black men are working there and it is a calling really, there is no money, we are like a gang... we work together because there is no voice for black people, no publication for them. Here, with the Drum, we have a role to play. A drum roll! Ha, ha, not so funny, yes?'

Intriguing, a German with a sense of humour! And now with a mission: how to face bold new political realities looming in a small office in Johannesburg. Finuala studied him with interest, this fresh-faced young man. He always carried with him a portfolio of electrifying photos.

She owned a box camera and took cautious pictures of her son. Nodding happily the youthful photographer praised her, not even remotely condescending... 'jawohl, Frau Finuala, may I call you this... you have ze talent! All you need is ze quick eye and ze good light... to appreciate *das Ding an sich*...the curiously entertaining, outstanding, unique property of each subject...and, do not be afraid, you press, and immediately you are becoming surprised how you catch 'things' that fascinate not only you but also others. Talking of interesting: I am getting pictures of a young black lawyer called Mandela...Ja? You hear ze name?' He nodded vigorously.

'He is stepping in the public eye...'

Finuala grinned. At last! Someone who made her laugh, however unwittingly. A fresh, new voice, even if it was a German one. She'd heard more than enough about Germans and it was mostly not good. But *this* young man…when *he* stepped into the room she felt stimulated and taken right out of herself. Under the tutelage of someone like Jürgen, so eager, so refreshing, all the way from Berlin, well, anything could happen. He always clicked his heels, leaned forward to kiss her hand on arrival and then again… on departure.  'It is the custom, in Germany, Gnädige Frau', he informed.

'How lovely, do come again,' she heard herself breathe, and really meaning it, while wondering if that nail varnish she'd  once used was still somewhere…..

And so he did, again and again, to enjoy Frau Finuala's hospitality. He'd appear, seemingly from nowhere, in his VW 'beetle,' often unannounced, basking in her admiration, while passing on welcome instruction and tips for taking photos of her son: 'it must be action, it must be life, close-up, a 'blitz' of reality, messy, falling over, crying, not just sitting in the playpen, that sort of usual and dull thing…'

'I'm saving every penny to buy a better camera,' she told him, while he suggested he might be able to arrange some typing jobs for the magazine: did she own a typewriter? 'Yes, gut, that is ganz ausgezeichnet', extremely excellent. 'Is it only Germans who will classify things as *extremely* excellent'...she wondered.

'As long as you can get scripts back to the office- perhaps Julian can drop the papers off, ja, you know how tricky it is, with ze deadlines and so on. You will have remuneration for zis... perhaps.'

She smiled. She was content; this was just what she needed. No-one had any idea how much she'd been missing the stimulating existence left behind in Stellenbosch, those invigorating daily lectures, typing reports, as well as the influx and contact with studious and articulate people. It became increasingly clear that Jürgen's company did, from time to time, make up for at least some of that.

***

Father, mother, small son: they were not exactly chasing gold, here, right by the richest gold-mine in the world. Even so, day to day routines brought stability at last; a security of the body, if perhaps not quite of the soul. Something which was never far away, politics, now became the un-easiest of predicaments. The Defiance Campaign begun in 1950, hung over white and black people in equal measure. Whites with a conscience wondered how the plot would unravel without bloodshed... now and then there was condemnation from other parts of the world. Trevor Huddlestone, a close friend of Drum Magazine and also superintendant of St. Peter's School in Johannesburg, (a place which educated many talented black South Africans), spoke his mind in open criticism of the government. Effects of the still unofficial Apartheid, the built-in discrimination, and economic reasons, had brought on plans to demolish Sophia-town, the very place where so many of the black intelligentsia lived. Even the thriving multicultural conurbation in other parts of Johannesburg was changing: from time to time black people were bundled up and moved further outside town to other townships. Politically conscious South Africans shook heads, got involved, perhaps, but mostly kept their heads down.

***

As soon as they could the young Cape Town-ians escaped from central Johannesburg into suburbia, to an area called Wychwood. This brought with it a tiresome journey each day for the head of the household. But here were open fields with trees close by, and Finuala was delighted to have a small walled-in garden with a high palm tree peeking out well over roof level, waving its fronds in the Transvaal breeze. Masses of white and pink flowers, Bauhinias, grew by the entrance and all this was close enough for pushing the pram to small shops, far away from the din and grubby shambles of town.

'Do I have 'green fingers' she wondered as she planted, for the first time ever, a packet of nasturtium seed. It was time to find out. Occasionally friends from earlier, more troubled times, but especially unstoppable, eager Jürgen, emerged from that exhausting centre of Johannesburg just to breathe the cleaner air of Wychwood.

'Aha, yes, liebe Frau Finuala, you and your wunderbares cooking, I will come many miles for that, especially ze Gateau Ganache; I have ze *sweet teeth*, is that not how you South African people like to speak? Or are you English?'

He inspired, her, to say the least. An intuitive response was to ask for views and suggestions about her early attempts at photography. 'I could not be in better hands,' she told herself. And she was learning more than others realised. For several months the young man drifted in and out of her now less predictable days and ways, calling at unexpected times. Finuala helped him by correcting his English, and by explaining all she knew about black people, the Zulu's, Bantu's, and Bushmen, about Afrikaners, about fears, hopes and feelings of white people in Africa and the built-in restrictive 'mores' which 'foreigners' like him would never be able to understand. Deriving great benefit from each other's company she and her young friend learned quickly, avidly, even greedily.

'I miss my work in Stellenbosch, you know', she'd remind her husband, when he came home from work in the big city, 'stimulation, youthful intelligent people milling about...' and to this, the un-easiest of many predicaments, Julian, concerned and vaguely guilty, showed some touchiness, pointing out he *had* been trying to bring occasional interesting guests...and 'of course, Fin, I see how you perk up when I bring colleagues, even those who stir things up with endless political fears. I am doing my best. You are getting plenty of information about the wider picture, literary giants, chatter about Todd Machekiza and Bloke Modisane, the latest books of Nadine Gordimer, and now there is your young German friend...'

Finuala had been trying to keep up as much as possible but, as she'd (just the other day) realised: 'shot in the foot' again: 'soon there will be *two* children, Mrs. Goodkin'. She'd smiled at the doctor, pleased, in a way, but kept this new development to herself for a while.

Reading was still *her* thing: she made use of a primitive local library, exchanged books with friends while Jon was too young for a nursery school, and soon she met other young mothers, mostly wives of affluent men, lawyers, business people, who all cultivated the friendly Sunday-by-the–pool–in Africa culture, often with that obligatory braai-vleis.

'How pleasing, these get-togethers,' she wrote to her mother, 'young children enjoying idyllic half-naked days by the pool, playing happily in the shade with other healthy youngsters, young parents discussing politics: ultimately the only topic these days. Besides, Sundays are mostly the servants' day off, so it is relaxing to pass the time in an uncomplicated way. Too bad I'm pregnant again, still, its months to go...and now, with our new friends who like us to come and sit by their pool...we 'Capetown-ians' can even afford a Bantu maid, our friendly Betty, with such superb references! We are so lucky!

Finuala trusted her Betty. A bare little room with the usual facilities at the bottom of the garden was there for servants to stay overnight, or even live in, if and when necessary. On the whole, young Betty, from the outskirts of Sophia-town, preferred to get back home, where she had caring duties of her own: an ailing mother.

But because of Betty's presence Finuala and Julian did occasionally get out, even though 'Fin' was soon back in voluminous smocks. Her man took her to theatres, films and concerts. Life had become more tolerable. Getting through a second pregnancy? Nothing to it: one has a maid, one has friends, little Jonathan was on his feet, becoming sensible. What lay ahead was predictable: even though life was not quite what they'd wished. Predictable, predictable..., almost as threatening as their old pet hate, 'conventional', still, they both looked forward to another child. Long days stretched ahead, with the sameness of daily routines. Occasionally old friends from Cape Town came, sometimes stayed overnight, even Ailsa visited for a few days. She too was about to leave home, become a married woman.   Yes, life was both: predictable, conventional. No getting away from it.

And then, at the appointed time:  please do meet Jon's little sister: Victoria! Quite the opposite of her earnest brother she was golden-haired, grey-eyed and quietly quirky from the very first moment.

Now a mother of two, Finuala grappled with new tasks and also braced herself for the issue of the christening. She was as wary as ever when making contact with Catholic authorities. 'Why am I doing this?   Is it just to keep Mother content?'

When Jonathan had been christened, still in the early Cape Town days, parents arranged the whole thing; while Julian was still thousands of miles away, finding his way around the new job in Johannesburg.  At the time of that Cape Town christening the name 'Jonathan', (son of Saul and friend of David) had been suggested by Julian's religious Papa, sanctioned of course, by the absentee father. It would have been nice to have the family there.  Money and time were tight in those days.  She closed her eyes, remembered how the tiny man-child had derived little pleasure from the ordeal, had cried himself crimson, where-upon that well-read uncle Frank had informed everyone that 'Jonathan' was a variety of American desert apple. Too late, the deed was done.

On that very occasion, after the drenched infant had been calmed, the priest prayed elaborately over Finuala, (some sort of cleansing ceremony to remove the *stains* of motherhood) while she, kneeling before him, bristled inwardly at the idea of having to be purged of this God-ordained process: ('what *is* all this, could this be what is known as a 'Churching' and what exactly am I being purged of? Is there some guilt attached; what *is* this forgiveness to be dispensed? Why had no-one warned me?'). Finuala was overwhelmed by a deluge of unexpected antagonism.

***

'In Ireland new mothers are considered to be attractive to fairies...in danger of being kidnapped by them', Finuala's mother leaned over her daughter and grandson, tenderly stroked their damp curls after the 'Churching', and said: 'it's usually done on the fortieth day after confinement, this special purification of the mother. But of course dear, that 'fairy thing' ...it is only a local superstition. Don't fret Fin!'

Finuala raised her eyebrows, but managed a mocking smile.

'Oh God, you, and your strange Irish world, Mother! Still, Julian and I would like to visit there sometime, Mum,' she added, just in case she'd once again caused offence. 'One day, when we are rich. For the moment we can only live for our happy and glorious Victoria, and darling little Jon, of course.'

Finuala's almost forgotten doubt: that magical purging of guilt in the Catholic confessional, had re-surfaced, briefly. Now she inclined her ear, managed to exchange her frown with a forced smile. 𝕬𝖚𝖉𝖎 𝖋𝖎𝖑𝖎𝖆, 𝖊𝖙 𝖛𝖎𝖉𝖊, 𝖊𝖙 𝖎𝖓𝖈𝖑𝖎𝖓𝖆 𝖆𝖚𝖗𝖊𝖒 𝖙𝖚𝖆𝖒...and 'forget thy people and thy father's house...' were also flashing through her retentive mind.

'Yes, Victoria! What a splendid name: surely a guiding light, an omen, for such a quirky daughter; she has a sparkle about her already....,' was Julian's contribution. The entire family had come up to Johannesburg for the event. After another 'Churching', again part of the ceremony... 'just a blessing, Fin, relax, honestly: this is no ritual purification, although it draws on the symbolism of the Virgin... there now, let me put my lace shawl over your hair,' her mother soothed; she always was the one who remembered exactly how to get through these Catholic rituals.

What was it about the Catholic Church, constantly, tediously grinding on about guilt? When sins can and must be first repented, only then absolved? An existence without a stain on one's character, that's what it seemed to be about. She imagined rows and rows of purged, pure, unspotted souls, gleaming like polished silver, in heaven.

'I should at least *try* to be submissive,' thought Finuala, suppressing her school-girl doubts. 'This will have been a blessing; it was, in all likelihood *just* what I needed, cloven-hoofed as I am,' she told herself. Just for one brief moment she felt suitably tamed and subdued...

\*\*\*

That grey dawn call: Here it comes again. It is the toughest one.

'Is there any point in sleeping in the same bed with Julian, at this time in our lives? He insists I do, God knows why. I'm not in any frame of mind for closeness and so on, with leaky 'bosoms,' on call again for feeding my offspring every few hours'.

Sliding, struggling, Finuala staggered from crumpled sheets to the adjacent 'baby' room, barefoot and barely conscious, while the miniscule female body squirmed, kicked and boxed the air, desperate for attention. 'Jon was far less troublesome,' she remembered. The sun barely up and this infant had perforated her mother's exhausted dreams with squawking and extremely grating demands for room-service...not forgetting a competent nappy change: a dangerous business at this time of day however large the safety pins are.

'Plop, there goes another smelly nappy into the special soaking pail, with a lid, thankfully. Dear Betty, so efficient with all the extra washing. Julian has promised us a washing machine soon, although we're still up to our ears with Hire Purchase.....'

'There now, keep that light low: my theory that Vicky goes back to sleep more readily in a darkened room is sound; I believe, the sun is not quite up, but birds are beginning to welcome the day while my daughter and I stagger to the window, jointly sink into an armchair, her little eyes tightly shut as she suckles, grizzles, grunts and snuffles. Just let it all happen. I close my eyes. Will I be allowed to creep back to bed? I feel that intriguing, deeply embedded pull of vaginal muscle, hm,....that best-kept secret of breastfeeding. It almost makes up for everything. One's only and fondest hope: more sleep. Some mothers keep their babies by their bed, *in* their bed even. I could never do that to my husband. He has a responsible job and needs his rest. Besides, I can take a siesta in the afternoon, he cannot. I am a damp, leaking, feeding machine, a slave to my daughter's needs. Just look at this creature, now gurgling sweetly, so content...

It only takes about half an hour before I'm allowed to collapse into my own bed again. Those birds, how they chirp and chatter despite the foggy dawn!

I dive back into deepest, blackest unconsciousness: heaven, more sleep, there never is enough of it. Julian sneaks out, quietly (he believes), grabs his coffee on the way. Sometimes I hear him switch on the engine of our very own VW. Yes, he's finally given in, learnt to drive. My turn next. Back, back, into my sleep, my dreams.'

The maid comes in before breakfast gets on with 'things', sees to Jon in his nursery's own toy-strewn bed while Finuala stays where she is for as long as she  can. And after that? Well, another day, like all the others.

The long 'daily-ness', regular as clockwork, ends around tea-time. Then, two hours after tea, when the sun is setting, when the crickets whirr and grate, Finuala changes her rhythm to devote herself to the return of the conquering hero from the heaving metropolis.

The maid will have gathered up the debris of another day, but the wreckage of Fin's thoughts is not so easily pushed aside. Each day there are renewed torments: it had seemed so urgent, that need to marry Julian, after almost six, or was it eight years... of boy-and girlfriend—now she wondered why they did, or rather, why she had. He had so many other things to think about.  But for her the feeling that life was over gathered momentum in the daily unchanging commotion of little people, *her* very own demanding little people. She decided to tell Julian about her misgivings:

'Our son already enjoys his tiny life in the nursery school nearby, you know, that *Tom Thumb* place. I've met one of the mothers: Cecily, quite a withdrawn woman, she will come tomorrow for a chat... I feel she is also experiencing dangerous thoughts; perhaps it is some hormonal thing, do you suppose...?' Finuala confides. Julian hears his wife but has little idea what she is talking about.

'Should you not be truly fulfilled and happy now, isn't that how it is supposed to go, normally, I mean, with motherhood and having a home? It's what you wanted, Fin... you've changed your mind?' But in *his* mind he was already rushing off, thinking of other things, work, challenges, new colleagues, projects, complex and much more interesting problems.

***

Five o'clock. Another day come and almost gone, count-down to bath and suppertime. Day and night, again and over again, how unstoppable it all was. Then silence, the ultimate luxury, perhaps a few pages of a book until Julian appeared with re-enlivening chatter and news of the big world. Another day, sherry on the stoep,...

hidden from distant prattling of neighbours' children, later the news, crackly news, on the SABC. Or the gramophone, or reading… that's what one does after supper. Dull, really dull! But there was a big bonus: one had moved into the safe suburbs, away from and out of the dangerous big city……..

'And tomorrow? How will it be? Bad things seem to be happening out there. Like the planned removal of all those poor Coloureds from Sophiatown, just because the place is so close, only four miles west of Johannesburg city centre. It's finally happening! Right, we know, the place is a terrible slum: it is to be razed to the ground. But the inhabitants will be re-housed elsewhere'.

Husbands and wives all over Johannesburg discuss daily events in town. Why don't the coloured people like it? Fear and tension, a permanent worry and bad feeling of impending trouble, soon one will be afraid to go out at night. Doesn't our Betty live there?

In the morning Fin walks with Jon to the nursery; he is two already; she takes the pushchair along in case he gets weary. He pushes the pram, she guides it along. Their joint progress is commendable. Laudable…. 'Oh, hallo there, how are you, Cecile?'

Two young mothers have arrived outside Tom Thumb nursery school, pleased to deposit their offspring. 'Had a rough night? You look terrible! I'm expecting you at three, is that right? Look forward to that, do come, whenever you like. 'Totsiens, see you then, Cecile, we'll pick the kids up before tea.'

At last, Fin has befriended someone: delicate, dark- shadows- under-her-eyes-Cecile, a girl from Paarl, of Huguenot extraction it appears, with gleaming, smooth, black hair. She speaks proudly, in a slow, deliberate, sing-song voice betraying a traditional Afrikaans-speaking upbringing. Her unusually large three-year old seems to have attached himself to Jon. How did she manage to produce this huge child? She is dainty and small, like Finuala. They could be sisters. Cecile dresses simply, almost to the point of asceticism, each day the same trousers and a plain-coloured T-shirt. She always arrives in her VW. Everyone here buys these German Beetles.... 'the local dealer must be a millionaire...'Finuala jokes.

Cecile pulls a face, mutters wryly... 'ag, yes, maybe....'

While pushing the empty push-chair back home, Finuala wondered: 'should I bake scones for tea, make an effort, bring out the best tea-service, that (unwanted) gift from my sister... 'perhaps Huguenots prefer South African things, like sticky Koek-Susters? I should have asked. Better go for meringues, yes, people like those.

At home in her carrycot, on her back, Vicky kicks, jerks, earnestly observes and communicates...with a shiny brass doorknob. 'She's done this before' Fin thinks, 'seems to like shiny things. The doorknob brings greater satisfaction than the rattle or even her new cuddly toy. Perhaps Vicky believes it to be a big golden eye, steadfast and interested in only one thing: herself. This is how we women begin to fool ourselves.'

Fin picks her up. 'Time for your second feed, my precious... what a 'smiler' you are today, my baby!' Vicky has attached herself to her mother's breast for the second feed, smacking her lips, gurgling happily. Finuala adores her daughter, rests the child on her shoulder, gently rubs the tiny soft back in time-honoured fashion, not conscious of the fact that the infant has just spewed up her entire second breakfast in a wide arc over her mum's shoulder, right across the room onto the pine floor. Betty, the maid from Sophiatown saw it happening, hurried over making reassuring clicking noises: 'ag, meddam, my friend's baby do it all the time, some babies do dis, dis nothing bad, moenie worry nie, its 'o-rrite', dey grrow out of it. Dit is called 'prrojectile vomiting,.....meddem, babbas, dey can't help it...'

'You're really good with her, Betty, I'm so lucky to have you! You can go home early today, the master will be very late tonight.

'Yes, Meddem, thank-you, Meddem, here you are, mei babatjie.'

'So much better than 'house-boys', these young women', thinks Finuala. 'I ought to be more grateful, although the 'boys' are faster cleaners. Nevertheless, I still seem to find a lot to sigh about'.

\*\*\*

She stopped for a cup of tea on the stoep....re-living the embarrassment last weekend, a relaxing afternoon with those new friends by their swimming pool... another warm Sunday, all of them loafing about on that freshly mown lawn, drinking cold beer, wine, gin and tonic, relaxing, browned skin under sunshades...a heavenly day, really... apart from trying hard to make a good impression...that's what I was thinking at the time; new and interesting couples had appeared …well, new to us, obviously, and all was fine until, God, it doesn't bear thinking about it,… until *our* Jon had wriggled out of his tiny swimsuit and, crouching in the safe shallow end for small children, delivered himself of a healthy bowel movement! By the time one guest noticed and called out… it was too late.  Our hostess, pretended to make little of it. Of course I rushed to the spot, yanked out my dismal child and trawled about with bare hands for most of my son's well-formed 'poo-poo,' as the child announced proudly after the event. Needless to say no-one wished to swim for the rest of the afternoon, quite understandably, and there were no servants on duty, it being Sunday. The husband of our hostess, a good-looking chap in dark glasses, smiled enigmatically, all the while engaging in serious discussion on race relations with his colleagues, all men. Bringing out further bottles of chilled lager from the fridge, the men completely disassociated themselves from the entire palaver….'

'Yes, of course it is pleasing and restful by the pool, it always is, but only if our Jon doesn't disgrace himself. Will we ever be asked back?'

Fin was discussing this mishap with Julian after the event, back in their small and completely uninteresting house, with its nasty hot corrugated iron roof and that unfriendly high surrounding wall. Increasingly conscious of their own circumstances, to say nothing of her regular shopping in the cheapest stores along with coloured people... she showed her displeasure with life. Julian glanced at his wife, shrugged his shoulders, raised his eyebrows...looking resigned and helpless.

*** 

Later, re-living the pool event in her mind, Fin whipped up eggs for meringues and mixed dough for scones in preparation for her guest. So therapeutic, a pleasing distraction: a visitor to look forward to! 'I will consult Cecile, who was there when it all happened, whether she believes Irene was actually quite upset and only *pretending* not to mind...like all diplomatic, polite hostesses should.'

As soon as Cecile came she managed to put Finuala out of her misery:

'.....but Finuala: pool filtration is quick and effective. You must forget it,' was Cecily's well-reasoned advice. As wife of an architect herself she did have, however, high standards when it came to homes and décor...so trying not to crumple her nose, nor be critical in any way, she was able to make a surreptitious assessment of the décor in Finuala's modest home.

A few plain pots, a huge Toulouse Lautrec poster, bright yellows and red, ('I adore this artist)', Cecile glowed, 'and that pleasing woven rug, so very artistique...where does *that* come from?' From time to time she glanced outside, noted her child was behaving admirably. The huge three year old was galloping about clumsily 'riding' Jon's much-loved shabby hobby horse while its owner watched warily, unused to such a large visitor and to sharing. Fin was waiting for screams, fights and disasters that might soon befall them both. So far so good, all was going well.

'Ag man, shame,' Cecile nodded, 'our little people have so much to learn, don't they, and we must learn too, the hard way, to be good mothers, all the time, *every single minute*. Did you hear about that ghastly misfortune?' She stressed her words, having changed the subject, and, hesitating, spoke with deliberation: 'I think you had already left yesterday, Finuala.  Jacques was telling us about it.'

'Ah, I thought his name was Jack! Is he French then,' enquired the eager hostess. 'I should have known from that accent... but yes, you were saying, Cecile, not another misadventure? By the pool? Not again?' Cecile frowned, looked serious and shook her head, while trying to keep track of the children.

'No, no, nothing to do with the pool. 'No, something truly horrendous happened to one of *their* family... only last week.' Preparing to speak, the guest kept a wary eye on the small boys outside:

'A cousin of Jacques', she began, 'up in Rhodesia, newly married to a sixteen year old who was chosen for him in Beirut, an arranged marriage... (yes, can you believe it,' she nods, 'they still do that there...,) well anyway, he and his young bride soon had a son, and at that toddler stage, just like ours'... they both glanced at the boys romping about... 'just the other day, this young mother was pressing her husband's trousers, removing a stain with cleaning benzene, and after she'd put the bottle back down on the floor, and stood up again to scrub and remove that stubborn stain, she heard her child spluttering, coughing and fighting to breathe and by then the two-year old was choking, terrified, gasping and squirming and then went limp in her arms. Dead. Imagine! She had not noticed him pick up the bottle, take a swig. The toddler thought it was *his* drink.'

Frozen, eyes vacant, both young mothers stood, helplessly picturing and re-living such a moment. Like wooden dolls they moved into the garden, heads turned fearfully in the direction of the resounding, healthy noises from their sons. Finuala, still holding both hands before her mouth, had tears in her eyes, imagining improbable dangers that might threaten...and that unknown child's face, she saw it: red, frightened, gasping, a little chest straining for air, choking noises, small fists, fingers rigid, reaching out to a mother who had picked him up, shaking him, running with him in her arms to the houseboy, screaming for help, panic and terror, unable to think clearly, and that impotence, the fear and guilt, her child still whimpering, but becoming still and limp...

'Please God, don't let this happen, I would die too, I'm sure, from the pain of seeing my child suffer!' The young mothers looked at each other. They found no words. Completely drained,

Finuala made her way to the kitchen, pushed the kettle across onto the hotplate. The fire was still on. Both women were trembling. Streaming eyes admitted they more than understood such agony.

Finuala decided she liked Cecile very much, hoped they would remain friends, meet regularly...certainly see each other on Sundays by the pool and after nursery school.

A firm bond had been formed.

# Seven

Sicut cedrus Libani multiplicabitor in domo Domini....

'I would like, just once, to take a look at a cedar of the Lebanon! What have we got here? Endless Palms, Blue Gums, and well yes, Jacarandas, they're nice in October. But the romance of a Cedar's powerful growth, branches spread wide open...the bond one would form, such a welcoming beacon for dark-eyed sailors of the Mediterranean,...yes, so romantic.....and look at this, here it is, my old Missal, buried in my wardrobe....almost guiltily... I open it, well, it does happen to be a Sunday. And here is a line about cedars. Almost at once comes that guilt-thing...about not going to Mass. Always looking over ones shoulder, well, one knows, that's how the church operates. I will not be bullied. Alienated? Some sort of despair, and now guilt? You may strike me down, God. Yet again: it *is* Sunday but I will not go to Mass. Like a naughty child, stamping its feet: that's how I feel. Pathetic really, creating a spoil-pretend-drama from absolutely nothing. How predictable life has become....'

Later that day, ominously, or by coincidence, during yet another sociable Sunday by the pool Finuala hears about this very same tree from her host, Jacques,  a name she spells 'Jack,' in her head. Synchronicity... that's what it was! Cecile had already told Finuala all about this man: Jacques, who pronounced her name: 'Ceceel'. She too visited this famous 'watering hole' on Sundays, for quite a few months already. Finuala had been informed their host came from the Lebanon; very wealthy from importing (or something). She knew no details, but he also worked in some connection with the mines in the University Science department... 'the Lebanese, they speak French, you know, they are Catholics. Well, Maronites, actually, some sect who speak Arabic, Aramaic, something exotic like that.  He was at Cape Town University, studied Science first, then Literature. And how he loves books!

You went there too, didn't you?'

Finuala allowed the question to float by, remembering she might one day soon have to explain, admit the truth, about her own happy years at a mere commercial college and her job in Stellenbosch; not quite as glamorous-sounding really, now, in retrospect, but at least it was something... (where exactly was this Lebanon?)

***

'The valleys and mountains in Liban,' recites Jacques, relaxing in swimming trunks on a deck-chair. He raises both hands over his hairy chest, like a half-naked priest in a ceremonial position. Totally incredulous, shaking his head, he declaimes: 'the cedars.....yes, and ah....the size, the sweetness of those apples, the grapes in the vineyards....and snow on the mountains... while on the same day you can dive into the turquoise waves of the Mediterranean...I mean, is this not true paradise? And strolling amongst the grandeur of ancient Baalbek...up on the fertile plateau behind the mountains of Lebanon, the splendour of antiquity, immense marble pillars, ornate marble structures gleaming, beaming their mysterious history into the bright sun: you must see to believe it...and there, on the slopes of the hills, stand those wondrous, famed ancient cedars, like sentinels of this magical small land....' His hands have come to rest on his chest.

After this poetic outburst he looked around into the eyes of every one of his listeners, savouring the effect of his words; an entertainer before a select and willingly enchanted audience.

Who were these stunning people, what was this civilisation that had bred such skill and enterprise? Finuala was mesmerised.

Dressed in a skimpy white bikini she lay on her towel, sunbathing, and now intoxicated by the expressive enthusiasm of her host. Born right here in Johannesburg, this intense man with a furred chest, who claimed to come from one of the foremost families of Lebanon, a noble clan, (my name is Mansour Jacques Haddad, but call me 'Jack') and who behaved like a prince while making the women surrounding him feel they had noble blood themselves. What was Finuala to make of this splendid creature: his dark velvet eyes, his enviable long lashes, built like a god himself, (a pity, his legs were so short, well, shorter than Julian's) so benign and full of intelligence and powerful gentleness?

Later, chatting about books they were reading, it was at his suggestion he and Finuala picked up their soggy towels, draped them around their bodies, and padded along into his mansion. He announced: 'I will show you my study stacked to the ceiling with books of French and English literature, also my collection of Khalil Gibran's work, you have heard of him? No? You love poetry?' Indoors, still barefoot, she stood transfixed on the cool tiled floor, gazing jealously from shelf to shelf, lips parted, her eyebrows up.

She pointed to Andre Gide's *La Porte Étroite*: 'I read it just the other day; such a powerful book', while he examined her over the top of his reading glasses. Aware of this scrutiny she tried not to look back. They stood, wrapped in their towels. She realised books meant a great deal to him, while he had gathered the same about her.

They smiled at each other, both hoping in subtle and innocent ways, to become good friends.

'Hm,... more to this young woman than meets the eye', he told himself, (just as she'd hoped he would): 'well-read, so interested in me *and* my books, so fragile, dark-haired and delicate, like a Lebanese princess herself.' He was aware and had always felt badly about his own five foot 'eight-ness,'....nearly every one of his men friends towered over him: all those blond, rugged, rugby-type South Africans...but with her he felt just right, powerful, masterful.

'Yes, well, this little lady, quite adorable! And so well read. Strange name,... hm,' he thought. He caught himself staring. So as not to overplay his cards he placed a book on a different shelf, pushed others around, anything to hide the sudden surge of lust and desire to conquer this female. Finuala blushed, nearly asked, but then lost courage, to borrow one or two of this impressive collection. The blonde he himself had chosen, statuesque, sombre, sober and mostly silent, had now also come into this inner sanctum and suggested, rather pointedly, with a resonant voice: '...shall we make the tea, Jacques?' This was Irene, his towering, good-looking wife. 'We have no help today.'

'Why yes, my dear, I'll carry the trays', he called to re-assure her. Just coming to help...won't be long.'

'Irene sings in the church choir,' he informed, quietly, after Irene had gone, and then stared admiringly at Finuala's painted toenails. Leading her out he gave his guest a confident wink and a smile.

***

'Another dinner-party, Irene, do let's invite them over! You hadn't met Julian, had you? He's keen on music, like you; you may find him pleasant to talk to... you'd get on really well. An obliging colleague, bit of a dreamer, well, keen on classical music, things like that. He doesn't swim! Unusual, don't you think, for a chap from Cape Town. Hydrophobia, perhaps? Some people are like that. One assumes Finuala usually comes here without him, because of his other interests. They have two children. He uses his weekends to practise the piano somewhere. Dead keen on Chopin: there are rumours he is planning to put together an opera performance at the office, a circular has been passed round, asking for singers and musicians, to come forward, members of staff in the science laboratory, doing all manner of research for the mining industry. The firm does support these ventures; good for everyone to relax together in this way'. Jacques checks with his wife; 'you did like him, didn't you, Irene? Clever chap, and sensitive. Used to be an officer in the Air Force! Let's keep it a small party though, not a huge crowd.'

'Fine.' Irene sighed, raised her shoulders, frowned, checked her diary, then sighing again, suggested suitable dates. 'Hm, let me see. We'll ask them first, then decide who else needs to be invited and fix a date that suits everyone. Perhaps Cecile and that architect husband could join us. Will you be around during the next three weeks, Jacques?' He nods appreciatively: 'You're an efficient lady, oh wife of mine!'

'And a good mother', he thinks to himself: 'she produces one daughter after another. Three already! Strange that. One would *quite* like a son.'

***

Three weeks later, despite stifling humid heat, perspiring guests were tucking into Irene's dinner; delicious, as always, only the best of everything, finest wines, imported cheeses, a party in full swing.

It was a hot night in more senses than one: calypsos were the rage these days, with their strong African roots. Harry Belafonte's new hit recordings were heard wherever one went and tonight was no exception.

'Did you know, Finuala' the host gasped as he pulled her out on to the terrace, 'Calypso was a nymph; it is a Greek myth...perhaps she knew the Lebanon...she held Ulysses captive on some island for ten whole years, Cyprus perhaps...while her husband was travelling the seas,...now how about that for a good yarn...?' Jacques, who knew the steps, somewhat out of breath, was trying to entertain his guest. As well as being a literary 'savant', he believed he was obliged to seduce Finuala's limbs into the required rhythm, to pass on the correct movements. He was a more impressive mover than she was, despite or possibly because he'd had rather a lot to drink.

'So authoritative, so masterful, he coaxes me into the correct positions, pushes me in all the right places, a man with experience, I suppose he's used to manoeuvring his large wife, anyway, I just wonder who taught *him* to move like that!' Finuala is out of breath: Yes, Jacques, I think I've got it now, yes, see? We've danced a long time now....a good dance, yes, really pleasing! Thank-you, thanks...'

Hot and embarrassed, sweat was running down her back and her face felt damp too. 'I do think we should stop now, Jacques.'

The man seemed oblivious. She could smell his armpits.

'Good, that's it, well done. Harry Belafonte, we love you even here, on the other side of the Atlantic...and look at poor Irene: she looks weary. Julian must be telling your wife about his Beethoven Sonatas, judging from his body language...what a shame he refuses to dance' tried Finuala. 'Doesn't Irene do this dance?'

Jacques ignored her question. Intent on bending Finuala's body to his demands he shouted: 'Isn't this good, Finuala? This is more fun than I've had in years.' All she could think of was how her socially inept and inhibited Julian would never rescue her in this situation, nor would the architect with his Cecile, and least of all the long-suffering housewife, all of them clinging to their wineglasses, unwilling, or too embarrassed to intervene. Champagne flowed: Jacques' thirty-fourth birthday was intended to be a relaxing celebration. Clouds had been gathering though, and yes, here they were: distant flashes, first rumblings. The air felt heavy.

'One of our Transvaal rainstorms, not long before we'll all be inside, did you see that lightening'...remarked Cecile, 'not so very far off, this will put an end to sexy dancing but that's how it is here, saved by February storms--- well it all adds to the drama. It will cool things down a bit.'

'I do hope so,' replied Irene, staring into her glass of red wine. Jacques had had too much to drink, was dancing suggestively. She tried not to look at him, the birthday-boy, hard at work...embarrassing his guests. 'Hot, humid pre-storm weather can be a torment,' she said.

Fin was still trying to pull away, but birthday-boy would not have it, clung to her. She could feel him, his arousal pressed against her. 'Thank goodness it is dark out here on the terrace--he now wants to go to the pool for a swim,' she realised, 'now, yes, right now,' .... 'but I'm afraid of the lightning... another time, Jacques, not now, it's dangerous, let's go back inside, join the others. Besides, I haven't brought a swimsuit.'

'Swimsuit? No need for that,' he said firmly, 'it's dark, come on, let's go!'

Finuala, no longer waiting for right moment, tried to pull away. But the Belafonte record needed turning over. Saved by sudden silence and the approaching storm she escaped and sat down next to Julian, trying at once to enter into the conversation with Irene, who, elbows on the table, had propped up her head, hands behind her ears, as if to say, oh no, please, no more about Beethoven Sonatas. The cool Nordic goddess looked sour, could barely keep her eyes open. At that moment the black cook, or was he the waiter, (they looked so alike,) brought a tray with coffee, wearing immaculate white gloves. Dirty plates now cleared he gently closed the door to the kitchen. His duties were probably over for the day, his gloves would be stained and the storm, well, it appeared to be taking a different course. Transvaal crickets resumed their chattering stridulation, filling the dark domed African sky above and around them with thin irritating streams of sound. Conversation was flagging.

They all distant drumming. Where did that sound of drums come from?

Later, on the way home, eyes shut, seated next to an untypically silent Julian she pondered the trouble with dinner parties and with marriage: 'it's all too predictable. Everything loses its edge. Julian and me, we've known each other for well over ten years. I'm very fond of him, but I'm ashamed to say... of course I enjoyed Jacques's fumblings, re-invigorated, re-invented... galvanized: I'm still a desirable woman, not that gradually abandoned drudge I thought I've become. In all honesty', she piped up, bravely, 'I did enjoy myself tonight.'

Her man, too weary to respond, a little befuddled, found his way home, driving with extra caution through considerable puddles: her 'poor Julian': so clever, always busy with something or other...and now this latest obsession, the horn, long neglected from the days when he came to work in Johannesburg:

after a long rest at the back of the wardrobe, polished up and re-explored; this man who was now disturbing the neighbourhood with inept sounds, but hoped he would soon be good enough to play in some amateur orchestra in town. Well, good luck to him, what can one say... those old longings for a musical career still rankled and forced him to spend his free time away from home. He didn't much care for dinner-parties, plainly. All those plans for a performance of some unknown forgotten Mozart work, 'King Thamos,' something like that, no-one has ever heard of it, creating a theatrical event...those were the things that motivated him; why push away such thoughts? All it means to me: he'll be home late even more often than he already is.

I must, I really must, find some occupation for myself when the children are asleep. I read and read. They aren't babies any longer, they hang about asking 'when is daddy coming' and I am the one who must keep them entertained. Was I getting into 'hot' water this evening? No, of course not. Just a bit of party fun; Jacques was the birthday boy after all. He taught me to do the calypso. I know men get very aroused when they dance with women, a compliment in a way. She broke her long silence: 'I suppose we'll have to invite them back sometime, what do *you* think,' drawing Julian out of *his* own reverie...'were *you* having a good time then? Did you hear the distant drumming, a threatening sound, I always think, don't you?'

'Don't be silly, Fin, it was very nice, food excellent, and yes, I heard the drumming.' He spoke without special enthusiasm. She decided not to press him. He frowned, concentrating on the road ahead. 'There seems to be some roadblock ahead, something's up...I heard there was going to be trouble with policed road-blocks, to do with that Sophia-town problem. Irene mentioned it at dinner when I was telling her about *King Thamos...* in fact she offered to help with the sets. I will need all the help I can get.'

'King Thamos is more important than a roadblock. Music, that's all Julian ever thinks about'. Finuala decided to leave it at that, replied: 'King Thamos, whoever he may be...that's good, darling...'and sighed instead, now unable to stop her yawns. They were almost home. Betty, who had stayed in to baby-sit this evening would go to her little room, glad to get some sleep at last.

There was no more drumming that night. Julian slept instantly. Finuala listened to the crickets for a while, but soon fell asleep too.

***

February, 1955, an unusually cool morning for summer, rain, drizzle, still dark. Just before sunrise, only a few miles west of central Johannesburg, heavy trucks rumbled into the outer edges of the slums of Sophiatown. Policemen, whole regiments of them, waited for a signal, then teemed into roads to be cleared; there were two thousand men, armed with knobkerries, rifles and revolvers. They jumped off trucks, hammered on doors, shouting, banging.

Terrified women, still in bed, angry men, piercing screams, shocked children now woken, were dragged from their pitiful shacks, forcibly loaded on trucks along with their possessions. Shocked from deepest sleep small children sobbed, clung to their mothers, unable to understand. With wide-open eyes they watched homes, houses, shacks vandalised, smashed to pieces. There would, could, should be no chance to return.

Some tried clinging to their demolished houses but with the efforts of so many police and soldiers, all heavily armed, resistance was soon quelled. Traumatised citizens of Sophiatown were loaded like so much cattle onto trucks and driven to Meadowlands, or other townships, where coloured people would be living.

The SABC presented crackly news about this event.

Destinations of these South Africans were registered. Groups of people previously classified as blacks, coloureds or Indians were now forced to live in separate townships, told to report to the native Resettlement Board where individual families received two loaves of bread and one pint of milk. There was a slogan: *New homes for everyone!* Belongings unloaded and dumped on bleak doorsteps of new homes were proof that new lives were about to begin. Poor shabby Sophia-town, duly emptied, would, in time, be flattened to the ground. It had existed on prime land, only four miles from the centre of town. The process of removing all traces of the old shanty town would probably take some years.

*** 

On the morning of that fateful day many white South Africans felt uneasy. Finuala discovered she was without help. How could this be: Betty had not appeared today, with all the washing piled up and she hadn't even phoned to explain... unheard of, 'one can't rely on these blacks and coloureds, always the same old story. Honestly...!

Still, Betty is probably having a tough time.'

So Finuala telephoned Cecily to hear of a similarly absent servant. What was going on? She managed to speak to Julian, who reported the centre of town was blocked off, there was a huge police presence; he would probably be very late getting back. What an upheaval, what a nuisance! And this was only the first day. The transaction would take years according to the police. Better to look for another maid as quickly as possible. One who lived closer by.

Finuala had switched on the radio. An announcer was telling the story of Sophia-town's origins, just one lifetime ago. Was it not all to the good: the slum would soon be razed to the ground, the inhabitants were already re-housed. At last! The government was finally doing something positive. Well, of course one wouldn't want to be chased out of bed early in the morning, like those poor devils had been, but surely they'd had plenty of warning. Why were the slum-dwellers not grateful? They were re-housed after-all, for free? What were they complaining about? There were slogans: 'We shall not move' or 'Over our dead bodies'. And the view of most whites: 'Our government has quietly got on with the whole necessary business. In the end, surely, this will be all to the good.'

But the attempt at drawing a veil had failed: from the rest of the world there was an outcry.

The history of Sophia-town was brief: it had belonged to an investor who bought the land, all 237 acres of it, in 1899. The area was on a ridge of lithified sediments from the first seashores of an ancient sea. In those days white people had dreams and aspirations: the investor hoped to sell the land to white men and to establish a new suburb to the west of Johannesburg. And indeed, the land was soon sold to a white man, Herman Tobiansky, whose customers in turn were white men. Now the proud new owner named the planned township after his wife, Sophia, and the streets after his own children. Things moved fast in those days.

Twenty years on most whites had moved, leaving the area to black, coloured, Indian and Chinese families. For half a century it was a vibrant part of the big new mining town. Then, increasingly it went to seed. End of story. But now there was another black mark on South Africa's copy-book it seemed.

Today all Finuala could think about was the absence of 'her' Betty. She called friends, chatted with neighbours. Others too were missing servants, seemed paralysed by their absence. The usually quirky, smiley Vikky was tearful, refusing to amuse herself in the playpen. Jon should by now be walked to the nursery school. Soon he would be starting proper school and then his sister would take his place at Tom Thumb....

Was it actually safe to go out? Everyone felt uneasy: there was both fear and anger due to the intervention. There'd been no further announcements on the radio. Finuala dialled Irene's number. To her surprise, and pleasure, if the truth were known, it was Jacques who answered.

'Goodness, Jacques, I thought you'd be at work; may I speak to Irene?' He enquired immediately whether Julian was on the road yet. Yes? Had he phoned at all? No? There were rumours the roads were closed because of unrest in town, but, anyway... 'how can I help, Finuala?'

'No, no, it's fine, thank you Jacques, I was just wondering: have *your* servants arrived this morning?

'Ours live on the property, so there's no problem; too bad your maid is caught up in all this'; she heard him pause for a moment, then: 'I could come over, give you a lift to the shops and the school, Fin...whatever you wish, yes, I'll be right over.'...and before she could say anything he'd put the receiver down. Ten minutes later a car-door slammed. She heard the creaking gate.

Now the man stood before her, smiling sheepishly.

'At your service, Madame: your knight in shining armour.' He stood to attention: 'Let's have a coffee and discuss our little problem.' Then, with a raffish smile: 'I'm here to help-I am your willing slave as well as general rescuer of damsels in distress.' With a rolled–up newspaper in one hand he hit energetically against the other.

'Too much pent up energy,' Finuala thought to herself; nevertheless it was impossible not to appear friendly. She studied his expression as he repeated: 'truly at your disposal, Madam. Where do we start?' He was beginning to look awkward.

'I suppose Irene knows you've come over?'

'I'm on my way to work, and perfectly able to get you and your son to Tom Thumb and you to the grocer and to drop you off again afterwards. Going to work is a moveable feast in my position, and things are obviously more than a little irregular today. Allow me, Madame Conley, I am glad to be of service.' He sounded agitated.

'But Jacques, what will Irene say?'

'Goodness! She'll say nothing! I'll tell her later. She was having a swim when I left. I'll tell her this evening -you phoned while she was in the pool. Don't be ridiculous Finuala, I'm trying to be helpful!

It's clear you don't trust me. Quite right too. I will come every morning to help you, if necessary, until your maid returns. I don't have to keep such regular hours as your husband. My tasks are more flexible. It will be my very great pleasure, *madame*!'

Finuala felt foolish. Soon they were driving off just like any normal family: Vikky on her lap, Jon at the back, the pushchair folded in the boot and Jacques beaming broadly in his role as saviour and conqueror. First they dropped off little Jon.

'No, really Jacques', she insisted, when he discussed the next part of the round-trip, 'thank you, but I will walk home after picking up food at the grocers.' He revved the engine, switched it off looking disappointed, then sat waiting for a while staring at the shop entrance until she began her return with Vikky buried good-naturedly under groceries in the pushchair. Again he offered to run them home. Finuala, flushed and touched by Jacques's gallantry, a friend in need...a true gentleman, agreed. All was well. It was warm, the groceries were cumbersome, some things might melt a little, and of course she remained a responsible, virtuous wife.

'Hope to see you all on Sunday, do feel free to come over, use the pool', he smiled soberly, as he drove off, and then: 'I like those earrings, Fin. He had called her Fin. Just like Julian did. 'They really suit you'. His compliment resonated all day, cheering her up while she went about her tasks.

'How kind he is, what a useful man! I forgot to ask if he might lend me some books. I must tell Julian how thoughtful his colleague has been.'

***

My private notebook:

𝔄𝔡 𝔇𝔢𝔲𝔪 𝔮𝔲𝔦 𝔩𝔞𝔢𝔱𝔦𝔣𝔦𝔠𝔞𝔱 𝔧𝔲𝔳𝔢𝔫𝔱𝔲𝔱𝔢𝔪 𝔪𝔢𝔞𝔪: I've not written in this for some years. Since 1951, before I was even married! Six whole years have passed. In fact I'd quite forgotten it existed, still in that old handbag, ostrich-skin and out of fashion now, the one I rarely use and in any case, we don't go out much. As I was tidying things I found it. One does a lot of tidying, especially now when both Vikky *and* Jon go to school. We really should have a cat. In my aloneness I have turned to my old notebook. A lonely person's last straw!

Our Betty has vanished with the Sophiatown upheaval and will probably not be replaced. I have nothing to read at present but that is entirely my own fault, I could borrow books from Jacques who appeared this morning, unbidden, in such a helpful and friendly way. What an epiphany, his arrival here! He *was* unusually attentive and very tense today.

Julian, now branching out in all directions, has hardly any time at home…he's committed himself to sing with a large group of singers and to conduct a 'scratch' orchestra as he describes it, all amateur players, something to do with the University. Strange how ecstatic he becomes when presented with a handful of musicians. He realises this himself: it is because he has been prevented from the pursuit of *his* talent. Is it a real talent or just a need to feel important? I would never say this to his face. He has this vision of himself, coaching, conducting, waving his arms about before a large group of people all admiringly dependant on his every twitch and command. I thought him to be quite shy, not at all someone who shows off. But I am proud of him. He still has no piano. Only that dreadful horn…

I talk to myself most of the day. Homesickness, that's at the bottom of it: how lovely it would be to see old friends, have a drink at 'Forries', walk along the beach at Muizenberg. Dear God! I miss the sea, I miss the mountain. I miss the future, the one I thought we'd have. A different future has come, everything, not just the landscape, is flat here. So, we are at least trying to keep up, adjust, in our quiet Cape way with our smart new friends in the Transvaal. Julian often returns very late; he needs to stay on because of rehearsals which mean so much to him. When he came home late last night he gave an account of the first rehearsal with the choir, somewhat shaken to find Jacques standing before him, in the tenor section. 'Fancy meeting you here', said Jacques, allegedly ill at ease. How perceptive Julian can be.... 'Jacques is hiding something', he said. Julian promptly scanned the sopranos for Irene, but Jacques informed she preferred the church choir closer to home. 'This is for more serious singers committed to the hilt with dedication and loyalty. It's been going for quite a while…anyway, nice to have you on board.' With that both men turned away to study their scores of 'La Forza del Destino'.I would feel so like the 'odd woman out' with all these singers running around at night. Besides, how could I, there is no babysitter at the moment.

Instead, I turn into a grey beast of burden, …sicut era in principio et nunc et semper, et in saecula saeculorum, as it was in the beginning, and now and ever shall be, world without end: house-work gets one down; spoilt I suppose…quare me repulisti, why go I sorrowful…abandoned.  I am aware that thinking in this way is like an unstoppable stone which rolls, gathering speed, sooner or later causing irreparable harm.  I could just as well go off singing at night, but let's face it: I'm not inclined that way. Besides: the children…Five uneventful days have passed. So nice to chat with Jacques the other morning. Since then he has telephoned, offered me free and frequent use of his library. All I must do is write down every book I take out, he stipulates.  Irene has instructions to let me in. I'd better stay on the right side of her!  He tells me she has taken up weaving, has a room with a large loom and baskets full of thread in glowing colours. There she sits patiently, like the Penelope of old, undoing her work every evening to start again on the next day.

I've noticed the calm ways they cultivate with their little girls, 'but', Irene whispered the other day, 'my husband wants a son. He wants many things I am in no position to provide,' and raising her eyebrows she left it at that. I did not press her. It seemed a very private thing to talk like that. What did she mean?  I tell her about the problems our Jon is having:  the endless waking up at night, quite often with breathing difficulties.  Could it be asthma? No-one else in the family has this complaint. And that awful eczema: our doctor has given me a disturbing list of possible causes, house dust, mould, or fungi, and now, to add to my discomfort my housekeeping is under scrutiny. Scrubbing, pushing a Hoover around, etc. has never been my forte. If anyone is stressed it is me, with the permanent anxiety of living on a plateau rather than at sea level. Jon would probably do better back in Cape Town. I do so long for the place. Writing things in my notebook feels so therapeutic.'

\*\*\*

'Vikky is sensible enough to go to Tom Thumb now, don't you agree', Finuala asked, sipping coffee, studying the half-woven tapestry on Irene's loom. Irene had abandoned her loom to escort her husband's special guest into the library. The women nodded, sizing each other up as women do, noticing re-assuring flaws, imperfections. Even when most fluent, in full flood, women can't help assessing other females as if they were opponents, both operating on several levels simultaneously.

'They do a wonderful job at Tom Thumb Nursery', claimed Irene, 'two of our daughters are already eager to move on, almost ready for the Convent. Very strict, those Irish nuns, but with high standards academically... our children adore nuns, talk about becoming nuns themselves; just a phase of course, I hope, still, one never knows! '

'Ah, well', said Finuala, 'at first it will be just for the morning. Then I'll bring Vikky home for a good long siesta.' She sensed Irene was a woman with standards, probably quite religious, demanding, with high expectations, though not someone to have a giggle or let ones hair down with. 'She must be wondering why her husband invites me here to borrow his books. I too would be just a little wary in *her* shoes.'

***

That quiet time after lunch always was the best time for reading, during the siesta ...but the day had been disturbed: a call from Jacques, he *must* talk, sort something out *once and for all!* Finuala immediately had cold feet. Now what? Was it something to do with his books...a smudge, a tear, or was he going to make a pass at me? What if someone saw him arrive in his car, what would neighbours think? If this is what *I* fear it might be, we are in dangerous territory.'

'Why are you not at work,' she asked when he arrived. 'I am not well', he replied. 'I need your help.'   He looked flushed. He stood before her, threateningly, breathing deeply, almost angry, like a beast about to charge. 'I had this primordial dream', he said.

She noted his twisted face,  heard him recite, staring at her, his hands now cupping her head, 'last night, in a dream, I saw these eyes… like those  of an angry elf, you were sitting naked on my chest, eyes boring into me, but all I could think of was your flesh, your legs wide open and your sex sliding up and down over me and then I had an orgasm,  groaning and waking my wife, who asked if anything was wrong….'

Fin,  forgive  me,  forgive  all  this,  I'm overwhelmed by my body and my restless mind, I can't get on with anything until you let me make love to you.' He stood before her, his face was glowing red, his hands were shaking and his forehead was damp with sweat. 'You're not well', said Finuala, 'you have a fever. Either that or you're out of your mind. Sit down!' Aware of his power and aggression the more she refused him she repeated firmly: 'sit down, Jacques, I will make a cup of tea!' He groaned, but obeyed like a child. She bent forward, touched his hot forehead with a cooling hand but in one brutal move, he pulled her on his lap, cradled her like a parent soothing a squirming infant.

'Fin', he pleaded, 'darling,' now in a strangled pitiful voice, 'I can't eat, I can't sleep, I need you...please let me love you, I can't go on like this, we've known each other for two years already, or is it three, I've lost track; I'll be very careful,' sensing she just might give in, surrender to his fever, drown in this longing and urgency, as he struggled to peel off whatever garment he could find above and under her skirt. And she began to respond, irresistibly melting in an anguished but enjoyable sweetness; engulfed by his lust, swept along, she allowed herself to become helpless; the floorboards were hard but this frenzied impetuosity was exactly what she needed to make her own dull daily-ness, her depression, fly from that open window, over the Palm tree and away into the peaceful, quiet, pale Transvaal sky. Uncomfortably entangled on the hard floor, they heard one lonely bird chirping outside, then a car slamming on its brakes with much screeching, hooting loudly. They froze... but the car drove on, their heartbeats slowed, normal consciousness returned. 'This man is someone very special' she thought....while       increasingly       feeling uncomfortable on the floor. They looked at each other. He stroked her hair and she was touched to see tears in his eyes. Neither of them had any words.

∗∗∗

𝔄𝔪𝔬, 𝔞𝔪𝔞𝔱, 𝔞𝔪𝔞𝔰…she recited in her mind, barely walking, dragging her feet. Mothers with cars were stowing away chattering children and Finuala cadged a lift with Cecily to get her two back home. She was moving like a zombie, her mind engaged elsewhere.

Perfunctory hugs, then she sent them out to play in the garden, while she sank into a deck chair on the gleaming polished *stoep.* The air was still and hot. Her eyes moved from the high slatted fence, densely covered with a jungle of morning glory to the best feature of the trouble-free garden: their palm, at least half a century old; like a frazzled old umbrella its shade moved across the grass with the position of the sun. Finuala had often kept track of this shadow as the sun passed overhead.

For some time she had wished to see no-one. She'd been out of circulation for weeks. Twice a month a shrivelled black gardener, perhaps in his eighties, limped, hobbled in, to mow and tend the lawn. Later, squatting on his haunches, he tidied things up; there was little enough to do. She pitied him, brought a tin mug full of sugared tea, which he received with humble servility: 'dankie, medem, hm, lekker, baaie dankie.'

She was still trying to find a modus vivendi. There was consolation in plants. They were like loyal friends. Agapanthus, huddled together in large clumps of blue, her favourite giant fern in the far corner, were special features of the garden, not forgetting her very own thriving nasturtiums. She'd picked their seeds, put them in the salad, and now she remembered Julian's surprise, savouring the peppery leaves, while she'd even chewed the blooms to impress him. 'One can eat the flowers, see...and later on the seeds.' She'd demonstrated. Julian had shaken his head, not so readily convinced. Now, studying her garden, she sighed. 'I must speak to Julian. We will never see a cedar of the Lebanon, see anything, unless we travel. I need a change. I've absolutely had it. When could we take some leave?'

***

Two months later Finuala, Irene, and their men dined together. The topic of travel was launched, toyed with. Just recovered from what can only have been a miscarriage, according to her doctor, Finuala was currently regarded as an invalid. She felt awkward, avoided looking at Jacques. Both couples agreed: a holiday, that's what was needed. 'I know just the place we could all go,' Julian declared, unusually animated: 'a place in heaven,...no,' he smiled, 'by the sea, near the Tsitsikamma mountains. Be patient now, this is a long story: it's the only time in my life I've *ever* had a holiday, that's for sure; I was about eleven, twelve... we, the whole family, travelled on a miniscule train all the way from Cape Town to Knysna, it took about ten hours, then someone picked us up and squeezed us into a terrible old pick-up van;  I can't remember how my parents knew them.' Stretching his long legs, he pushed himself away from the table: 'there'd been occasional mention of a couple who left Cape Town in the early months of World War 2: a gifted English water-colourist wife and a German businessman with remote Jewish ancestry.' Julian sipped his wine, continued his account of this *interesting case*, as he put it: '*real* Germans were being locked up in POW camps, you know, immediately the war broke out. It's all so long ago, but I was very impressed by all this as a boy, imagining 'bad' Germans all locked away, safely. Two of these camps were actually near here, one outside Pretoria. Well, anyway, this 'German' friend, battling with the authorities, managed, just in time, to find documentation, proof, of his Jewish ancestors. Revealing he'd just bought a remote farm near Plettenberg Bay, there surely could be no reason to arrest him along with *real* Germans? It was an open-and-shut case: so he and his English wife escaped to their secret paradise, a simple farmhouse on the plateau, mountain-range vistas on one side, the Indian Ocean on the other….what I'm trying to get to is: why don't we all go there! It was a beautiful place. We could stay in those rondavels and have a splendid sea-side holiday?' Julian had surprised himself; only once in his life had he proposed holiday plans and that was the Hermanus gathering. Even Finuala had never heard this account of an alleged paradise.

'Good memory! Great. Another sign of your IQ, what is it, 165?' She looked at him, well pleased. 'The only time we've been away together was a showing-off-to-everyone- weekend in Hermanus with our 'varsity' friends, and later our two-day honeymoon, absentee leave from the Air Force.' Julian grinned: 'Yes,' he had now convinced even himself: 'feasible, probably affordable, and pleasing. What do we all think...., if these people are still there, of course? The farm was near Plettenberg Bay, they were called Kramer, something like that..... 'But Jacques shook his head: 'No way. Look at your Atlas, my friend! We'd all go mad driving such distances with young children. Our only chance is Durban, and even that is a considerable journey. I suggest we go to Natal, by train. Let me look into it. Besides, our wives have to be spoilt a little. Sitting in cars for days with restless kids, in the heat, just imagine...terrible! We're not bloody Voortreckers, you know!' Irene gave him a stern look ...Julian had to bow to practical good sense, and admit, tongue-in-cheek, but only to himself, 'of course, the man is right, annoying, but right. What luck he works in a different department of the research laboratories. We'd be endlessly locking horns about things...but fine', he nodded, 'you know best. Let's do it. Good old South African Railways.'

'I'll make enquiries', said the ineffable Jacques, 'I know people in Durban. We could rent a romantic beach cottage, they might even lend us a car...the place will be self-catering and there will be plenty to do and enjoy. Leave it *all* to me'. The 'all' was musical and long drawn-out. Julian glowered at him.

It was the wives who instantly imagined all those things that might go wrong: unbelievable tropical heat, stinging blue-bottles in the sea, high waves, sharks lurking in them, sunburn, cockroaches, mosquito-bites and then those endless days with nothing to do. Not really believing anything would come of it, they both soon changed the subject. Finuala knew Julian cared neither for humid heat, swimming, nor for cooking. Already in agony picturing the entire scenario he grimly kept his counsel. Only later, when they were alone, he spoke his mind: 'that man is so overbearing, how does Irene put up with him,... still, to be fair, the train journey, a much better bet; he was right there.' Julian liked to give praise where praise was due. He studied his wife's face; yes, poor thing, she'd been looking poorly ever since that miscarriage. Later they parted with polite nodding of heads, leaving the matter open. Still, Julian knew when he was beaten. It seemed inevitable, they would all be going, it had to be by train and then they would find a pleasure seekers city, bustling, subtropical, a sultry paradise. He sighed. He was a peace-loving, patient man.

'There is, allegedly, a Nature Reserve, a beach called Brighton Beach, but the kids can also be taken to amusement parks, to an aquarium and to a snake park. I could sit about reading, bring scores and study them; I have an operatic text to translate. Even if I am chewed alive by mosquitoes, if scorpions tweak my toes, I will not complain. I must not spoil everybody's fun. I will ride on rickshaws, wear a hat, drink huge amounts of cold beer, lose my figure (and the will to live).' Fin smiled fondly at her man.

'No, no complaints….of course, Fin, it's *you* who needs a break. I will look after the kids. At least, with Jacques and *two* women, conversation in the evenings might be stimulating,' Julian was trying to see the bright side. He was not at all sure about Irene, felt he barely knew the lady. 'And isn't that Indian Ocean full of sharks? I'm told the sand slopes deeply into the warm waters of the Indian Ocean.' He imagined sharks, lined up, glistening sharp teeth, lurking.

'When you lot go swimming I will sit and read. Bliss.'

Slowly, stealthily, the pleasing adventure got going: they began to feel like a very large family, all filled with happy expectation and caring, helpful feelings ….all but Julian, who knew how to keep his thoughts to himself.  As fate would have it,  things turned out differently: father and son bonded instantly, set about collecting bags full of shells, spent hours arranging them according to size, shape, texture and colour, 'as boys do', and then there were further hours looking for missing links, exercising masculine logic, wishing for order in all things.  Jonathan had not had one single asthma attack. They did get caught out by the sun's rays but also spent much time bonding and recovering together from nature's unkindness.

And then it came to be, an unforeseen epiphany: by a seemingly burning bush glowing at sunset, exhausted children safely in their beds, grownups drank wine, took turns to wander off, now euphoric, unsteady in the moonlight along the beach, Julian with Irene, Fin with Jacques...they chattered, laughed, and teased, getting their feet and garments wet from wandering along the lapping waves. Just *one* evening of amicable, light-hearted inebriation, of melting passive near-consent, then it was Jacques who broached one further step: to switch partners in the bedrooms. Initial searching looks into meandering eyes of partners and then hurdles were pushed aside and all barriers broken. Without question, this proved to be undeniably daring but also pleasing. In fact, even back in their own beds before morning, so as not to confuse the children, it was unquestionably aphrodisiac. Improbably re-invigorated and content, both couples came to life on the next day, amicably filled with visions of themselves as actors in rehearsal for a black and white Nouvelle Vague film. And so it proved to be something they wanted to experience again and again, until the holiday came to an end: under those balmy skies, a return to pagan innocence, or even just the illusion of it, a return to paradise for once.

All this helped keep the peace for ten memorable days.

# Eight

_Misereatur tui omnipotens Deus:_ may almighty God have mercy upon _thee_....miserere mihi, _Domine_ ....have mercy on _me._ If only I were still in touch with my religion, with peace and that innocence I once had, knowing who was the 'physician of my life'. If only!

A 'plenary indulgence', that might be the one and only thing left. But I am sure none of us are evil, as the church would have it, always trying to keep order in the world. I now feel so close to this man, who has cleverly engineered the situation all four of us have got ourselves into. He means well. He is not a bad person. Others might say he was. Of course, _his_ three daughters will never know. _Our_ offspring will never know. And his own dear wife has found a new dimension to her dried up existence: she sings more lustily in her choir and, surely makes ever more splendid, joyous, richly coloured tapestries on her loom. No-one is suffering. Neither Julian nor Irene have shown any sign of minding, quite the opposite.

\*

Finuala had flopped into the only deckchair out on their veranda; she was alone. Since their holiday her strength had returned, she'd even gained some weight; not really a welcome revelation, that.

'We've discovered the secret to quiet contentment' she reflected,...fixing her gaze on languidly waving palm fronds overhead; today they looked resigned, sorrowful. She did feel terribly tired. Some bird or insect was fluttering about restlessly, constructing a clay nest in one of the corners of the corrugated iron overhang....which was now sheltering her from the ferocious sun.

'The heat is determined to melt our roof.' She shut her eyes.

It now seemed months ago, planting that Bougainvillea, still only three feet high; 'I'd hoped it might grow quickly, provide some shade: its flowers might soon appear and they'd be my favourite deep wine-red colour. Strange, I've never noticed any activity up there. But then I rarely sit outside gazing up at a roof. So many things happen in one's home and one never notices, until a bolt from the blue, some moment of discovery comes. Like that black day', she shuddered reliving the memory, 'the squalor, the shock!' It had been triggered by Julian's only domestic chore: clearing out the debris of the wood-fired stove in the kitchen; he did this on a regular basis, usually on the weekend,... the children had been playing outside.' Fin's eyes were tightly closed. She frowned re-living the ghastly event:

'*What is this*?' she'd heard Julian call out in a voice she'd never registered before: 'not one, but *two*, thrown in here...by lover-boy, I suppose?' She remembered closing her eyes for a moment, then getting up and hurrying indoors. Her placid, calm, peace-loving Julian, turned nasty? He seemed beside himself and she was afraid: she'd never seen her husband so indignant, so offended, out of reach and out-of-love. What had so set him off? He'd been poking around in the burnt-out ashes and picked up first, one condom, then a second one with a stick...and then he dangled them before her; she didn't know what to say, where to look, hoping the children would not come running in. They'd both stood, stared and then, wordless, he'd flipped them back in, slammed the door and left the house shouting: 'It's an outrage....Clean this up yourself!'

His parting shot! The words seemed to bounce back from every wall in the house. Still holding her hands clasped in front of her mouth she sensed a gloomy, dark silence around her. The children were still out of reach, she did hear occasional shouts outside. They were playing 'jumping down the steps,' a routine competition with the children from next door.

'They must have moved aside to let him leave,' she thought. 'What did he say to them, where had he gone? So he *did* mind, after all! What have I done? When will he come home? I want to explain: it is surely better this way; I mean, one would rather not be pregnant.'

***

Julian returned, several hours later, looking drawn, and exhausted. 'I'm really sorry and sad', said Finuala and spoke softly and slowly and caringly about the state of their marriage. They ended up in bed together; it all began to feel less threatening; he seemed to have recovered his senses, found an even, quiet, resigned equilibrium. But what were his true thoughts, feelings? At one point he muttered: 'Of course he should use condoms if he *must* come to see you, but tell him I don't wish to have to deal with them when he's finished'.

For a while she was reassured… Julian seemed reasonable and calm. Later it all welled up again. Pale and tense with repressed disgust and fury he hissed at her: 'You tell yourself this behaviour is honourable? You must imagine I am an amnesiac! What right does *he* have to leave the laboratories when the rest of us are slaving away while he comes calling here? I thought it was just a holiday thing?' He paused for a while, staring out into the garden. Then he said:

'This is outrageous. I must report his behaviour.'

'Don't *you* use condoms when you sleep with Irene,' Finuala queried, trying to deflect his rage, and fearing Jacques' future. Through gritted teeth came his reply: 'no, no, she takes care of that sort of thing,'…and all Finuala could think to reply was a muted 'oh,' not wishing to prolong the squalor of it all, or to stoke his rage…

His last words, turning out the bedside lamp, were: 'It's all the same to me: you have your freedom; do as you please. From now on we will both be free.' So there it was.

But Finuala, stuck in the escalation of events, felt unexpectedly trapped. While going over it all on the next day she sat watching a small bird dangling a worm from its beak. The creature, fluttering near a nest under the roof, was bringing food to its children. Distracted for a moment she was able, for a short while, to push Julian's threat aside, but she knew she must face up to the truth: their relationship had taken a most serious knock. A powerful avalanche of nastiness: that's what was now coming her way, still hidden burdens, troubles, impossible to avoid. It would disturb her day and night.

How she longed to speak with Jacques, to find out whether he and Irene were experiencing similar reactions. How did they put up with each other? It now seemed wiser to stay clear of Irene. Finuala was surprised by herself but also by Julian. She wanted him to mind, but in a different way. Not in that conventional way. They used to talk about this, years ago.

'We've both forgotten. We *did say* we would not be *conventional*....' all that high thinking, it seems it no longer counts?

A great chill had set in. Finuala wondered if there was a way to change how one looked at it all: 'We don't want to break up our families. It was about 'borrowing' someone, not taking them away. None of us have lost our allegiances so badly that we can't return to that original place, that simple innocence where it all began when we were still new to each other.'

'Oh no,' replied a small but more insistent voice, 'don't be daft,' as her mother would say, 'that old way is lost forever. Come on, you may as well face up to that.'

'But', Finuala tried to reassure herself, 'my furthest horizon has only ever been to earn respect, learn, and to enjoy the intelligence, the privilege of understanding one another. We can change the way we see all this, become true, responsible friends, all four of us.' 'Yes, but,' the little voice insisted: 'try imagining Irene's feelings, Jacques' reaction and all the consequences of this new arrangement. And also the truly unnerving thought: our children catching on, despising us, or worse, even suffering for it.'

***

The following day just happened to be a huge one: Vikky's first day at school. Her small, solemn face and quick sparkling repartee showed everyone that the Conleys had a daughter to be proud of. At first she clung to her mother's hand firmly as if it was the adult who needed support. Then, shown to a colourful circular table, five other little faces studied the newcomer while Vikky's own eyes were already darting about in her new surroundings. She let go of her mother's hand and looked around expecting miraculous events.

'I thought she'd have a desk to sit at, as I did when I was a small girl,'...said Finuala to the teacher. How education had changed: children were learning by having fun, by discovery; no more hideous rote–learning.  Even the strict, fear-inducing nuns *she* remembered had been trained to believe in 'new' ways: to be oneself: assertive, open, to see the world with fresh eyes. No 'repeat this' and 'repeat that, no dead learning, memorise this, recite your times-tables, instead:  bold shapes and colours, surprising objects to touch and explore, discover, tactile and fresh, even in this convent school. I like it! Vikky is only little, but so independent. Good as gold with the nuns; my best little girl. And how she adores her dad!  Father and daughter doted on each other.

\*\*\*

Julian sold his horn, got far more money than he'd paid for it, and now also cleverly earned a handsome amount of money from translating a German scientific tome into English. The result: a gleaming grand piano which took up most of the living-room.

Well, he deserved it. At last, a real piano in the house!

Neighbours, fortunately, were fulsome with compliments, and the children marvelled at daddy's long fingers flying across the keys. On Sundays, when they went off to swim at Auntie Irene's pool Julian had a good work-out with all his favourite Chopin studies. His children soon got used to hearing these accomplished sounds, even began whistling some of the tunes they remembered. Fin would nod approvingly. Then, before leaving, she'd tell him there was salad and an avocado sandwich: he might like to sit on the stoep later.... 'we'll be back when the children have had enough, you know how they love it there, by the pool.'

'Greetings to dear Irene and Jacques,' he'd mumble starchily, not bothering to look up. Not even smiling. He had his Chopin, and now even thirty–two Beethoven Sonatas, all to be explored, one after the other.  His musical life, right into his late eighties, seemed to be mapped out for him.

*** 

Stretched out by the pool Finuala gazed at her three newly chosen books from the magnificent library indoors. Conscious of nausea, and the overpowering wish to be back in bed she wondered whether those dates in her calendar were correct.'  Here it was again, that feeling, mixed with dread: 'it couldn't possibly be true, could it?  Have I missed a period? Dive in, swim like mad, twist, kick and turn in the water, the cold water will clear it all away; I've forgotten to have breakfast, forgotten dates, time, that's all it is.'

Rising awkwardly, her head spinning, she flopped back into the deckchair, then flustered, flipped over and fumbled with a few pages. 'This overwhelming need to retch!' With no time to get to the bathroom she executed a whirligig stumble across to a shrub, convulsively vomited behind it, masked by the noise of a flock of squawking birds. No-one had noticed, she hoped. 'Of course I'm not pregnant. Surely not? Something I've eaten perhaps. Yes, that's what this was.' But within a week the medicine-man confirmed: 'Congratulations, Mrs. Conley: indeed, yes, you are in the early stages of pregnancy.'

Like all good Catholics she rose to the challenge. While imagining a smallish, dark-haired boy, with dark eyes and velvety eye-lashes she realised how such a thing might give the game away. As her uncertainties multiplied, doubts flourished, she'd wake up in the early hours and worry.

'Pull yourself together, Finuala Conley', she told herself: 'whatever it is, as long as it's an easy birth, you will be ready for another child. With overwhelming love and delight, even! Especially if,...well, who's to know?' All this was an excellent excuse to employ a coloured woman to come twice a week for some serious house cleaning.

'Do you suppose it's mine?' enquired Julian, with a look of concern although he knew, she knew and Jacques would soon realise that, for a time, it would be impossible to tell. She raised her shoulders, her eyebrows and heard herself say:

'Why yes, of course, darling'. But flitting about in her head was: ' Deliver us, deliver us, in time of our tribulation, in all time of our wealth; in the hour of death, and in the day of our judgement...freely one must abstain in a spirit of penance from something licit and pleasing, but nevertheless verboten, taboo!'

Occasionally a German word brought back memories of the German photographer from Berlin, the man who had, long ago, taught her to be bold, to seize the moment. Fragments floated across a screen in Finuala's mind, while she tried to imagine how memory worked: like that church Latin, which was gradually fading away now, although, '𝔟𝔢𝔫𝔢𝔡𝔦𝔠𝔱𝔞 𝔱𝔲 𝔦𝔫 𝔪𝔲𝔩𝔦𝔢𝔯𝔦𝔟𝔲𝔰' had just returned. Certain things were best left forgotten, undisturbed.

*** 

'So? What *is* new in this world?' During the now rare occasions she and Jacques could be together alone, even if it was only during precious moments when she was deciding what books to borrow this time, staring absent-mindedly at a shelf of 'poetical' works in his splendid library.... she heard Jacques encouraging her:

'There *are* others, you know, beyond the splendours of Shakespeare and all those bards of the British Isles, the 19<sup>th</sup> and 20<sup>th</sup> century poets, the miraculous ones...'

But Fin had already opened an unusual leather-covered booklet at random: *It has died in me, as it must, every idle earthy lust, the curtain falls, the play is done*...she read. Her interest was aroused. Smiling wearily she asked: 'how appropriate is that?' But he only shook his head and countered with words of the same poet: *they loved each other beyond belief, she was a strumpet, he a thief...*

Jacques looked at her: Finuala had managed a cynical smile.

'Sit down, Fin, be peaceful for a few minutes, here, sink into this leather couch, Danish leather, very soft...'there, oh beautiful one, gently, relax, and I will tell you about the writer of these lines, a man who lay paralysed on his mattress for eight years. He was dead a century before our children were born and even now he delights us and the world with satirical wit and irony....Heinrich Heine, a German Jew, a prolific poet who wrote the prophetic remark *'where they burn books they will ultimately burn people.'* Ironic, don't you think?

'How amazingly awful', sighed Fin, her pupils dilated in the cool dark interior of the house, 'thanks to you, Jacques, one makes new discoveries: European poets. I've never even thought about German poets. Are there many? He was about to reply but she interrupted: 'by the way.....I dare say you might be interested: I have just decided to absorb as much romantic poetry as I can lay my hands on, and for a good reason: my next baby will be born, thanks to you, with poetic understanding, with a sweet and caring soul...and yes,' she hesitated, looking up at him, 'I *am* pregnant.'

He studied her, his dark eyes filled with tenderness: 'If it is mine, Fin, we will have something to remind us of our love for ever. Forgive me for wishing it, but how would we know? I do so hope it might be! *A loving heart is the beginning of all knowledge*, a chap called Thomas Carlyle wrote that. I like that. Even better, Plato knew, hundreds of years before the others: *at the touch of love everyone becomes a poet*...all I've done so far is scribble a few hopeless lines- about liberation, and race....they will be published in the Drum, a few months from now... I am quite pleased with myself! After today's wonderful news I will write another poem...just for you.'

'You never told me, Jacques, about all your talents', she said, 'I had no idea; how lovely!'

Most 'Sunday' friends, accustomed to spending time in Jacques' library, had benefitted from his willingness to lend them his books. 'Jacques, our trusted literary guide,' they said. 'Such a civilised man'!

It was 1961.

***

One who seemed, at this time, to care the most was Julian: distracted only by his new toy: a film camera.  This instrument/ toy/tool was to capture unusual events such as newly born babies and was in part-ownership with Jacques. These two men had made their peace and become more than just used to 'sharing.'

A newborn daughter blinked, smiled unflinchingly from snug soft pillows in her pram, straight into a glittering lens pointed at her. She was proving to the world that she, already a female of substance, was ready to take on whatever unusual challenges would come her way.

'The cutest, sweetest honey-bunch we've ever seen...'everyone huddled around the pram, studied the new family member who appeared to be squinting with a friendly smile, (no, she's got wind, said Finuala.) 'Wind, Mummy? How did that wind get inside her,' Vikki worried. 'Couldn't my new sister be called Dympna, like my own lovely nun at school?' Finuala mock-crumpled her forehead, pretending to study Vikky's now so very earnest face.

'But, my sweet, how about a more usual name: also starting with D..., let me see, do you like... Dulcie?' Quick as a flash Vikky replied: 'But that's not *so* usual, Mummy,..it sounds, so... dull...See?' Befogged from getting back home too hurriedly from her hospital bed, Finuala was now obliged to give a coherent explanation why a Sister Dympna and a *baby sister* Dulcie would be quite different sort of 'sisters'. Vikky, resigned, but not convinced, crept onto her daddy's lap for a cuddle but also, with earnest, coherent and feminine logic for reassurance she would not be losing her own special place in *his* heart. He did so understand her tiny doubts and feelings. They were becoming so very close. He needed that, almost as much as she did.

'What *will* become of them all,' worried Finuala. 'What a strange thing: I am the mother of two daughters: two future mothers, and here we are....part of that long chain of daughters, generations, over and over again. First my daughters, then my granddaughters, will they remember me? How much will they know, and what will they think about us?'

But there was little time for introspection: In a letter to her own mother she complained: 'our biggest concern is Jon; he looks terrible, lately his eczema is worse, the asthma attacks are something awful, worsening... despite drugs and the inhaler, prescribed by our dear doctor; no-one else in both our families has had this problem, isn't that so? You haven't heard of anyone, have you? He's loved, he does well at school, and he and Vikky are now particularly close... we do so long to come down to the Cape to see you soon'.

Brother and sister shared magical secrets: Vikky's and Jon's secrets were so special, no-one could remotely begin to guess them. They understood 'things'...clever scientific things, for example: how to cut glass.

'We so like to do wicked, dangerous deeds together: like etching signs into window-glass ...we have our own special secret sign. We used Mum's ring, the one with the little diamonds. (We did put it back later.)The sign is right in the corner, hidden by the curtain. No-one must ever know this secret, OK?' Jon made Vikky and also the coloured maid swear they'd never tell a soul. Being the older one, he was in charge of their games. Vikky adored him. This boy, examined by specialists at the children's hospital in Johannesburg, heard his own anxious parents complain how terrified they were to have to see him suffer, and how they would come running, appalled, helpless, sensing those muscles around his airways tighten and swell; 'we stand by, doctor, chilled with fear, hold him, although, eventually, the drugs do help, but the nights are sheer terror, his sudden inability to breathe.' Jon carried about with him not just his own fear but also the weight of the worries he was causing his parents. An earnest, almost grown-up look was gradually replacing his puzzled little boy's face.

'Where does this horrible thing come from? No-one, absolutely not one other person in our family has it.' Doctors promised to do their best. Day after day and also in the night, the Conley family was on constant alert.

'Our poor Jon, he should be taken more often to breathe clean air, to the sea, to mountains. We should arrange another holiday with him. Three years have passed, can you believe it, since the last one. Yes, another trip, down to the coast, away from Johannesburg.'

Fin and Julian, Irene and Jacques agreed while lounging about in that grandiose garden near the pool: they would repeat the previous memorable time, perhaps an attempt at renewed innocence, along with a truce between all parties concerned. It was the sixties, after all. There were invisible forces between them, pulling and tugging this way and that, hidden currents and a new outlook with fearsome consequences still hidden from the world.

1965. Julian, buried in amateur music–making, was especially flattered by the request he might stand in for someone to conduct a choral society…. a newly formed group of singers, all amateurs, like himself, dedicated devotees. Was this a step in the right direction, his dream come true?  Might it occur again? The answers were 'yes', and yes, again. Impressive in a dinner jacket or even in tails Julian was the archetypal admirable sight of a picture-book conductor. He formed new friendships and it was a small step closer to the life he'd always dreamed about…well nearly. Spared many of the predictable events of family life his new hobby kept him away from home on a regular basis.

This seemed to be what he loved best, there was nothing to match it, and certainly better than endless evenings at home.

There was still no television in South Africa, the government banned the medium for fear of instabilities, political unrest. White South Africans were doomed to continue living in their own bubbles of deception, selfishness, mistrust ..... but also increasingly, fear.

One made one's own amusements.

After a recent joint holiday by the sea, again spending time with Jacques and *his* family, a close and happy event, Fin pottered about, pregnant yet again; it felt as if she'd only just recovered from having Dulcie. Two years after the last yet another daughter made an appearance. She was Sybil, soon known as Sybs...

*** 

Still a young woman, but now a mother of four, Finuala, like all mothers, practised and invoked the art of self-preservation. There had been growth, there was understanding, but now her life, in its determined onward flow, in the passing of time, had become a compromise in that relentless progress of those who have known, in successive states of their existence, to keep every one of their cards truly close to their chests.

Some might call it 'karma'.

Seemingly unstoppable, in that very flow, in the wake of events reasonably well controlled, for an immeasurably long time, there came one unexpected moment which stopped all reason, all hope, all understanding.

Finuala and Julian were to come face to face with forces from hell.

# Nine

'A call, Mr. Conley, urgent... quickly, please hurry, your wife...'

A secretary, agitated, was signalling from the doorway into the laboratory. Julian looked up, frowned and shook his head impatiently: '...we're in the middle of something, do ask her to call back later,' but then, taking another look at the young woman, he somehow realised he'd better hurry to that phone straight away.

When he grabbed the receiver he heard gasping, choking and Finuala's sob, 'come quickly'...it was all she managed at first. He heard her voice, disconnected words, 'the ambulance, they are coming, he's lying there, on the floor, I don't know what's wrong, I heard him fall, he'd gone to the lavatory...I dragged him into the passageway. Jon, he is unconscious', she was struggling, her voice strangled, words faltering, in short gasps, he imagined her, clinging to the receiver, alone with the unconscious boy,... he heard her sobbing. Too agitated to drive Julian was driven home by the office secretary. Progress was slow. Having broken every traffic rule they arrived at the moment when an ambulance-man and his assistant firmly shut the doors of the ambulance. The assistant, about to return to the house, turned back when he heard screeching brakes, seen some-one tall ('the husband, presumably,') hurry towards them, one of them raised his hands as if in doubt, 'like a blessing' thought Julian as he approached,... 'can I see him,'... but the older man shook his head from side to side: 'your wife, Sir, she is inside, she really needs you. We are so very sorry, we stayed as long as we could, but now *you* are here....'

'Breathe,' Julian reminded himself, 'breathe!' His heart was beating fast. The gate wide open, he took those familiar steps through their small garden; he sensed the usual warmth from the paving stones, then the glowing red cement floor as he climbed five steps, he noted the fright of a small colourful bird fluttering past... while he, barely conscious of his own progress, half knowing... half hoping it might all be some ghastly mistake, slowed his steps. He saw his wife, collapsed on a chair by the table, slumped forward, her head on her arms,... 'Jon' he heard ... 'how can this be... Why? Where is he gone?' Jon, Jon, Jon. They took him away. She looked up staring at Julian with blind eyes. Shivering, her mouth remained open. Someone had put a glass of water in front of her, the ambulance men perhaps.

'What has happened? He was fine this morning, when I left with the girls'....asked Julian, now stupefied with fright. He put an arm around his trembling wife. Her upper body was slumped over the dining-table, her lips seemed to move, but she could not form words. Heaving, convulsive animal sounds came from deep inside her body as she clung, bowed over, to an empty mug in her hands. 'My Jon, our boy, Jon, he's dead...only half an hour ago. Jon has gone,' she whimpered in a vague monotone, retracing events in her mind, hesitating, faltering, searching, 'why, why, why.... I don't know why,' her heaving, choked breathing, groans from the pit of her stomach were more frightening than those of any night terror. Julian, too terrified to touch her, to interrupt, tried to follow the mangled sounds which she made with each breath: 'the drug-an attack- his drug did it-I heard noises- he made sounds I'd never heard before, horrible, horrible, oh God, why, -I couldn't do anything -in the lavatory, strangled noises in his throat- a crash, I rushed to him- too late....the men took him away. God! What is this punishment? I can't bear it.' Again and again she repeated her litany. Julian tried to hold her. Hope extinguished...he too had lost his strength, as they clung to each other, in shock, unable to speak, in an immeasurable state of emptiness, side by side, numbed and lost. 'I am cut in half, I want to die...' she whimpered.

A while later Jacques appeared in the doorway. She looked up at him, then through him, as if he were invisible. He too had jumped into his car when the news spread from one person to the other in the department. Now so near his friends, tears in his eyes, he could find barely a word to say to them. 'Is this our punishment?' went through his mind. 'Strength, dear friends, be strong,' was all he got out. Everything, absolutely everything was changed, for ever.

Trouble heaped on trouble, sorrows multiplied: in the following months Finuala's parents passed away, one after the other. With their deaths followed inheritance: family belongings and money for both Finuala and Ailsa. The sisters, their families, saddened and sober, were now a little more comfortable. But the irreparable loss of her first-born had changed Finuala: she now pressed Julian to start a new life, to leave behind everything to do with

Johannesburg. Their strongest connection, the one with Jacques, Irene and his two daughters, had already been all but severed: Jacques would be returning to Europe for research, abandoning his family, for very long spells. 'Although I think I might have to come and go', he told Finuala. 'Just short, friendly letters, from time to time', he urged, 'please, to remain friends in a civilised way. Not like those stupid ships that pass in the night; believe me Fin, you can count on me, I am always there to help, whenever possible, if there is anything at all I can do... it goes without saying, we are more than just friends. Fin, I will not forget. I will always love you.'

'We must return to the Cape. We must wipe out memories, buy a new and better home, take care of *our* parents,' Finuala pleaded with Julian. He agreed at once.

# Ten

While un-packing our baggage from Johannesburg, I re-discovered that battered old 'notebook' of mine. How disconcerting to come across my former troubled memories: this so-called 'friend' from my past; it had got mixed up with some box files of Julian's. Strange, and quite irresistible, I must take my pen and write:

'𝕭ene fundata est domus meum supra firmam petram. I admit: I copied this word for word from my battered missal. Strange:it fell open on just this page. To be re-grounded on firm rock has been our greatest need at this time of shock and loss and it's the *firm rock* which appeals, when I consider our new home. *Not* that so-called house of God.

Almost a year has passed. I've gone through denial, even anger. I've fought depression and now, with everyone's help, we're *learning* to accept our terrible loss. We've come home, to our beloved Mountain, to good memories from the distant past. We love it, just as we did before. More, even. If ever there was a firm rock, this is the one. Vikky and her sisters, 'the inseparables' we call them, all of us have slipped gently as snails into a new, perfectly shaped shell. Even Julian appreciates his return to home territory, that feeling of safety, in a place so known, its plants, smells, birds, the winds, the seasons. To find the house of ones dreams instinctively, without even thinking about the location, this too came as a pleasing surprise. Looking back on the dull criss-cross of modern suburbia outside Johannesburg, (small wonder we barely ever truly felt at home...) could it have been something subversive like that which unsettled our Jon with his breathing difficulties: simply not feeling well in his skin?, Now, back at sea-level, we savour this paradise... the familiar vegetation, and yes, the sounds and the smells of the Cape. Earlier plans about house-hunting had imposed that contemporary, bold, Le Corbusier style, but then we walked into this old double-story home, and well, it not only suited our purse, but is halfway between where we both grew up...in the heart of dear Rondebosch.

We have an ancient oak, a cool, lush, sloping lawn; two urns frame the steps up to our stoep: instant contentment. We find ourselves nodding and agreeing. We love being here. Only one thing has changed: most houses (not ours) now have high-security fences and locked gates. Cape Town people seem to be afraid. It was not like that here, before we left....

What still hovers over us is our nightmare of Jon's dying, despite all I've said on the pages before. We avoid talking about it. The return to our roots helps us to be at peace, more readily than we could up in the Transvaal. The trees, the birds, our mountain, and the cloud of happy memories containing parents and friends will help us to be healed. Julian has found work similar to the experimental laboratories in Johannesburg and as far as his music-room goes everything is in its rightful place, at last. He's even agreed to manage the garden…as it is small. (We shall see.) Yes, this is exactly what we want. Well, almost. Inevitably memories of Jon return and then we cling to each other, Julian and I. There are also duties we have towards *his* ageing parents, although this is something we share with his brothers and their wives.

The girls have adjusted: they love their new home, a place with stairs and many rooms, big and small, and secret nooks for many cats. Ours is a household which understands the mysterious minds of cats. We have only superior beasts with noble pedigrees. Vikki, Sybs and Dulcie: all three adore cats; they bring them into their lives and make them part of their own existence. 'Psss, psss, psss… Gremin, Tatiana,' are the first sounds each morning, when the beasts are lured to the children's beds, they sleep curled around the girls' shoulders, ankles, knees. Their names, from Russian opera, were instigated by Daddy of course. He's already joined a local choral society, with weekly rehearsals in Long Street, near the Lutheran Church. Performances? You bet! These people take themselves extremely seriously. Ensnared yet again by the possibility of conducting, something Julian so loves to do, he has committed himself, stimulated to be involved with such events. 'Such a pleasing change from work'…he proclaims, looking transformed and animated. Well, why not. If he so loves it.…

In a small study upstairs I have a built-in wardrobe with many shelves for my cameras, typewriter, papers, photographs and other important things. One shelf is special: I've rescued two of Jon's most valued possessions: his football boots, mud and all, also a pair of his dirty socks… and those shells he collected in Durban with his Dad. This is all I have left of my darling Jon. His things have a shelf all to themselves. When I look at these possessions of his I remember the sound of his croaky voice, the puzzled-eyes-look on his face when he used his inhaler…but also the love we experienced together. Would it be easier *not* to keep such things?

Occasionally I think of Jacques (and Irene), wonder how they are. I think of his well-stocked bookshelves, but it's fair to say I have no complaints about our own Rondebosch library, practically around the corner. I will…no, I *must not* be dishonest: I would welcome at least *some fragment* of news from Jacques. Sometimes, in a heightened state of awareness, I feel him looking at me the way he did. He had such strength, such powers of persuasion. I could feel his love. I pray we will hear from him, or both of them, one day. Of course I would not make the first move. And, speaking of enlightened thinking: today, as a reward, after staring at the clouds tumbling from the greyness of the mountain I moved my gaze down and here, close to our veranda, was a Cape Sugarbird…right before me: a miracle, all that blue and yellow and those incredible tail feathers swooping along; an omen surely, to see such a thing! How can living creatures be so beautiful? I didn't dare move, besides, there is no film in my camera!

If only I had the talent to write a poem…I am too feeble even to imagine an opening line. How do poets reach into their hearts to distil words and thoughts for eternal delight? A very good photograph might surely count, just as much as a poem? I have started using colour film, an expensive hobby, but reassuring: holding fast something memorable or beautiful, even though it is only on a bit of paper…. And *our* lives? Stable, I suppose. Old friends seem to have gone away. There is nothing else worth recording in this, my now so very ancient notebook…

'Ye gods, what time is it?' A sudden bang of the front door has woken Finuala from deepest sleep. She checks the ticking clock by her bedside. The light is still on, her book had slipped to the floor. Quiet footsteps, coming up the stairs! Of course it is Julian, back from his rehearsal, I recognise his special '*trying*- to- walk- quietly' steps, but at one o'clock in the morning?

'Where have you been, it's so late? Is everything alright?'

'Yes, yes, sorry to wake you, I was held up after the rehearsal, some woman suggested I should help train the chorus and so we had a coffee and talked about this idea for a while. There is a chance I might take over more of the rehearsals... go back to sleep, Fin, I'll tell you in the morning.

Just a quick shower, won't be long, close your eyes, back to sleep....'

***

On the following morning, while dressing, Julian pulled a letter from his jacket pocket and handed it to her. 'Oh yes, nearly forgot, this is to us both...from Jacques. He hopes to call, when he comes to Cape Town on business.' Julian studied Finuala's face; her eyes flew over the familiar handwriting. 'I'd forgotten to give it to you....'

His face, his voice were non-committal.

'Show no emotion whatsoever', she thought, her heart racing. She tried to fathom Julian's expression. It seemed guarded, eyebrows raised, chin up, while he checked his tie in the mirror before going down for breakfast. Later, having breakfast, he studied the girls and told them: 'well, he...they, are, were, such old friends! *You* know, you surely remember him, that Uncle

Jacques, the man with the swimming-pool and Aunty Irene? When he comes to Cape Town I'll invite him to come to our house for supper if you like, inspect this new home of ours, and say hallo to you... and you.... and you as well', nodding and smiling at each of the daughters in turn.

'It will be interesting to hear how they are getting on, don't you think,' he continued, 'and also *their* little girls; what am I saying, they must be almost teenagers by now; we will hear news about them all.' Julian, savouring the first of many cups of coffee, was now ready to leave, hoping to beat the rush of cars driving to the front of the mountain. 'Tonight I'll be home, but next week looks terrible, rehearsals, meetings and so on. Let's hope he's not coming until the week after that. Fin, could I have that letter back, I'll call him from the office, fix up something.....' 'Look at this, Julian,' she'd been studying the familiar handwriting, 'it seems he now works mostly in America. He only *visits* Johannesburg and....Irene has some new 'friend'. Goodness, things *have* changed, they actually live apart! *And* he's given no home address!'

'Yes, yes, must rush, you know, the traffic, leave it to me, Fin, I'll figure out something through the office.  See you this evening…bye everyone, I'm off.'

He was not certain what he felt. He did *quite* like Jacques; they'd been colleagues after all, for so many years.

***

Alone again, her feet unusually light, there appeared to be a radiant glow around everything. Baffling glimpses of furtive joy, seen only with the inner eye, helped Finuala tackle her daily tasks with renewed energy.

Everything seemed charged, changed, cheering.

'At the touch of love everyone becomes a fool,' she reminded herself, remembering her admirer saying just that, an eternity ago. Plato, wasn't it? Yep, those old Greeks, they certainly knew a thing or two.

'Our gardener comes tomorrow: he must mow the lawn, re-shape the hedge. And we need new bedding plants, but Julian has the car… next weekend then'. Later, passing by the large oval mirror in the hall, the one inherited from her mum, in which she'd seen herself since she was three foot tall, she caught a glimpse of a fat, mousy, troubled, forty-year old frump. Oh dear.

'Yes, a hair-cut, long overdue, that's what is required. I've let myself go: a livelier, richer, perhaps a darker shade? And shorter; it makes one look younger.' Finuala straightened up, pulled in her stomach. 'Which of my least ancient garments are still fashionable: that A-line skirt with the wide leather-belt and a crisp blouse...no, my Chanel-look-alike suit.... and some new, smart shoes?'

Secret fashion parades took place while the girls were at school (dressed in their little uniforms) while Sybil was safely tucked away at nursery school. For a few hours each day Fin planned, well, not actually doing anything, just *trying* to observe herself as others might, (who am I kidding,) 'if and when Jacques comes to see us,... or is he really just wanting to see me? What nonsense, I must pull myself together. Still, I suppose it is time I tried to look elegant again.' Just one simple, non-committal letter from Jacques had been the catalyst.

Or a wake-up call?

Fin was not alone: fate, mostly fair and generous, had granted Julian an equally galvanising experience. After one of his rehearsals a smiling young woman, trim, sporty and well-spoken, had approached him in the coffee-break...introduced herself as Frances, and asking for advice,... bowing submissively to undoubted superior wisdom, acknowledging his musical insights and experience,...on a *small* problem to do with her own vocal range: she, (a curly-haired sporty, blondish soprano,) was considering a move into the alto section, but only if *he* felt that would be appropriate, not without *his* sanction of course? Within several minutes the scheming lass had cast a spell on the mesmerised conductor. She was a scientist, she revealed, 'without family ties and keen on the violin although not yet *very* accomplished, and all things to do with classical music in Cape Town, but especially fond of walking and hiking and swimming and bird-watching'.... 'and talking', thought Julian. Of course he was flattered to have been targeted by this intriguing, intelligent creature. He peered around to see if others had noticed the frontal attack by one of the more attractive members of an otherwise rather elderly chorus. No. No-one was taking the slightest notice; they were all sipping their tea. 'You should consult the chorus master,' he suggested, 'but let's meet for a drink afterwards. So we can talk.' And so they did.

He drove very slowly that night, taking the curves on De Waal Drive with conscientious care. Having now befriended an attractive would-be alto who lived on the rump of the 'Lion' in Tambours' Kloof and who drove a VW like all the nicest people seemed to do, he now knew she was, it seemed, unattached. Julian felt light, bafflingly alive, even after an extremely busy day at work.

'More than likely the effect of a powerful gin and tonic', he told himself. The temptation to look away from the narrow elevated mountain road, down and across the sparkling carpet of glittering lights on the plains to the north, was compelling, but also a death-sentence. All caution thrown aside he took quick looks, allowing his automatic responses, his subliminal consciousness, to guide him safely back to his own front door. It was a test, this risk-taking, this tempting fate; at the same time he became conscious of new energies and an amazing surge of renewed interest in what the future might hold.

When he drove up the driveway he saw the light in the bedroom still on; 'She's reading, as usual', he thought. Julian took a deep breath, stepped into the hall, flung his briefcase on the chair and called up to the bedroom, 'here I am, back at last.' This is what husbands do, when they come home late at night, he reminded himself: good, honest, devoted husbands.

'He smells of something I don't recognise, but it's too late to remonstrate', went through Fin's mind. Amiably, thoughts elsewhere, they both smoked the pipe of peace.

***

Some weeks later the 'old friend' from Johannesburg arrived and was promptly invited to dinner along with new neighbours and also with Frances, the singer from the choral society. 'Uncle Jacques' appeared, to much acclaim, bearing spectacular flowers and fairy-tale gifts for the children. The older two gathered round him, little fluttering angels in their nightgowns, remembering him, and his swimming pool, not even remotely shy... a pleasing and moving moment.

Sybil was already asleep.

'You gave us sweets and treats in Johannesburg,' they seemed to remember. 'You always dived into the pool. You had loads of books in your house. We went on a train to the sea-side.' He kissed each child, examined innocent faces, held their hands. Dulcie was four, Vikky was eleven and the sleeping Sybil was two. He was even taken to the nursery to see her. Vikky, however, turned away, after only one polite moment, claimed she had homework to do.

'She's very bright,' Fin explained, 'very responsible'. 'Of course, just like her mama', replied Jacques.

'How short he is…and now so corpulent,' Finuala noticed.

Soon, seated by the oval dinner table, close to the terrace, the glass doors were pushed wide open to reveal the Southern Cross sparkling in the dark-blue heavens, vying with polished silver, flickering candles and finest, white German porcelain on a damask table cloth. Finuala's daily help, now dressed up as waitress, served at the table; the food was exquisite. The hostess still could excel herself.

'This is the first real dinner party in our new home' she announced. Seated by her right was Jacques, the guest of honour, on *his* right a dark-haired, streaked-with-grey matron, the neighbour from the house next door, then Julian, doing his best in his role as host, on *his* right the curly-haired Frances, from the choir. It would be Fin's task to field an as yet unknown quantity: the almost bald outdoors-type neighbour, Jan de Groot, who, fleshy, wrinkled and covered in large brown freckles managed to monopolise the conversation with his knowledge of gardening, his anxiousness about trees and plants growing too tall, spreading too far, ever in danger of spoiling their view. He wasted no time in eliciting promises from the host.

'Yes, yes, of course, we will take great care about all such things' assured Julian, who did not have the remotest idea what the man was talking about. Diplomacy intervened: Finuala asked if there was any possibility they might share the neighbour's wonderful gardener, perhaps only for one day a week? Cunningly she achieved a tiny connection....trying to get on the right footing with neighbours who proudly expanded on their very own black man's virtues and talents: 'Ag man, he's mos been working for our family since years and years,' their heads nodded simultaneously and appreciatively...while Jacques and Finuala communicated with looks alone. Fin, tongue-tied, conscious of being watched, didn't feel free to speak to him in the way she might have liked to, the way she used to.

Challenged tonight by three new acquaintances, Julian quietly hoped the young woman from the chorus, seated on his right, was taking particular interest in *his* own talents and achievements. Subtle, quietly observant, the young woman gave nothing away. She had immediately picked up an undoubted closeness between the hostess and this quixotic, amusing scientist from America...or was he from Johannesburg...with *that* accent, or from some foreign country? She was confused.

Host and hostess, both constrained, were on their best behaviour. For a short while, after general topics were exhausted, the rules of good behaviour still applied. Nagging, busy tendrils of specific views and bigger less common issues had, of necessity, been kept in check. But excellent Cape wines gradually loosened tongues. The new neighbours, Mr. and Mrs. De Groot, were already destined to suffer the fate of an unwanted filling in a sandwich. Unstoppably, *the* general topic in Cape Town turned to Mandela's incarceration on Robben Island.

'Mandela,' Jacques was striking out: 'have you heard this strange statistic: when the man got to his cell on Robben island he saw a white card on his door: it bore his name and the number 466/64...he was the 466th prisoner, now, in 1964 and he was exactly forty-six years old. What was it with the fours and sixes? Could there be some deep significance?'

'Yes, verry curious,' the neighbour rolled his R's. 'And it's a good thing they've locked that skelm up, don't you agrree...? A momentary hesitation followed this remark. De Groot felt he had done rather well, since he was an Afrikaans speaker.

'Oh well, he's been there before', Frances added, 'but only for a short while. He'll come out again. Other important people have been locked up there.' She hesitated, looked around...... 'remember Makanna, that tall strong Xhosa, who was banished by the British, after he'd led thousands of warriors against them in Grahamstown.... he actually drowned when he tried to escape. We all learned about him in Grade 8, didn't we?' The neighbour studied the faces around him. Frances was smiling, so the neighbour nodded, pulling a face as if to say 'serves him right', and raised his glass. Frances was now congratulated on her knowledge of history. Both host and hostess nodded approvingly.

But the new neighbour had the bit between his teeth: 'This Mandela, he must stay there for ever. Us South Africans, we can't have such a man tell us what to do in *ourr* country. He may be clever but us white people, we will not listen to men like that....those *blecks*, they are all Communists, you know, and the ANC too, all of them just trrying to brreak us down......' Flushed now, and sweating profusely he pulled out a handkerchief, wiped his brow, noisily blew his nose...then, unstoppably: 'that Mandela, the way he entered Court during the Rivonia Trial, dressed in his rridiculous Xhosa leopard-skin *kaross,* not even in a suit and tie, and all his supporters shouting *'amandla*! ...that man, he has nothing but contempt for white justice. And us whites, we are mos thrreatened by his culture... ag, yes, man.'

Finuala tried to catch Julian's eye, hoping he might come out with the 'right' thing at this moment. This was no longer a comfortable conversation. An awkward silence had settled on the proceedings. In the end it was Jacques who picked up his glass, pushed back his chair, stretched his legs and looked at everyone in turn ending with the neighbour. Calmly he explained:

'*my* family originally came here from the Lebanon. It was half a century ago.' Then, with a sigh, he looked from face to face around the table and stated: 'It's the *invisible wall* syndrome...' Leaning forward a little he stressed the 'syn'.

'I can tell you this: we, our family, have not found it easy to become South Africans: the disparities, inequalities, the subsistence level of blacks and darker races, and the lack of legislation to set things right, yes, even some of my own family,... I'm thinking of a cousin who looks very Mediterranean, you know: curly black hair and a good suntan, he gets suspicious looks in this country, people think he is a coloured man, he can feel it and is very nervous about it. And when we speak French, English and Arabic, and now also Afrikaans, up goes that 'invisible wall! My cousin has even taken to wearing a gold crucifix on his jacket, for fear of being thought an Arab or a Jew. Try to imagine that.' Jacques looked the Afrikaner in the eye: 'We know how it feels and we really believe things must change, right from the roots up... this Mandela is a saint and a martyr for his cause, and us whites,' he looked from guest to guest, 'must open our minds now. Now! Not tomorrow, now. At once!'

Finuala smiled up at him, stirred and touched by such brave, disarming revelations. The neighbour, disgruntled, frowned across the table. If he'd been some furry beast he would by now be growling, showing his fangs, ready to pounce. For some moments the guests remained very still, embarrassed.

'Mandela has behaved like a courageous, heroic figure....' This was Frances, challenging her host's new Afrikaner neighbour.

Elbow on the table, his hand holding his chin, the man shook his head sadly, saying: 'ag, nee, mense, you jes' don't understand. Dis will never work here, dere are too many of them, dose 'blecks',...countless billions of dem all the way up into the North of Africa, jes think about it.' His wife stared at her plate, silent in a cocoon of embarrassed, unexpressed doubts; whichever way she looked things were becoming unimaginably difficult, troubling. Easily intimidated she must have felt it was best to leave this topic to men.

The guests had blazed a trail, had made their mark, while appreciating their hostess and host, who had so far kept the peace. 'Somehow we must get through all this without trampling on each other's' already painful corns,' thought poor

Finuala. By now everyone knew where they stood. With politics as crudely divisive as in South Africa it was becoming an art to guide dinner-party discussions to digestible conclusions. The neighbours, carefully drawn to less loaded topics, now faltered and crumbled as soon as they began to speak. It was all very hard work. Finuala looked at her wristwatch. What she really wanted was to talk with Jacques, while Julian was hoping to get to know more, (even everything,) about Frances, who seemed so steady, so sure and un-phased.

'Still,' the neighbours said later, when they were safely back home, 'interesting people...these new *'mense'* next door, but, ag, you know, much too liberal! Look, their lights are *still* on. Perhaps they are now talking about us and that irritating Mandela...

Ag man, you know, we could ask them over when we have our next braai, even if they are too *kaffir-loving.'*

***

Finuala received a long telephone call on the following morning. It was Jacques, thanking her for the meal, followed by a confrontation of cold clear male logic: 'you know how much I care for you, you know I've moved away from Irene, let's put the record straight: I will always love you, so why are you still with Julian?  It is obvious to me how attracted he is to that blonde girl...they have much in common and she could hardly take her eyes off him: come on darling, you yourself told me that even Jon was probably not his child, nor is Vikky and you know as well as I do about *our* daughters...who, it has to be said, even look like me, both of them! You are so illogical.  Why must you cling to Julian? Have you really told him everything? Why don't you tell him the truth? He's not right for you. You were childhood sweethearts, yes, I know, but look at you now. How long have you two been together, twenty years...twenty-five?

You and I, you know we are right together. I shall be spending time in America now. I will keep in touch. I will write. I miss you. Life gallops on, who knows how little time is left for us. What are you doing with your life? He's had his share of you; isn't it my turn now?

My flight leaves later this morning: please, Fin ....think carefully'!

***

Finuala has collapsed in the garden, on a bench by a bed of day-lilies. The bees look for honey; mesmerised she follows their progress, their tenacious search…. and broods over Jacques' almost angry call.

𝕵𝖚𝖘𝖙𝖚𝖘 𝖌𝖊𝖗𝖒𝖎𝖓𝖆𝖇𝖎𝖙 𝖘𝖎𝖈𝖚𝖙 𝖑𝖎𝖑𝖎𝖚𝖒: 𝖊𝖙 𝖋𝖑𝖔𝖗𝖊𝖇𝖎𝖙 𝖎𝖓 𝖆𝖊𝖙𝖊𝖗𝖓𝖚𝖒 𝖆𝖓𝖙𝖊 𝕯𝖔𝖒𝖎𝖓𝖚𝖒…the just shall spring as the lily; and shall flourish for ever before the lord. 'This brief encounter with my ex-lover has cooled my ardour. Memories have dimmed, especially now, under Jacques' pressure, such as it was.'

'What are you doing with your life,' he'd demanded on the phone. 'He has a nerve! I am close to Julian. We know each other better than anyone else. We were hardly more than children when we first met, now over a quarter of a century ago… And yes, it is true, he neglects me in his compulsive need to be part of the world of music, this maddening hankering of his. But a God-given talent must have its way, it seems. I do understand that, even…well, I feel sorry for him. Often. Well, sometimes. He's probably not as good as he thinks he is, but who am I to judge? All I do is read, garden, listen to records, plan interesting meals and put the children to bed. I should get a part-time job, but perhaps not quite yet. The children still need me.

And yes, I saw it too: he does show an interest in that Frances: well, so be it, but the woman will have enough sense to understand he has a home and a wife and all these children; she will soon look elsewhere if she has any brains...at least, that is what I believe will happen. Anyway: she's no spring-chicken either, probably past that dangerous urge to procreate. Whenever I allowed myself to give in to an admirer I seemed to conceive; ironic, that, and certainly not planned. How does one hold back in the face of senselessly impassioned and desperate lovers? Searing incidents, and in earlier times long correspondence, offers of marriage, from three others, while I had already promised myself to Julian, who was always away, or too busy.... well, occasionally I caved in, not wanting to hurt anyone too much, perhaps that was stupid and vain, and careless, *things* could always have happened, I know, but then, afterwards, it always felt so pleasing to be back in the arms of someone so clever, so trusted and tried....someone I'd known and admired since we were both schoolchildren.' Scenes flashed past her mind: the night on the beach with....and that determined politician at the Adult Education Centre... and the photographer, now *he* was charming, and all those impassioned letters, now mouldering away in folders, it's all I've got, plus a heavy dose of guilt. Even so, I've tried to keep my memories of these uncertain, even confrontational men...often crazed and beside themselves...yes, slightly uncomfortable but now just memories, vivid, some fading... I'm lucky really and sorry to have hurt them. The hardest one to give up was dear Julius, he was such an artist! Someone told me he soon found another girl after I'd abandoned him.

Do I still love Julian? I believe I do. But is it still *that* love? Of course not, how could it be after all this time. And now Jacques still swears he loves me, claims Julian and I are only being dutiful. What does *he* know? We do care: it is the love that changes. First, it is hard to come by; then, just like precious metal, it becomes tarnished. But it shines up again. And its value remains the same; or increases! And we've been together for twenty years. Twenty years! One can't just push that away? Many couples split up nowadays. But I've made up my mind: I will remain his wife, just as I once promised in church, for what it's worth. Besides, the children love him.

\*\*\*

In September 1966 Verwoerd, South Africa's prime minister, was stabbed to death by a white parliamentary messenger. He had been, with the support of Strijdom, the great master-builder of South African apartheid and his views on black men were the basest imaginable. The years that followed were filled with events leading to change in South Africa. Inevitably tensions in the country grew and with it the fears of most white South Africans. The all-powerful police seemed ruthless. South Africa had allies in Great Britain and even in the United states, the state was strong. But despite, or because of, increasing unrest in other parts of southern Africa, in South West Africa, in Angola and Mozambique, in the Rhodesia's and Tanzania, there was an exhilarating and growing movement towards freedom. It was a world-wide thing, that famous 'wind of change.'

It was not only happening in Africa.

Finuala and Julian's own boundaries were also opening, their habits and expectations developing away from constraints reaching back to distant times far beyond even those two world wars in Europe. As their children grew, barely realising all was not well in the world around them, they gradually discovered the anomalies in their own home. 'Where is Daddy tonight?' It's not his going–out night again? Why is Daddy not here with us? He's always going away......'

Fin loyally tried to cover for him: 'His work,' she said, 'his rehearsals, his other friends He needs to have some fun, after all that work in the office.' But children are quick to notice anomalies.

Vikky especially dreaded seeing her Dad's tweed jacket. For some reason she knew, when he put on that tweed jacket he usually disappeared for several days. A way of life had developed as the years passed: a father who went elsewhere for several nights every week, even away on holidays, and then to endless rehearsals and concerts on other evenings, so that Mummy was left behind doing everything alone. The girls had become used to it really. It was only whenever he reappeared that all seemed, was, as it should be.

Waiting for him, but on the receiving end of these excursions, would be many years of impassioned expectations increasingly buried in the bosom of an unhappy spinster: Frances had fallen in love so desperately that she kept in the background for the remaining fifteen years of her fruitless life, never giving up hope her lover would abandon his family in their 'nest', their hungry beaks wide open for his attention. For there they all were, waiting for him: he'd hurry back to them, embrace them warmly, while the lonesome spinster waited and hoped, longing to have even just one little bird's mouth to feed. Somehow this never happened.

'I can't understand it', she complained,' please darling, have a fertility test...I've tried so hard to have your baby, maybe there is something wrong?' Julian, sympathetic and puzzled, considered this suggestion, but somehow there never was the right time. Was he too busy juggling his life, or just too afraid to hear such an answer? Frances' only consolations just happened to be bird-watching, but also playing her violin in amateur orchestras, and singing. She would go off on her own, whenever Julian returned to fulfil his 'paternal' duties. She knew only too well the story about Finuala's children: two of them more than likely, no, certainly, those of Jacques, an earlier one uncertain. As the years passed Frances lived in hope, desperately, but no babies appeared. 'God is punishing me,' she told herself guiltily,' I remain a barren woman.'

Almost two decades passed. During this time Julian found himself trapped in a web so complex he saw no way out: courageous, foolhardy, yes, all the while blindly improving his balancing act over the lives of two anguished and deeply disappointed women.

Julian spent holidays in Turkey, in Greece, in Paris with Frances, they played quartets, both struggling with instruments they hardly knew, (he had bought himself a cello and taken a few lessons) they sang in choirs. Very occasionally he thought he'd almost found that longed-for equilibrium between 'work' and Frances, between the little daughters and his lawful wife and between his now far too numerous other commitments. The only thing he never could say was 'no'.

Frances gave him an almost life-size pottery sculpture of a black seal balancing a ball on its nose, a jeux d'esprit, a delight for the children. The symbolism was surely not wasted on Finuala, who, in the spirit of noble resignation and forgiveness put it in a place of honour in the music room. Dusting it from time to time she must have interpreted this gift as clear proof that even the loathed Frances understood the ridiculous situation they'd all got into.

Like some superhuman Romeo Julian flourished while Finuala bore the situation with stubborn bravery and anguish in equal parts, but not without making at least one unusually prudent move on the chess board of her life: for a while she too got involved with the choral society, but in a managerial capacity: all three children were forced to sit through endless evening rehearsals and concerts, as she claimed not to approve of babysitters. Tired, bored, unwilling, three desperate fidgeting small girls stared up at an ocean of singers while their mother was rushing around 'organising' behind the scenes and their father, now called a conductor, appeared to be waving his arms about in time to the music.

Their presence caused comment, speculation and discomfort all round. But it was, or had been, Finuala's most desperate and most cunning move: the children learned to hate choral music, but at least Daddy did *have* to go home with them. To save face. In the eyes of at least half the strangers on the stage they remained his family, whether Julian liked it or not. Checkmate to Finuala.

It was during this time she received an unexpectedly sizeable letter from Jacques. His handwriting was exceptional: huge, each capital letter almost an inch high, and each page almost one foot long, a graphologist's dream. He'd called on them briefly, he claimed, since the previous time: he was moving to a different job, in his capacity as industrial scientist; there were openings in America and London. Although she was used to receiving letters from him, this one immediately caught her attention...demanded single-minded absorption, concentration. He stated he'd telephoned twice, having received no answer, he then called a mutual friend who said 'they are all away, returning on Saturday..' He'd tried again on Saturday, still without luck...so...*the reason why I am writing is really to try to get some communication to you because I hate the telephone at times like this. Since our weekend together* (they'd had a weekend together?) *and especially since I have been away, I have been thinking a lot, almost all the time in fact, about the best thing to do. You are so right: things have changed, changed completely without anything dramatic appearing to have happened. The holiday I spent with Irene was very remote and cold in the sense that my mind was not there. There was little privacy during the whole time since it was a tiny cottage....and full of Irene's cousins and families. A sort of imprisonment more than anything else,...which is plainly ridiculous.*

*I remember you saying that now wasn't the time for drastic changes since there is the business of settling me into the new job and so on, but I do feel that we have got to do some preliminary sorting out, if only to prevent decisions being taken for us or events getting out of control. You could of course say with some justice that we could and should have moved years ago, and what have I been doing all this time? True, and I regret it, very much indeed. Ten years, more, not exactly wasted of course but some of that time we could have lived together.*

*The lesson I have learned is that we must act soon or we shall fritter away our remaining time. (The other lesson I've learnt is how much I love you and how unique it seems, corny words perhaps but true nevertheless....)*

*What then are we to do? It seems to me we have two main choices, either to try to live within the present farcical situation but insisting on being together for a much greater proportion of the time...or to break away and live together. The first idea is surely only really possible if we can make a workable foursome with Julian and Irene; scarcely possible now or likely in the future. To attempt it otherwise would be impossible unless Irene were to find someone else (which is a distinct possibility; more of that another time). But in that case we might just as well go for the second idea which is very much to be preferred anyway.*

*Assuming that the Frances/ Julian affair goes on it is only a matter of time before one of them (probably Frances, who would not like to be seen in a bad light socially) makes known their version (and justification) to mutual friends. That will happen inevitably, it's only a question of when, and the timing will suit them and not necessarily us. That being so surely the best thing to do is to plan for ourselves; at least plan even if we can't act straight away.*

*The main question is what effect it will have on the girls. That really is something you must know much better than I do. You have said that they like me, are very fond of me, but if it came to living with us, with Julian away, what would their reaction be then? I suppose it's a bad age for them to have that sort of a jolt. They will soon be grown-up. But then perhaps it would be preferable for them in the long run, to living with you and Julian as things are. What do you think?*

*There is one question. <u>That I have to ask you.</u> We have known and loved each other for ten years, even more, but your experience of me as a person to live with is not all that great! Well, do you want to risk it? I must go and catch the post, will write later. Love Jacques.*

Finuala's heart had hardened. It did flutter a little, at first. 'Yes', she thought and dreamed, 'oh yes, I want to live with him, and with my children.' It did feel so consoling. She was soothed and flattered. But with such a huge challenge and possible disappointment in the fore-front again she was soon overcome with indifference, overwhelmed by a complete loss of appetite, a wary weariness: it had all become too improbable. Enraged by Julian's recent suggestion, even request, to sell the house, split the profits, so he might move to another place with Frances, Finuala turned into a fury of vengeance: 'I will fight you tooth and nail, both of you,' were her embittered words, and 'don't ever ask this question again.'

Poor Frances, equally incensed, turned up un-invited a few evenings later, rang the bell, pushed the door open and stormed into the dining room where Julian and Finuala were entertaining a group of friends from the choir. The children happened to be out, spending the night with friends.

Frances, who knew most of the guests, moved directly towards the table: demanded to know why she was not included, staring wildly, madly, in some heightened state, at everyone seated around it. Her arms reached forward, swept blindly, pushing plates, glasses, cutlery and food, everything on the floor, she chanted her mantra 'why, why, why'....now leaning against the wall behind her. Her body, her troubled mind, were in torment. Food and wine, plastered on or dripping from the walls, the stunned guests around the dinner-table ducking and turning this way and that, crying out 'calm down' or 'have a heart, Frances,' ....the nightmarish rebellion of Frances had only just begun: she was unstoppable, at the end of her tether, she no longer cared: a virago blinded with rage, she seemed to have lost her mind.

One guest had slipped away, was quietly using the telephone on the landing to call the police.

Rampaging, raging, her screaming and accusations continued until two officers stepped into the house to find a battlefield of broken china, stunned guests and two screeching women...who only stopped when the men in uniform actually stood between them. Silence fell. No-one was arrested, no-one was hurt, the dining room resembled a bombsite. Immobilised by such unleashed forces, Julian had kept well out of the way.

'This woman wants to kill both me and Fin,' he feared.  He knew only too well how crazed Frances could become. To be an onlooker must have been bad enough: Julian had not dared move, stood helpless, keeping clear of the fray as best he could. This was no time for heroics, as far as he was concerned. Bubbling up of fury on *this* scale had never happened before. In her heightened state, eyeballs like cracked glass, Frances' strong, muscular frame was more than ready for a fight. One can only imagine what other reactions there were, both externally and internally, less visible ones. One of the older visitors, a legal person of some eminence, felt he had enough gravitas to block the onslaught, to calm this outraged, unhinged tigress. With the help of a stiff whiskey he and his wife managed to soothe and sedate Frances and now, benumbed, spent by her own fury, she allowed them to lead her to their car without saying a single word, staring dumbly before her while she was driven home.

The remaining guests made statements to the police, helped clear the mess, tried to make light of it, having experienced the shock of their lives. Julian was silent. He knew about such outbursts; in the past years Frances' anger had often proved to be an aphrodisiac, even a necessary one. Now, craven, crestfallen, he stood in his own home, unmanned, useless, humiliated. There was no way forward for them any longer. This sordid event, his weakness, his endless prevarication, had finally created a permanent barrier.

'It's all my fault', he muttered bleakly, weak and finally defeated.

Finuala felt a forgiving surge of pity. It soon passed. It seemed the pair of them, she and Julian, were well matched in their misgivings about each other, constantly opening up new misery... almost as if they thrived on it.

Even so, the balance of power had shifted.

# Eleven

*Lava quod est sordidum...veni lumen cordum,* wash sordidness away, fill our hearts with light... Balance...that's what it was about... for more than one decade Finuala balanced apparent calm and peace with deeply embedded daily ordinariness. She stayed in touch with her sister who had settled in the Transvaal, still fond of life in Pretoria, and who knew surprisingly little or perhaps even nothing about the troubled marriage of her sister. Finuala valued and somehow managed to remain an exceptionally private person.

Family gatherings were limited to summer-holidays, occasionally in Europe, and more often, at Christmas. Even in her fifties and early sixties Finuala spent time earning extra cash in the almost forgotten capacity as a top-notch secretary. Generous to a fault she had little reason to earn money other than wanting to spoil her daughters and then even her first grandchildren. She bestowed lavish gifts, cooked gourmet meals and ordered choice wines. She went to posh hairdressers and bought smart clothes. All her cats were Siamese with exotic names and elaborate pedigrees. With generosity and apparent contentment this model grandmother savoured her independence, got out of the house, befriended new colleagues, while also building a collection of stunning photographs.

Many shots were taken during holidays with her sister in France and Italy, but mostly she was immersed in the awesome beauty of the Cape, its harbours, ships and water, the plants and fauna, always tenderly inspired by small animals and delicate scenes of valleys and hills. Finuala's work, finely judged, showed she was an artist; she must have had the same gene as Ailsa's, but lying dormant; buried beneath everything were her own complex talents and drive. It seemed she had, at last, learned to see the world with fresh eyes but also to stand on her own two feet.

She and Julian had an 'open' marriage. Despite the terrifying tantrums of Frances Julian maintained a discreet relationship with her *and* his official wife; there were also occasional romps with others, a potter, a singer, a plain but clever scientist from the Soviet block. The Russian lady-scientist he met at conferences abroad but the relationship appeared to be 'of little consequence'.

Finuala took this in her stride. She had more important things to worry about. Her life with Julian had become a simple arrangement of mutual support: shared memories, both painful and tender, laced with polite interest. Former passions spent, vanished, evaporated she spent lonely evenings watching John Thaw as Inspector Morse, masterfully solving mysterious crimes. Was it a coincidence the hero so resembled her still lawful husband?

Occasionally, in passing, she might have opened her missal, immersed herself in a few pages, perhaps re-absorbing, brushing up, Latin vocabulary, possibly speculating how Anglo-Saxons had become so civilised. Her own Latin *cornucopia*, (yes, even *that* word, a horn to drink from, the horn of a goat by which the infant of Zeus was suckled,) continued to please her, reminded her of consoling sounds from the past, voices of her mother, her sister, her teachers, those years of innocence and dependence and ultimately even the fascination of having been part of something immensely bigger than herself, but alas, with those prescriptive guidelines she could no longer hold on to. She did not even try to return to her religion.

Numbers of noble cats slithered around her legs, clambered about, languidly clawing, destroying whatever furniture took their fancy.

Nevertheless, they remained a consolation, as did exotic plants in her garden, along with skilled photography and fine books, visits to and from relatives, food, wine and friends. It appeared to be enough. Finuala and Julian's attempts to nudge their memories into a place where no one trod or even looked had succeeded: a past abandoned but not forgotten; something one might perhaps confess, one day, but only to the initiated. It was only God who knew. Their past remained a discrete and private thing.

This is where one might question whether repressed anger or guilt can unlock, trigger destruction and disarray... not only on the outside but also inside a human body, to say nothing of the soul? Was anguished rage a necessary release? 'Bottling up' anger, might this do harm to internal organs, locked as they are into the troubled system of a responsive living structure? The human brain is the most complex organism in the world.

\*\*\*

Grown to adulthood Finuala's three daughters brought new life, new ideas, made successful marriages. Just as these children had fast-forwarded into the future, into the world of computers, mobile phones and the ever-present media, there unfolded the start of a rainbow of events Finuala had hoped to see, embracing them with all her heart. As the years raced on she had entered, not just into her children's futures but also wholeheartedly into that 'rainbow nation' Mandela spoke of so fondly. But then, by the time there was one grandchild, celebrated, loved and preserved in a splendid photo album, Finuala began complaining. There seemed to be a backache; she took painkillers, her doctor was non-committal. Her sister came to stay, brought help and support but the pain became unbearable and Finuala returned to her doctor; Julian intervened at last, made complaints, demanded a second opinion. A new doctor sent her straight to hospital. There was a cancer in the spine spread from the liver, too far gone to be cured. Somehow the truth, not quite spelled out, hovered, shimmered in a threatening haze of improbability. Heavily drugged she asked for only one thing: poems; it was her old love re-awakened: a thirst for soothing thoughts and for the greater picture. Julian informed Jacques in America, who flew back to the Cape to call on Finuala one last time, before it was too late. Vikky sat by the bed, day after day, reading poetry to her mother. The younger daughters did their share. The dying woman was not afraid; but she did ask for one poem over and over again. And then one more time:

*Death stands above me, whispering low- I know not what into my ear:- Of his strange language all I know, is, there is not a word of fear...*

Even through a haze of drugs she seemed moved by the mystifying language of death: a poet called Landor...*not a word of fear, not a word.*

Vikky, the eldest, remained with her mother for several days, the other two took over from time to time. The passing hours launched themselves each day like an avalanche, at first imperceptible, even innocent, seemingly cumbersome, but soon they speeded up, until one day, still heading off to work as usual, Julian had no idea that his wife, prayed over by a Catholic priest, had, in the presence of her eldest daughter, closed her eyes for ever.

It was 1992. Her suffering had been short.

No-one is ever prepared for it, that day of 'tears and mourning'...lacrimosa dies illa, qua resurget ex favilla....

How often would she, or indeed all Catholics, have heard or read those much sung words, while not *truly* taking in the inevitability lurking in the process of dying.

Jacques, arrived from America, bought the entire contents of a flower shop to fill Fin's house with scents and colours, as if to counter his own pain with an excess of living beauty. He borrowed vases, buckets, tins from neighbours along the entire road to present immense numbers of glorious blooms... to numb and stun and deflect the hurt of all those left behind. During the church service a choir, under Julian's baton, sang like peaceful angels fluttering gentle gossamer wings. They sang, they sang, again and again, angels all of them, trying to soften the nightmare of this loss. And Fin's children, alone with their burden, clung to each other, no longer hating singers, but also no longer able to console their mother, and, for the foreseeable future, unable to ask those questions which could and should, but might never be answered.

***

Now three daughters and nine grandchildren can turn their faces toward her, like sunflowers to the life-bestowing sun. For what they did not yet know was that a correspondence of hundreds of letters, in crumbling cardboard boxes, had been stored by Finuala at the back of those impossibly high shelves in her study. Her children, her grandchildren, had loved her. Years later, when they read those letters, they began to understand all.

She always would be their mother, their grandmother; her story would be handled with glacé gloves, and her judgement, her need to achieve the impossible, was marvelled at.

For a while the girls and Julian clung to each other....*veni lumen cordium*...and suffered, feeling her abandoning absence, that bleak darkness, just like that of the daily sunset behind their beloved mountain. In this case there was no hope of any sunrise.

Like an exotic soon- to- be- fading bloom, a mystery had opened up with layers and ever more layers of delicate, translucent petals all representing questions that could never be answered. These gossamer petals float uneasily over my desk, (hers once, I am still conscious of that) and they come from enigmatic places. I imagine Fin's inscrutable smile. I somehow feel I owe it to her: to give an account, as undistorted as possible. Do I know her, just a little, by now? After all, we are both lapsed Catholics, we've loved the same man, lived in the same house. Nevertheless, Fin's choices remain an enigma.

\*\*\*

An epoch had ended; Finuala's children inherited the inevitable long period of readjustment. Their own lives were overflowing with work and husbands and children; they now met annually to remember and celebrate their mother, to have a meal with the man who had brought them up. Re-assured and gradually strengthened, they still desperately needed to reminisce when they could all be together.

At this time the whole world was watching our country's new beginning, our re-birth. It all sounded so easy: Mandela was free! Around South Africa there was soul-searching, but, above all, rejoicing. A new world was coming into being. No one knew when Mandela would be Prime Minister. No one had any idea what he might achieve.

On several occasions Jacques arrived from America, made contact with Julian, and brought gifts, mostly generous sums of money for the two younger daughters. Now in their thirties and mothers themselves, both of them bore an uncanny resemblance to him. I noted their delicate shyness when they accepted his affection, indulged his interest and tried to find shared memories: 'We have this film Dad made, remember, when we were little, all together on holiday…we must set it up for you…..' and there they'd appear, the two families with defenceless children in swimsuits, blinking in bright sunlight, shells on a beach, adults drinking wine, self-conscious, apologetic faces smiling foolishly, half-blinded into the lens. Proud of them all, interested in their activities and filled with admiration in this now quite hopeless way, the only way Julian knew to console himself was by keeping alive the affection, the memories he had of the woman with whom he had been linked for a lifetime.

And Vikky? Well, she remained warmly protective of her sisters, always sympathetic, being a good many years older, but standing somewhat apart as Julian's child; she did, after all, resemble him in so very many ways. So did her own son, an irresistible toddler, already reciting poetry, astounding all who heard and saw him; a genius, perhaps, talented and clever just like his mother, or indeed, he'd certainly taken after that admirable granddad of his.

Then, suddenly, a flutter of uneasiness: further insights from intimate discussions with their mother's devoted 'friend' Jacques: 'Vikky was allegedly the child of some *other* friend; a photographer,' he remembered,...'that wild German boy who worked in Johannesburg for a while, whom Finuala had known for only a short time...anyway, that's what your mother told me,' he assured them: 'why should she make this up? She'd been badly hurt by Julian...some affair of his, she no longer saw any point in fidelity; I thought you knew? Well? Didn't you?'

There was blank astonishment all round. Julian was puzzled. But then, ever the peace-maker, he weighed his word: 'what difference does it make *who* the father is? These are Fin's children and we are a family, aren't we?'

Vikky smiled her Giaconda smile. She knew how to hide beliefs that go deeper than thought. She, of all people, has an insight into hidden troubles: she works with disturbed people, she understands the need for therapy. As an outsider

I sensed the damage done to her by her buried fears. This brilliant, amusing woman was now someone else one found oneself worrying about, loved and admired as she was by her own children, her sisters, her adoring 'papa', and , one hopes, her troubled customers.

Bravely Vikky took on the disturbing task to seek out, confront this well-known photographer...himself a married man and not remotely warming to an exhumation of some almost forgotten sexual encounter. During a secret appointment, stirring their cups of tea in a depressingly seedy tea-room in Sea Point, the subject was declared not exactly null and void but quite simply closed: there was not the remotest spark of connection between them. He stood accused.... but then he shrugged his shoulders and seemed concerned only about his own wife who was under no circumstances to know about this, ('she is troubled already, deeply disturbed for other reasons'). Vicky, repulsed, felt both sickened, helpless and totally lost.

She spoke of this sobering experience in a cloud of unfathomable loneliness. 'He still has a faintly German accent. You know, I'm just so miserable' she added. 'Who *is* my father? I certainly didn't care for that one.' Eyes shut, seemingly in sorrow, she turned her head from side to side.

Only later she shrugged and smiled, in her inimitable 'knowing' way.

I knew, I could tell: she'd come to terms.

# Benediction

## 2007, <u>Rondebosch.</u>

My only contribution to all this 'knowing' came on the day, when, in a wild, bold moment, I urged Vikky to do a blood test: 'Let's put an end to disturbing speculation: Of course Julian is your Dad. And if he isn't, which, surely, is improbable, just look at you two, I mean, you are so alike, so close, so on the same wave-length... it makes no difference. Besides, even the neighbour said, just the other day, *aren't they alike, Vikky and her dad*! Furthermore: he's filed an application to remain your Dad, whatever happens.'

Joking about such things was easy. I had long convinced myself there was absolutely no question, although I did feel hot and my face was flushed. So this is what one does: a ridiculous toothpick-like-cotton-wool swab of sputum taken from the inside of the mouth... not even a blood test for such a cataclysmic event... is the current, brilliant and *certain* way of identifying DNA. Just a bit of spit is enough to change ones entire view of existence...for a modest sum of money paid to some laboratory. That's all it takes to change lives. First knowing, then absorbing. And then the crux of it: to believe the result! Still, nowadays one exists filled with trust in the miracles of science.

Just to remain in our safe, known, old-fashioned world I lit a candle, put on a pleasing CD, trying to turn the event into a ceremony: one which was meant to heal, to support, to release all doubts, the sort of thing hippies, or, by extension, even good ex-Catholics might wish to do. 'There now, rub this swab inside your cheek...and then, straight into this envelope. Soon we'll know the truth.' Father and daughter both do this; they have earnest, resigned faces. We are, were, all three of us, feeling self-conscious. As if we might possibly be interfering with something divine and pre-ordained, this business of *still* needing 'The Truth'.

'That's alright then, well done', I told them, trying to sound wise, and confident, hoping my benediction might help push away remaining uneasy feelings. Had I, in some barbaric way, disturbed nature? Self-conscious and embarrassed, although I was only an 'un-official' supervisor, a bystander, an observer, I felt I might have unleashed something threatening. That's how it seemed to me. I reminded myself to have no feelings, no emotions:  I was an 'organiser,' just someone trying to help to reveal 'The Truth.'

'And now, how about a glass of wine……'

Some days later the official answer lay before us: 'No match in this DNA'. The result was/is/remained, negative.  We looked at each other. Negative? Unbelievable! All three of us, gloomily embarrassed, continued looking at each other, haplessly wishing we'd never done this. I'd so believed they needed to know. And now… that they did?

Testing the waters, after a while, I felt I should at least offer an apology, take the blame: 'Dear God, I'm so very sorry.  It's all my fault.' No-one remonstrated. Then, after an uncomfortable silence: 'Of course it makes ab-so-lute-ly no difference'. Heads nodded, voices went up and down, stressing the same syllables, in that sing-song everybody uses to show ab-so-lute belief in something that is un-fort-un-ate but regrettably true. Yes. True.

'Of course, of course', we assured one another. But then again, perhaps somewhere, lurking, hidden away, subconsciously, just a little, it *does* or did make a difference. God, this is hell', I thought. I felt terrible. Shaking my head, lips squeezed together, I fathomed (too late), I should have kept out of all this.  But then, in the end, at last, something useful did come of this: Julian finally revealed that his mistress, Frances, so hated and abhorred by all three daughters, had already suspected he was infertile years ago, had begged him, nagged him, to have a test... a sperm test, that is. 'Yes, why not,' he'd agreed, probably irritably, in those busy days, when he was running around juggling a double, treble, quadruple life, one with his mistress, the other with his family, another with work, and then his music. Always a procrastinator he'd simply never got round to it.

Ah! Poor Frances, weighed down, crushed by her solitary existence! For almost twenty years, two long decades, she hoped in vain. What unconscious, unwanted material was stored in that body of hers? What madness had slowly released illness into *her* later life?  Do some people not toy with the idea, this strange concept: psychogenic illness, derived from 'immoral', 'amoral' conduct, releasing potential toxins?  What and who defines 'morality', and 'guilt'?

Less than a decade later Frances too died of cancer: a tumour at the base of her spine which had attacked the bowel. The suffering was intense, drawn-out. Julian did offer to visit her in hospital. She refused: 'No, I don't wish to see you. Thank-you, but please, don't come.' Poor lonely, love-less, childless, man-less, and now dying woman....

Shortly after Frances it was Jacques' turn: also a cancer, this time in the liver, also attacking his spine. An unnerving similarity in the fates of three so closely linked people, their bodies ravaged by destructive cells, all of them destroyed by inescapable, private, lonely sadness, so soon, one after the other.

Might it, could it have been guilt? What nonsense! No-one in their right minds would agree with such thinking.

Is one even remotely aware of the power of destructive, deceptive, unhelpful beliefs? Some of those commandments, drummed into us by would-be holy men, might *they* be blamed for piling on such guilt? Do the last two sentences go too far? Who can, who will dictate the correct checks and balances? Is it even desirable to submit and believe such things? Where do our moral certainties come from? Who is in a position to decide what moral certainty is? Reading about stress one learns about opioid-like substances, encephalins, which numb the cells of our bodies, thus making them unable to destroy cancer cells, or any other invader: that so-called immune system.

Might this not be where the Catholic Church flaunts its trump card, its 'sweet oblivious antidote'? According to the church God forgives your sins at the moment of absolution, when an appointed official on earth, the priest in the confessional, assures you, the repentant sinner: '𝔢𝔤𝔬 𝔱𝔢 𝔞𝔟𝔰𝔬𝔩𝔳𝔬'... I absolve you. You are no longer guilty. You might, you will probably live eternally. With any luck even in heaven, that is.

Here lies dangerous territory for lapsed Catholics. Is this true or not? One learns, or tries to learn, not to be naive. Beliefs are in our minds; minds govern every part of our bodies. So, could this be the reality?

'Canst thou not minister to a mind diseas'd;
Pluck from the memory a rooted sorrow;
Raze out the written troubles of the brain,......

...and with some sweet oblivious antidote, cleanse the stuff'd bosom of that perilous stuff which weighs upon the heart?' And the doctor responds: 'Therein the patient must minister to himself....' 'Pluck out the rooted sorrow, cleanse out the perilous stuff.'

So much for Shakespeare's 'take' in Macbeth. But now a quote by Sören Kierkegaard, a somewhat vague consolation of religion:
'No-one loses his way so far
That he cannot find his way back to You.
You who are not just like a fountain
which allows others to find You,

But are a fountain which itself seeks the thirsty.

Finuala, might you have found this helpful, inspirational? In your younger days perhaps, while you and your sister, oblivious of the future, were fidgeting during mass? Probably not: such thoughts remain exclusively for those who truly believe. So here I am again, still caught up in my own, no longer never-ending future as I stand once again by the window of that small room upstairs. I close my eyes. I think about Julian. I see him, a field lying fallow, without hope of any yield. Might his wife, in her new state of self-awareness, have guessed this was so and did she try to protect him from this disappointment; after all, it was *his* fertility that was at stake? She *did* care about him. I hear the old house breathing, sighing: 'let it rest', it says. 'There is no more to say.'

Finuala's room is *my* study now, but also *our* library. Between us, Julian and I, we read and mull over huge numbers of books, mostly English but also French and German. Just like Finuala, I still love Latin. Julian and I agree that reading and knowing languages seems to be one of the most rewarding delights and consolations in old age. Just outside the window stands our ancient oak... still there, but only just. Please do note: I said *our* oak. Twenty years have gone by. I and it, we are, none of us, as strong as we once were. Sometimes I sit on the wooden bench in its shade.

'Now listen to me', I tell the tree, 'we must trust each other! You are not well, you have some fatal oak-disease; you are not alone, many Cape Oaks look terrible now. Might you be oppressed by nasty exhaust fumes, by electronic messages, by pollution? Has some immoral 'oak conduct' produced a potential toxin, some sort of oak cancer? No point pretending: I have looked it up, you know. But then, it may just be chronic oak decline, or dieback. This is a widespread and complex disorder due to a number of causes such as recurrent drought, which is stressful, and less obviously, a hidden root disease caused by fungi. First symptoms are pale or small leaves, or the death of fine twigs and whole braches... your demise, just like with humans, can take years. But then, unlike humans you might stabilise...you may remain a strong oak, for a very, very long time yet.' I listen. But there is only silence.

'On the other hand, you may have to be felled.' Now the leaves rustle consolingly, un-phased by my threats. Some are pale gold; they drop on and around me, unsettling me even further. Avoid swirling dead leaves, they remind one of dying, bring painful speculation, and memories, so many memories. Could it be oaks have souls just as we do? What is a soul? There are things here that need connecting. I must think, be alone. Best not to chatter on about such things at the next dinner party... friends will think I'm dotty,' I tell myself, 'they probably already do.'

***

Twenty years have gone by since I moved in with Julian. I have studied the troubled course of living passion in his family, the deaths of Finuala, then Frances and now, finally Jacques. In my new state of awareness it is cancer-cells which haunt: all three died from cancers near the spine, their bodies had become their enemy, cells growing on cells. One tries to find a link; but it refuses to add up. These mysterious processes, the 'perilous stuff,' all this needs connecting. But 'there-in the patient must minister to himself'...said the bard.

I hear my man practising, now with more clumsy fingers than twenty years ago, one of the slow movements of Beethoven's late piano sonatas... heart-rending modulations that go well with the sad reality of the oak which has endured so much history, sheltered so many generations below its protective spread branches. One occasionally sees 'nutters', who, with embarrassed looks, embrace trees. I admit I've tried it myself, feeling extremely sheepish. Finuala no doubt loved it too. The oak, I mean.

Perhaps this oak of ours already lived, even as a tiny acorn, when Beethoven was writing his passionate masterpieces. Could it be a tree resolves to become a masterpiece, just as we all try to... in our ephemeral way,' I suggest, aware that this is otherworldly and fey to say the least. Julian is studying me. He proposes we sit outside, drink a glass of wine. 'Poor old thing, she's alone too much, needs cheering up'... that's the kind of look Julian is giving me.

'I like to be alone,' I keep telling him. He and others seem to be incapable of understanding this requirement, this need. Ever the scientist *he* needs proof: he insists and thrives on learned papers, graphs and figures proposed and confirmed in lectures by doctors and professors at colleges and universities. While he reads, collates, studies, draws conclusions, my heart breaks to see our tree so unwell and myself unable to put things right. The garden, the old house, Julian and I, we've bonded in ways which are difficult to explain. It is as if we have always belonged to each other; a pre-ordained state. But now my own beloved Latin words, so carefully acquired, seem to be crumbling, falling from my mind; where they once stood there are gaps, words are lost, and their spaces remain empty. Unbelievably, Julian and I have both become old. One *tries* to understand: time is running out. It is elusive, both time *and* the understanding and acceptance of one's own end in time.

In vain one avoids the high winds.

And now even Mandela has died before us: his last rare appearances had shown a wizened, shrivelled childlike person, no longer with a twinkle in those wise eyes; they were beginning to look dull, opaque, uncomprehending. For long spells he lay in hospitals in a state of suspended animation. What did *such* a man feel about dying?

It was he who made us look at ourselves, our reflections, helped us understand the cruel, selfish, divisive, posturing meanness of all who have lost or never known the ability to love. Imagine architects, artists, sculptors in South Africa vying with each other, designing monuments to remind those still on their path through life of the Mandela who forged the way, the only way, forward. Even the youthful president of the United States had hoped to call on this ancient sage, to receive inspiration and benediction from a dying man filled with such wisdom and grace. It was not to be. A few months on, he has come again, but for the funeral of his inspirational hero. Mandela's monument should rise into the sky, fixed to the top of Table Mountain. It should last as long as the pyramids, it should glow in the dark.

Nothing is easy. Dying is not easy. Not for Mandela, not for Beethoven, presumably, perhaps not even for an oak.

Is there any soothing poem someone will read to me to discourage my own raging, fighting, for one more day, one more month, or another year? I don't think so. The ability to love, to forgive: one must not lose track of this gift. The next-best thing might be to enlist the help of psychoanalysis. True forgiveness, freedom from guilt, is hard to come by. Just thinking about it makes guilt come rushing in....engulfing just about everyone.

Before our eyes lie roughly sixty-four thousand words about someone who learned to love, to understand and forgive.  Here they are again, those sixes and fours, how spooky is that!

Has one done all one can to understand the mysterious sphinx, the one who drifted through gardens frowning a little, wearing exceptionally white gloves, looking to be loved, appreciated, wanted, even now in her darkly secret 'pure, unspotted' silence?

Silence is also conversation, according to an Indian sage.

# Vocabulary

| | | | |
|---|---|---|---|
| 22 | Bakkie | (Afrikaans) | Truck, van |
| 28 | Introitus | (Latin) | Introduction |
| 29 | Flectamus genua | (Latin) | We genuflect |
| 29 | Benedicta tu in mulieribus | (Latin) | Blessed among women |
| 29 | Ecce virgo concipiet | (Latin) | Behold a virgin conceives |
| 33 | Braai | (Afrikaans) | Barbeque |
| 35 | Boers | (Afrikaans) | Peasants |
| 36 | Gesel | (Afrikaans) | Whip, friend |
| 36 | Gesels | (Afrikaans) | To chat |
| 38 | Goggas | (Hottentot) | Insects |
| 39 | Boere-wors | (Afrikaans) | Sausage |
| 44 | 'Ag man, jy moet mos praat soos ons Afrikaners' | (Afrikaans) | 'You should speak like us South Africans' |
| 49 | Ora et labora | (Latin) | Pray and work |
| 77 | Eikestad | (Afrikaans) | Oak town |
| | | (Afrikaans) | Cape Dutch |
| 78 | Boeretjie | (Afrikaans) | Little peasant |
| 78 | Burgerhuis | (Afrikaans) | Citizens' house |
| 81 | Jou beste vriendin | (Afrikaans) | Your best girlfriend |
| 100 | Kali | (Swahili, Arabic) | Angry |
| 101 | Outjies | (Afrikaans) | Chums |
| 106 | Kinderkies | (Afrikaans) | Little children |
| 106 | kinderspeletjies | (Afrikaans) | Children's games |
| 101 | Mense | (Afrikaans) | People |
| 127 | Tota pulchra es, macula originalis non es in te | (Latin) | All is ripe perfection, there is no blemish |
| 141 | Puer natus est nobis et filius datos est nobis | (Latin) | A child is born to us, a son is given |
| 141 | Grossesse | (French) | Pregnancy |
| 151 | Tickey | (South African) | Three-pence |
| 155 | Tsotsi | (Afrikaans) | Street urchin |
| 155 | Tsotsi taal | (Afrikaans) | Street urchin lingo |
| 191 | Koek-susters | (Afrikaans) | Sticky South-African cake |
| 191 | Huguenots | (English) | French emigrants to South Africa |

| 199 | Sicut cedrus libano | (Latin) | Like cedars of Lebanon |
|-----|---------------------|---------|------------------------|
| 192 | Mei babatjie | (Afrikaans) | My little baby |
| 264 | Bene fundata es domus meum supra firmam petram | (Latin) | My house is well founded on firm rock |
| 279 | Skelm | (Afrikaans) | Rascals |
|     | Mos just |  | Indeed |
| 301 | Lava quod est sordidum | (Latin) | Cleanse what is soiled |
| 301 | Veni lumen cordium | (Latin) | Come light into my heart |
|     | Molto amabile | (Italian) | Much loved |
|     | Fin | (French) | The end |

www.ingramcontent.com/pod-product-compliance
Lightning Source LLC
Chambersburg PA
CBHW060534030726
47498CB00004B/1190